WWW.PASSAICPUBLICLIBRARY.ORG

3 2344 09277420 1

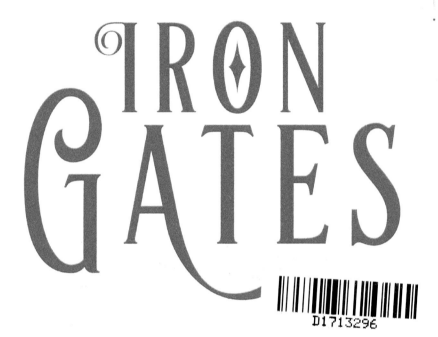

IRON GATES

D E B B I E   S T R O M

PASSAIC PUBLIC LIBRARY
195 Gregory Avenue
Passaic, NJ 07055   3|19

AYAL PRESS

Copyright © 2018 by Debbie Strom.
All rights reserved.

No part of this publication may be translated, reproduced, stored in a retrieval system or transmitted, in any form or by any means, electronic, mechanical, photocopying, recording or otherwise, even for personal use, without written permission from the publisher.

Distributed by:
Feldheim Publishers
POB 43163 / Jerusalem, Israel
208 Airport Executive Park
Nanuet, NY 10954

www.feldheim.com

Distributed in Europe by:
Lehmanns
+44-0-191-430-0333
info@lehmanns.co.uk
www.lehmanns.co.uk

Distributed in Australia by:
Golds World of Judaica
+613 95278775
info@golds.com.au
www.golds.com.au

Previously Published in the Yated Magazine.

For R. N.

CHAPTER 1

Almost there.

The English countryside rolled past my window, offering me a glimpse of the Mersey River in the distance. It was a small waterway compared to the vast Atlantic Ocean I'd seen from the deck of the ship, *Brittania,* and although I had enjoyed the journey, I was glad to be near the end of it.

Traveling after the war was serious business. I supposed I was on serious business, crossing the Atlantic by ship on my own and now, riding the train to Eccles.

My parents had been opposed to my going and our strained conversations still echoed in my head, filling me with regret.

"They need me in England," I had told them. "It's an opportunity to do my part, something I may never get a chance to do again. Please, you must let me go."

"It's too far from home, Judith. I'm worried," my mother said. "Across the ocean, not seeing you for a year... not knowing the people besides Aunt Arlene's cousin, but we know little about the others... traveling by yourself... it's just too much..." My mother trailed off, shaking her head, looking helplessly to my father to explain.

I jumped in. "I'll be with other frum people, the teachers, Mrs. Morgan, the girls, good people. It's not like I've never been away. And I'll write. The main thing is they truly need my help. How can I not do my part when they really need me?"

My mother's expression was bleak. "You've never been this far away…" she trailed off again.

"You can help here," my father said. "Girls need you here."

I felt my face set stubbornly.

"You're a good teacher. Why do you need to go halfway across the globe to teach?"

"It's different. It's not just teaching. The girls are away from home. They've lived through bombings and the threat of war, too close to home. A house mother can give them more support than a regular teacher."

"Yes, that's true," he said. "But others can support them. Why does it have to be you, Judy?"

Daddy's face was very close, his concern palpable. I looked at his worried eyes and whispered fiercely, "Why not me?"

They became weary of arguing, though I knew they still worried.

They let me go.

I hoped I could prove to them that their sacrifice had not been in vain.

* * *

The bustling Liverpool station had been chaotic and didn't provide a map or directions to the correct platform. I was jostled a number of times while I scanned the crowds for someone to ask directions.

I spotted a woman striding confidently and my instinct told me I could approach her. I ran to catch up with her.

"Excuse me… excuse me…!?"

She stopped and looked at me intently.

"Excuse me, do you know where the train to Eccles is?"

Her eyes quickly looked down at my skirt and shoes. "Come along. Quick."

She grabbed my sleeve and steered me with rapid steps through mobs of rushing people, while my suitcase and bag banged against my leg. I was propelled up the train steps by the woman's hand on the back of my jacket. She drove my jacket through the busy train, her forward momentum causing me to dodge passengers and luggage headlong in an unrelenting quest toward an undetermined destination.

"Here we are," she said, finally letting go of my jacket and taking my suitcase from my hand. She led the way into a small cabin car and stowed my suitcase under the seat. "An empty car simply waiting for the two of us." She laughed. "A rare find." She promptly sat down and made herself comfortable.

I hoped she didn't think I was helpless. At nineteen, I could certainly find my way through a train. Probably not as expertly as she, but I admitted that I had been somewhat lost and would still be lost, if not for her. Apparently, we were traveling the same route.

A bell clanged. "And not a moment too soon," she said, with a pointed nod. She regarded me with amusement. "For the same fare, my dear, you are granted an uncomfortable seat and a beautiful view." Her arm gestured toward the seat and her eyes twinkled. "May as well sit, it's an hour-long ride." She gazed briefly out the window and opened her bag to rummage its insides.

I slid into the window seat and took off my cap. I had promised my parents I would wear it during the trip. It felt safe to remove it now. A huge hiss of steam shushed by the window and slowly we began to move. We had just made it.

Almost there.

I put my bag on the seat and shrugged out of my jacket while I gazed out the window. Freight ships chugged through a canal and beyond that, I glimpsed a scattering of boats on the Mersey River. We slowed again and pulled into a station.

"Bootle!" A strong male voice called out. I chuckled. I liked the name.

We continued out of the station and traveled between high stone walls and under abandoned old bridges going nowhere. I could see evidence of bombings, although World War Two had ended five years ago. Numerous shells of buildings and large craters reminded me that England was still rebuilding. I experienced a moment of wonder, breathing it in. History was alive here.

The male voice bellowed, "Olive Mount Station!"

I continued to watch as the sun shone bright on canal waterways and barely moving barge boats.

Feverish mutterings drew my attention back to my seatmate. She was searching through her bag, scolding it as if it were a disobedient child. I suppressed a smile.

"Thank you for your help," I said. "I'm glad I found the right person. You certainly know your way around."

She looked up from her open bag. "I'm a native, born and bred in Manchester. Not saying how long, mind you. I can travel this route with my eyes closed." She laughed a musical laugh. Her eyes scanned my head. "No impropriety intended, but you do have the loveliest red hair I've ever seen."

The reason for my cap. My fiery crown, as my father called it, which he said matched my spirit. She stared unabashedly at my hair, her eyes sparkling.

"Simply lovely." She went back to rummaging and muttering into her satchel. I had an urge to tell her I loved her hat, the purple ostrich plume completely outrageous, but I held my tongue. She was dressed in a classic gold-buttoned, navy silk suit, a blouse with plume-matching ruffles cascading halfway down the front. Low heeled pumps and her satchel were in matching navy. There was something familiar about her. What was it? It had drawn me to her at the train station. She was capable, classy, refined, civilized and…familiar, somehow.

"Aha!" She pulled out a small knitted blue circle and a crocheting needle. "Hiding from me, naughty naughty." She held it up to me and waved it slightly, its yarn tail dangling. "Do you know what this is?" She shot me a challenging look.

It looked like a small yarmulke. I didn't dare say it. Maybe it was the beginning of a tablecloth. Or a doily. Or a hat.

"I… it's a navy, um, round…" Not wanting to insult her, I groped for words, "yarn…"

"You are Jewish, are you not?"

"Well, yes, I am. How— "

"Yes, indeed. I was correct. Your manner of dress and demeanor provided a definite clue. Sedate colors, modest attire. But then when I saw your flaming hair and oh-so-fair skin, there was the tiniest bit of doubt. But, I'm not often wrong. Well?

What am I crocheting?"

"A yarmulke, I think."

"But of course! Although in England, we call it a koppel. It's in its early stage. I'm fashioning it for my son's third birthday. My favorite child. But I say that about all my children." She laughed and I couldn't help laughing with her. "Now that we're train mates, we must introduce ourselves. I'm Shirley Weiss. A fellow Jew."

"Judith Mintz." Of course. Now I knew what had struck me as familiar. She reminded me of Aunt Arlene.

"You're American. And, correct me if I'm wrong Judith Mintz, you're on your way to Eccles to the boarding school for girls at Thornton," she said, while crocheting. "Certainly not as a student. You look a tad past that." She paused in her work, tilted her head and eyed me. "Not as a teacher, most certainly not!" She laughed and resumed crocheting.

"What makes you say most certainly not as a teacher?" Was I insulted? Maybe just defensive.

She set down her crocheting and her smile widened. "Well, the school is utterly and properly English. Thoroughly committed to be-ing En-glish," she enunciated the last two words, the syllables separated. Her teeth stayed together in an overly large smile. I felt myself fake-smiling back, but prickling inside.

"And...? Are you saying that people who are not 'utterly English' are not acceptable as teachers there? That sounds... elitist."

"How American. No, Judith Mintz, it's not a matter of what I say. And it's not a matter of being elitist, rather it's a matter of preservation. Of dignity and sanctity. Of regality. And although confusing, it's not only being English that is acceptable. No. At Thornton, only the English with equal *standards*, high standards." She saw my perplexed look. "A certain correctness, a refinement of speech and behavior... European principles and Jewish adherence. And..." her eyes opened wide and she gasped, "...you *are* going to Thornton to teach, aren't you, Judith Mintz? Oh my, however did you get into this complexity?" She laughed and looked heavenward, raising her hands in a beseeching manner.

I had to laugh. "I had no idea that being accepted was such an accomplishment. And honestly, until today I never thought of myself as an uncouth and unprincipled American!"

She laughed. "Oh yes! In England, that is what you are! But congratulations, Judith Mintz! Apparently, you passed inspection of the highest order. You're in!" She stuck out her hand and grabbed mine and shook it.

I laughed. "They've never even met me. My Aunt Arlene is English. She's a cousin of Mrs. Hannah Morgan—"

"—the headmistress of Thornton boarding school?!" she clapped and laughed. She leaned forward. "Hannah Morgan is a close friend of mine. What a small world!"

"Yes, it really is!" Her enthusiasm was contagious. "My aunt had heard from Mrs. Morgan that there was a shortage of available young women to live in the boardinghouse with the students. My aunt who dotes on me, apparently convinced them to accept me and arranged everything, including my trip. So here I am on my way to Eccles, their new house mother and writing teacher. And... I am an American." I put on my most humble expression.

Mrs. Weiss shook her head. "My, will wonders never cease! Well, my opinion is that they made a brilliant choice. It was meant to be and only good can come of it." She gazed out the window. "We're nearing the Eccles station." She looked at me and gave me a huge smile again. "I'm sure they'll be so pleased when they meet you. You know, dear, you do have "good girl" written all over you."

I blushed at her compliment. She was so warm and friendly. I wondered whether what she said about the boarding school was true. I hoped not. They had accepted me sight unseen, which to me meant that my credentials were good enough. After all, my father was a respected Rav, my mother a teacher. My brothers were in good yeshivos. I had been teaching for two years. Plus Aunt Arlene could be very persuasive.

"I hope they'll think so, too."

She clapped her hands together. "Of course they will. Hannah Morgan is a love. Oh, I am so pleased we met, nothing is by chance you know, Judith Mintz. You must promise to come and visit me at my home when you have holidays. Manchester is a mere four miles by train from Eccles."

"You wouldn't want an uncivilized American in your home, would you, Mrs. Weiss?" I felt comfortable enough to tease her.

She laughed an entire segment of music and tapped my hand. "Oh, I'm not one of those old school English. No, I'm a live-and-let-live-we're-all-in-this-together kind of English. And you know, Judith Mintz, you do possess the most charming red hair I've ever seen in my entire life. It would be my greatest pleasure to see it again. Soon."

"My father says it matches my charming personality."

"Oh I agree, Judith Mintz. I dare say Thornton School for Girls is in for a surprise." She reached into her bag and withdrew paper and pen and scribbled.

The train slowed. I heard the stationmaster call out, "Eccles Station!"

"That's me." I put on my jacket and cap.

"Here's my telephone number." She thrust the paper into my hand. "Don't lose it!"

I pushed the paper into my jacket pocket and dragged my suitcase out from under the bench. I turned to look at Mrs. Shirley Weiss. I wanted to see her again.

"I won't. Thank you. I'm really glad I found you." I hurried out.

"Good luck!" Her voice trailed after me, but I was banging my way out and down the train stairs, looking ahead.

CHAPTER 2

The Eccles station was small. I set my suitcase down on the plat-form and took the yellow paper flower out of my pocket and poked it into my jacket lapel, a pre-arranged identity tag so Mrs. Morgan could find me. Not that it would be difficult. I was the only girl my age among the few people milling around.

At the far end of the station, a woman in her mid-thirties appeared, a sturdy woman of medium height, possessing a frum demeanor. She fit Aunt Arlene's description perfectly. Beside her stood a tall, lean man with a bushy mustache, wear-ing a stiff, fitted suit and cap.

The woman saw me and strode briskly towards me, the man following. Clearly, this was Mrs. Morgan and I felt a thrill in my heart. I debated whether to approach her or just wait with my bags, but her purposeful stride took the decision out of my hands. She was before me in an instant.

She looked at the yellow flower in my lapel and nodded approvingly, her eyes bright as our eyes met.

She drew in a great, satisfied breath. "Good day. Do I have the pleasure of greeting Miss Judith Mintz from America?" She smiled warmly and nodded.

"Yes, Mrs. Morgan, I'm Judith." I was finally here. She took my hand and shook it and I was instantly comfortable. Much like with Mrs.Weiss.

"I thought so. I hardly needed the flower for confirmation. You are precisely the picture of the girl I imagined. Welcome to England, Judith." She released my hand. "Might I ask how your journey was? I heard there was a terrible storm. Were you caught in it?"

"Yes, Mrs. Morgan, I was. And sea sick for a day or two while the ship climbed and crashed." I laughed. "I might have done better if I hadn't stood looking out the ship's porthole the entire time. I just didn't want to miss anything."

She laughed. "Oh you are a spirited one. And look at you. Just arrived from your lengthy travels, crossing the ocean all by yourself and none the worse for wear." She chuckled. "I had heard this about you. My cousin—your Aunt Arlene—was chock full of stories about your abilities and— Alfred, please take Miss Mintz's bags to the car."

Alfred muttered into his mustache, hoisted my things and headed out of the station at a long-legged pace.

"The girls can't wait to meet you," said Mrs. Morgan, marching rapidly after Alfred. Apparently, nobody ambled leisurely here in England. I hurried to keep up. "They've not had anyone to supervise them adequately, expected you to arrive this morning, not your fault of course, just being that it is the first day and the girls are spirited as girls are wont to be after summer holidays…"

Alfred had deposited my belongings in the trunk of a black

car and hurriedly opened the passenger doors for us. Mrs. Morgan kept a constant, lively conversation going as we sat ourselves in the back seat of the car. Alfred shut the doors, got in on the right side, where the steering wheel was, and we drove off.

"It's only a short drive from the Eccles train station to Thornton. Your aunt Arlene and I are not merely cousins, but the best of friends Oh, since childhood! She and I lived near each other and grew up together in Manchester. Oh, she is a darling! This is Peel Street. Have a look over there, fairly new housing built alongside the railway. And over there, you can see the factory that produces the famous Eccles cakes exported across the world. We're approaching Liverpool Road and will be crossing the Bridgewater Canal Towpath up ahead, have a look. On your left in the distance are large estates that were built for the wealthy during the latter half of the nineteenth century."

"Mrs. Morgan, will we be arriving soon?"

"Yes, we're almost there."

"Would you mind if we discussed my schedule?"

"Not at all." She laughed. "What was I thinking? Your writing lessons will take place once per day from eleven o'clock until twelve-fifteen, Sunday through Thursday. We've decided it's best to form a combined writing session, although admittedly the class size and dynamics might pose a bit of a challenge."

"Combined? How many girls would attend a combined class, Mrs. Morgan?"

"All of them." She saw my face and laughed. "Yes. All twenty-five girls. It did seem like a brilliant idea when we thought of it. How does it strike you?"

I didn't know. I was a little stunned. "The mix of ages, I

think, might present a challenge. Thirteen-year-olds, fourteen-year-olds together with fifteen through seventeen-year-olds? I've never taught a mix of ages like that before."

"Yes, I understand and we can consider the arrangement experimental. It's not at all how we arrange the classes, you know, but perhaps it might work for writing. Juggling the dozens of studies in our curriculum, it seemed the only available option." She looked hopeful, waiting for my approval.

Would it really affect my teaching? Who knew? Everything I would do here would be an experiment. "I want to be of service to the school, Mrs. Morgan, whatever you need. I may have to adjust my lessons, but…" I was thinking aloud. After meeting the girls, I would have a better picture of what I was dealing with. "…I'll do my best."

"Splendid. With your can-do attitude, all will be marvelous. Now, for Shabbos I think you know, the girls go home except for Thornton Shabbos, which takes place mid-winter. And one more school Shabbos in the springtime."

"How do the girls travel home?"

"Good question. I make the arrangements for the teachers to travel with the girls. Oh, yes, and some girls can't go home, although generally there aren't many, but those girls must be placed by you, at friends or relatives. Please let me know by Thursday evening who they are and where they wish to go, so I can make the arrangements."

My mind started reeling. I needed a place to go myself.

"I require you as housemother, morning and night and…" she leaned towards me in a conspiratorial manner, "…I would look forward to enjoying your company for Shabbos, if you care to join me at my Manchester home. Wouldn't that be marvelous?" She smiled and her shoulders raised slightly, her head tilted. "You might think about it and let me know." She paused and gazed upwards, counting her fingers. "Have I forgotten anything?"

I wondered whether Mrs. Morgan had a husband or children in Manchester. I didn't dare ask. She wasn't old. Was she alone? Out the window, I saw a pretty park as we turned left onto a private road. Beyond the park I could see a small waterway.

"Mrs. Morgan, would I be able to go off grounds when I'm not needed?"

"Yes, of course, Judith." She clasped her hands and looked excited. "There's Thornton."

I caught a glimpse of a building up ahead, set back, mostly hidden by trees. Mrs. Morgan had called it 'Thornton'.

"Does the building have a name?"

We turned right onto a gravel driveway and approached huge ornate, wrought-iron twin gates held up at the sides by two rectangular stone blocks. Eight-foot hedges flanked the blocks and created a wall for what seemed like miles in each direction. Alfred jumped out and unlocked the gates and opened them wide.

"Yes. The home is called Thornton, like the park we just passed. The grounds and home belonged to a Sir Richard Thornton, an English nobleman, whose family had posted it for sale a few years before the war broke out. Our benefactor, Mr. Avrohom Strom, bought the home at auction and upon hearing of our plans to open a boarding school, graciously donated it to us. And now we have it. The perfect place in the perfect spot, don't you think?"

I did. "It is perfect."

"You'll see…even more perfect inside." She sighed happily.

We drove through the gates and then stopped for Alfred to relock the gates. The grounds were very pretty, flowers and carefully trimmed shrubs and trees of all sizes were artfully planted alongside the meandering driveway.

"Will I have a key to the gate?" I asked Mrs. Morgan.

"Certainly I have a key for you, only you must promise you'll guard it well. We don't allow the girls off grounds, except with adult supervision, and we keep the gates locked at all times. If you go out for a good part of the day, please let me know where you'll be. You do understand that I feel responsible for your safety."

"Yes, I understand."

We drove left on an angle and the building loomed ahead of us. I took off my cap and stared. It wasn't the hugest building I'd ever seen but it was ornate and lavish. Thick pillars supported the second story while wrought-iron arches, adorned with graceful leaves, connected the pillars. The front façade was covered in multi-hued stone and English ivy that climbed in intriguing patterns.

As we pulled up to the front of the mansion, I saw a two-story archway shadowing a wrap-around veranda and massive double entry doors of carved wood. Softly padded chairs and couches were arranged invitingly, hinting at infinite possibilities.

"Isn't it marvelous? I never tire of looking at Thornton." Mrs. Morgan sighed, then quickly turned to me. "One last thing. Just so you know, Judith." Mrs. Morgan laid her hand on my arm. "Oh, my Heavens…" she stammered. Her eyes were on my hair.

Her mouth opened.

Sometimes I would get that reaction.

"Sorry, I didn't mean to stare. My… my daughter had hair the same color… as yours." She looked away and seemed to struggle to compose herself. She looked back at me. "It's a beautiful color. I can understand why you kept it covered." She inhaled deeply. "Judith, I am so very pleased to have you here. I think you will do remarkably well. Just so you know…" She halted, clearing her throat. "It's an advantage to be prepared for, er, challenges, don't you think?"

She looked at me. I waited. What was she saying? "Right. I'll plunge straight in," she said. "Some of the teachers were opposed to my hiring you, I'm sorry to say. It's nothing against you personally, just being of the old school, it was difficult for them to accept an American as part of the establishment."

My heart sank. So it was true. Oh, no. Everything Mrs. Weiss had told me was true.

"I'm absolutely certain that when they get to know you, they will change their minds." She gave me an encouraging smile. "And I will stand behind you every step of the way." She gave my hand a pat. "I am your ally, Judith."

I struggled to come to terms with it. "I met Shirley Weiss on the train. She told me to expect this. I was hoping she was wrong."

"My friend Shirley! Another close friend. Oh, she is a dear. Your aunt and Shirley and I were school chums, our homes right near one another, oh the times we had…"

Mrs. Morgan was reveling in her happy memories while I was drowning in dread. "Mrs. Morgan, how many are there? I mean, opposed to me."

"Of the eight teachers..." she looked at me with deep sadness, "...four are opposed."

Oh, no. Half of the teaching staff. I took a deep breath and blew it out slowly. What was I dealing with? I tried to conjure up an image of old-world ladies, old school. Nothing materialized. I didn't know anyone like that. Did it really matter? No. I hadn't traveled all the way across the ocean to become involved in school politics. I had come to help. I reaffirmed my resolve that I would be the best house mother and writing teacher I could be.

I heard Mrs. Morgan say, "Mainly two. Come, let's go inside and meet the girls."

Alfred had opened our car doors. We exited and Mrs. Morgan led the way up the wide, rounded mosaic stone steps. Lions greeted us at the top. Were they old school? They weren't smiling. Probably.

Beyond the lions, to my left, I caught a glimpse of someone partially hidden behind a pillar. An imposing, strong-looking, tall woman in black stood still as a statue, staring at me. I quickly looked away.

A chill went up my spine.

I hurried after Mrs. Morgan.

CHAPTER 3

I entered a massive front foyer.

"Welcome to Thornton," said Mrs. Morgan.

Gleaming brown and white marble flooring cast glimmers from below, while from the second story, a three-tiered, circular chandelier bearing at least a million crystals, showered sparkles of light from above. My eyes darted everywhere, trying to absorb the grandeur. Uncomfortable red-cushioned seats stood along the walls. Most eye-catching was the centerpiece of the room, where twin staircases in red and ivory curved their way down from the upper floor's two opposite sides and curved until very nearly touching, then flared outward in graceful arcs onto the main floor.

I felt myself gape.

"This is Thornton's grand dining hall, one of my favorite rooms," Mrs. Morgan's voice echoed to my left. She stood under a ten-foot high carved archway. I came and stood beside her and gasped. The room was enormous. Its ceiling was lavishly embellished along the edges, a garden painted across its entire domed center. A huge chandelier hung down over the table, much like the one in the lobby, but this one held hundreds of miniature candle-shaped bulbs. The table was at least twenty feet long but looked average-sized or even small in the gigantic room. Its pedestal legs stood on a magnificent red and gold carpet that matched the eight sets of heavy, floor-to-ceiling brocade drapery and the twenty-some dining chairs.

"Is this where we eat?" I had finally found my tongue, although for some reason I had whispered.

"Not often. Such a kingly setting, how do you think it would affect our digestion?" She laughed. "No, we reserve it for Yom Tov and special occasions. Come. I'll show you where we commoners dine."

She marched off and I followed in her wake through a service door into a large wood paneled room, decorated with many leather couches, chairs and low tables, all in deep brown.

"This is the parlor, the room where we daven and on through here…" she led the way through a small corridor and pushed through a swinging door, "oh, hello Paula and Vicky, this is our new house mother, a young one, you'll like her." She chuckled.

The most delicious smells wafted in the air. Loaves of bread were cooling on the counters and my insides begged. The two cooks were flour-dusted and jolly-looking, wearing puffy hats on their heads and wide white aprons around them. They stood together and extended heartwarming grins.

"Hallo, love. You a good eater? You don't look like it," said Paula or Vicky, shaking her head at me and then laughing. "We'll try to fix that."

"What's your name, pretty red-haired miss?"

"I'm Judith. Your bread smells heavenly."

"Paula, fetch some nice scones for Judith, there's a love. She must be starving," said Vicky. "So you're the American?" She leaned in close and gave me an impish grin. Paula who was a bit taller and broader brought a large wrapped sampling of scones. My stomach lurched. I hadn't eaten anything at all that day.

"Guilty," I said, my hand up. "I see word has gotten out."

They laughed heartily.

"You can't hide a thing like that," said Paula. "Here you go, love." I took the package and involuntarily inhaled. "You don't look so bad." She eyed me good naturedly. "You're my first American."

"I say she looks right well."

"Nice hair."

"Very nice."

I smiled at their endorsements. This seemed like a nice place to visit, especially if I was hungry. "Thanks, ladies. I think I'll visit you again soon." I gestured at my package whose aroma was causing me to slightly swoon.

"We'll be serving dinner shortly like you asked, Mrs. M," said Vicky.

"Yes, marvelous. Speaking of dinner, I was just about to show Judith our dining hall." She swung the door open.

"Nice meeting you," I called to Vicky and Paula, who stood together, watching me go.

Mrs. Morgan led the way through a narrow hallway.

"Paula and Vicky were employed by the Yeshiva in Manchester but we snatched them away as soon as their services were no longer required. Not because the students didn't love their cooking. The yeshiva actually preferred to hire a male cook, and the students were positively devastated. Paula and Vicky were thrilled to join us."

"They do seem happy," I commented.

"Yes. A jolly pair."

Mrs. Morgan pushed through another swinging door and held it open for me. This room was beautifully wood-paneled, with lacquered beams across the ceiling. An extra-long, ornately carved wooden table, flanked by countless chairs, extended down the length of it. Two smallish round tables stood at the corners of the room, surrounded by four chairs. On a large expanse of wall hung a wall-sized painting of a summer scene, a grassy field dotted with fruit trees.

"This used to be a game room for the noble people and to my thinking, it is far more suitable for dining, don't you think? We have the table extended to its fullest length."

"Do the girls eat all their meals here?"

"Well, I dare say some of the girls have at one time or another absconded with a few scones and eaten them upstairs, but yes, this is where morning, noon and evening meals are served. And tea. We've firmly established that you're not British, neverthe-less, you're bound to love tea time." She laughed. "Let's go up. The stairs to the sleep quarters are right through this door."

"I suppose we don't use the magnificent dual staircase up front."

She laughed and went through a door at the end of the room. "Oh, no. Hardly. Unless we stage a ball, which I highly doubt." She laughed again.

I smiled. We were in a wide hallway, the entire length of its outer wall completely made of glass. The late afternoon sunshine streamed through and lit up the back of the building, revealing a wrap-around porch and beyond it a garden, large enough to be a park. Various benches and wicker chairs beckoned me to sit there, among the trees. It had been a long day.

"Lots of doors, as you can see," Mrs. Morgan said. I pulled my attention away from the outdoors. Mrs. Morgan held open a wide door which opened to a stairway. "The four classrooms are down this Sunshine Corridor, I like to call it. You might wish to explore the classrooms after dinner. At the farthermost point of this corridor, is a magnificent sunroom and whenever we spend Shabbos here, I unofficially claim it as mine." She beamed at me. "But more importantly, Judith, it is to be your writing classroom. Make sure and visit it tonight. The very last room. You will adore it! Now, let's ascend. These stairs were built for the servants." She leaned towards me, amusement in her eyes. "We are all servants, are we not?" She laughed.

"Mrs. Morgan, where is everyone?"

We ascended plush carpeted stairs of brown, red and ivory that were wide enough to accommodate three or four people. Carved mahogany spindles supported a railing, though Mrs. Morgan didn't use the railing. Paintings hung on the walls and I would have like to pause to look at them but it didn't seem like the right time, especially at Mrs. Morgan's pace.

"The girls are most likely in their sleeping quarters. There were no classes today and the teachers who greeted the girls this morning have gone home by now."

I remembered the ominous tall lady in black.

We arrived on the second floor, a wide walkway of polished wood and sitting areas.

"Here on the right of the stairwell are sleeping quarters for the teachers and their families when they stay for Thornton Shabbos."

I peeked in and saw three neat bedrooms tastefully decorated with matching coverlets, curtains and a small dresser or two.

"And here on the left," Mrs. Morgan said as she marched past the stairway across the walkway, "are the students' quarters. The girls apparently are... what—?!" She clutched her heart.

I saw a spacious room with rows of beds and a shambled wreck. Pillows were on the floor, quilts were half off the beds, socks and shoes were scattered everywhere and cabinet doors were open, garments in disarray.

"Oh, my gracious!" Mrs. Morgan had her hand at her throat. "What on earth..?" Her head darted from side to side taking it all in. "I don't know what could have come over them! Girls!! Girls!!! Oh, they must be about somewhere!" She looked at me fiercely. "This is not like them. The room is always neat and tidy. Something must have happened. GIRLS!!!"

Mrs. Morgan continued to shout for the girls as she walked purposefully to another door. The door led to another enormous bedroom, in the middle of which were standing the girls of Thornton, at attention.

"Girls! I've never...! What on earth possessed you? Please explain yourselves!"

I looked at the girls. They looked at us. Pretty and pale, the girls looked well-mannered, well-groomed, refined, obedient. And guilty.

"I am utterly astounded at the state of the room. Far, far beneath your standards as students of Thornton and as English young ladies. What sort of impression can your new house mother receive under these circumstances? First impressions last a lifetime sometimes, and negative impressions are terribly difficult to undo. I would hope that this behavior is not repeated in the future and you portray yourselves as responsible, well-mannered young ladies at all times."

She cleared her throat and took a few deep breaths, composing herself. I had the feeling that it was a rare occurrence for Mrs. Morgan to become so irritated. Although she hadn't raised her voice, her disapproval was palpable.

"Mrs. Morgan," said an older-looking girl with a serious face. She stepped forward, her eyes huge. "Representing my fellow students, I apologize for the reckless manner and activities that produced the untidy state of our quarters. In addition, we the senior students, should have contained any unruly activities and seen to it that the room was made tidy. Before you arrived. So sorry." She stepped back into place, her eyes cast down.

"Very well, Ruthie. I accept your apology, as representative of the entire group. And girls, it would serve you well to pattern yourselves after Ruthie. In more ways than one." She looked archly around the group.

Then her mood changed and she smiled. "Girls, this is Miss Mintz, your new house mother and writing teacher. You are to treat her with the utmost respect and strictly follow her direction. Dinner will be served promptly at seven and I'm confident that by then the room will be perfectly tidy. Let's put this incident behind us."

She turned and marched out. I was hoping for a longer

introduction. I looked at the girls. They looked at me. What now? Have them clean up the room? Learn their names?

"Miss Mintz, your chamber is this way," Mrs. Morgan called.

I turned and found Mrs. Morgan at the end of the hallway, waiting for me in front of a doorway.

"Here are your quarters. I hope you like them."

The room was small and cozy. Mrs. Morgan pointed out a single bed with a puffy comforter and matching pillow, a bureau with drawers and hanging space, and a soft arm chair. A washroom. And a window that faced the beautiful grounds. I breathed. "It's perfect."

"I trust you know your way around now, Judith. The next two doors are the girls' rooms. There is an adjoining door in between the two rooms. The stairs lead down to the Sunshine Corridor, the dining area to your left, the classrooms to your right."

I nodded, remembering the layout. I pulled open one of the bureau drawers and peeked inside. A bullfrog rested calmly within. I smoothly shut the drawer before Mrs. Morgan could see. I was getting the feeling that the English girls had much more spunk than I had anticipated.

"Mrs. Morgan, is your room up here?"

"Heavens no, Miss Mintz. My quarters are on the ground floor. I won't be hearing much down there, so..." she gave me a charming smile "...unless it's an emergency, I plan on sleeping through the night. Oh, and please have the girls in the dining hall for supper by seven. Just enough time for you to freshen up." She smiled.

She turned and marched away.

"Mrs. Morgan. One more thing, Mrs. Morgan." I hurried to

catch her. She paused at the top of the stairs.

"Yes, Judith, what is it?"

"Mrs. Morgan, is there a time I can discuss the girls with you? Their backgrounds, where they come from, who their families are. What their history is...?

"We'll talk after dinner. All the girls are from fine families, Judith. You know, I put my reputation on the line and brought you here trusting that you would be the right one for the job. I think you are the right one." She looked at me strongly. "You won't breach that trust, will you?"

"Mrs. Morgan, I will do everything in my power to honor your trust."

"Good. See you at seven." She marched down the stairs, her back straight.

I thought about what Mrs. Morgan had just said. I believed I could do a good job. I entered my room. I took a bite of the scone. Delicious.

I slid the bureau drawer open.

The frog was still there.

CHAPTER 4

It was time to speak to the girls of Thornton.

I walked down the hallway and entered the dormitory room. The girls were milling about, chatting. I cleared my throat. Everything stopped. All eyes locked onto mine.

"Hello. I'd like to begin again. I'm very happy to be your house mother this year. And I look forward to having you in my writing class."

"You have an accent," said a small dark-haired girl with braids. Some of the other girls shushed her and I caught her name.

"Yes, Nettie, I do. I think you do, too. Isn't that interesting? We both have accents. Do you know why?"

Another smallish, button-faced girl with bangs, raised her hand and spoke breathlessly, "Oh, I know! It's because you come from a different country and my mother told me that in no other country do they speak English, besides here."

I struggled to contain my smile. "Well, I'm sure there are some who would agree with that. What's your name?"

"Blimale."

"Well, Blimale, your answer tells part of the story. I come

from America, across the Atlantic Ocean…"

"Do you keep Shabbos there?" asked a soft-spoken, very small girl with big brown eyes.

I couldn't suppress my smile. "And what's your name?"

"Esther," she said shyly. "Everyone calls me Etty." I reviewed the names in my head, Etty, Netty, Blimale. These three appeared very young.

"I have a lot to tell you, Etty, but we must get ready for dinner. Briefly, we have Shabbos and Yomtov just like you do. We speak a bit differently than you, but the language we speak, we call English." I smiled big and nodded at her incredulous look. "It makes life interesting to hear different accents, I think. I'm looking forward to telling you about myself and I'm sure we'll have time for it throughout the year. Girls," I said to the group, "you needn't be afraid of me and run away in the middle of a pillow fight." The girls looked at each other, some giggled, their hands over their mouths. "I think that's good fun. Also, I wish to thank whoever placed a welcome gift in my bureau drawer. So thoughtful."

I quickly looked at each of the girls. Three girls blushed bright pink. Were they the ones? They looked too old to be catching frogs.

"I'd like to be a bit early to dinner, if possible, so I'll wait for all of you at the bottom of the stairs in fifteen minutes. And to put on a good show for Mrs. Morgan and any other staff members, we'll enter the dining room in pairs." A bit of murmuring ensued. "May I have a volunteer to supervise the pairing?"

A girl came forward, the same one who had apologized to Mrs. Morgan. "You're Ruthie, aren't you?"

"Yes, Miss Mintz. I'll supervise the girls. And in the name of all the girls, may I say welcome."

"Thank you, Ruthie. How old are you?"

"I'm seventeen years old."

She seemed very responsible and mature. "Are you the oldest in the group?"

"No, Miss Mintz. Two girls are older than I."

I looked at the group, trying to guess who they were. It was getting late. Fourteen minutes left. "See you soon. I'm relying on you, Ruthie." She nodded.

I turned away. A thought occurred to me and I turned back at the door. "Girls, you have a few minutes to clean your room. All blankets and pillows neatly on beds and your clothing straightened. I'll inspect it later when we return from dinner."

I went quickly to my room. I unpacked my things and splashed water on my face. I looked at my reflection. *So, Judy, this is it. What you begged for.* Hurriedly, I brushed my hair. *Just get them to dinner.* What happens after? I put down my brush. I walked down the hall. *I'll need to learn all their names. What about the teachers? They don't want me here.* I descended the stairs. One step at a time.

I opened the door. *Breathe,* I told myself. *Hold the door. Wait for the girls.* Will they come? I looked at my watch. The fifteen minutes were up. Now, sixteen minutes. Not a sound. I waited. *Please come.* Seventeen minutes. *I'm not going up there…*

I heard footsteps. Ruthie appeared, leading the group in twos. The smallest girls were in the front, the tallest ones at the back. I breathed. The girls descended with their heads held high. I nodded at Ruthie. It was a relief to know there was someone I could rely on. I backed up as they emerged from the stairwell. I put my finger to my lips and led them to the dining room door and we entered the dining hall in silence. I stood aside as the girls filed toward the table and stood at their seats.

Mrs. Morgan was seated at the far end of the long table with two other women who were dressed severely in dark navy dresses with high collars. Was one of them the woman who had stared at me? I wasn't sure. The two women appeared stiff and starched and wore wigs that were formal and tightly wrapped. I approached the table, wondering if I was meant to sit with them. The two women were as still as stone and didn't look at me.

Mrs. Morgan had seen us and glanced at a round watch clipped to her collar. She nodded.

"Good evening, Mrs. Morgan," I said, as I approached her. "The girls have arrived for dinner."

Mrs. Morgan smiled up at me. "So I see. Quite good, Judith. Spot on." She rose from her chair and announced, "Girls, you may be seated and begin dinner."

The girls sat down and the room became animated. There was salad and potatoes with gravy and chicken. Paula, I think it was, came in carrying a soup tureen and began ladling soup into bowls. Everything smelled delicious. I said to Mrs. Morgan. "I'm not familiar with the dining rules. Am I to sit together with you here?"

Mrs. Morgan opened her mouth to answer, but one of the women said, "It would be best if you sit with the girls." It was hard to tell which of the two women had spoken. There had been no movement at all.

Mrs. Morgan looked uncomfortable and coughed slightly.

"Ahem, well, yes, but perhaps not. In the past we've seated the house mother at her own private table so she can see to the girls, if necessary. Have a look, Judith, at the corner table, there. Rather cozy, don't you think?" She lowered her voice and moved towards my ear. "I would sit there myself if I could."

I looked where her chin had pointed and saw a round table with four chairs and a place setting for one. I liked it. It was good for me, a private place to observe girls. And teachers.

"Of course, I could squeeze you in nearby me, if you wish." Mrs. Morgan was amusing herself, I thought. Her eyes twinkled.

"Oh, that won't be necessary, Mrs. Morgan," I said quickly. "The corner table is fine. Thank you." I turned to go, but she touched my hand and I stopped.

She took in a big breath. "Alright, then." She blinked rapidly and breathed in and out. "Ahem…" She was clearly uncomfortable. "Ladies, this is Judith Mintz, who is our new house mother… as well as our writing instructor …as you know… oh…" She faltered. The women did not look her way, just stared stonily at the table.

Mrs. Morgan cleared her throat. She took my elbow firmly and brought me closer. There would be no mistake now to whom she was speaking. She rapped on the tabletop twice. I held my breath. "Mrs. Strassfeld, Mrs. Mark, allow me to introduce Miss Judith Mintz," she announced with firm, clear articulation. "Thornton's new house mother and writing instructor, who with *great* courage has traveled to join our establishment. I'm *certain* you good ladies of impeccable quality wish to *welcome* her."

Silence, thick and unyielding, sucked the air from my lungs. I wanted to disappear. A fire rose inside me and crept into my cheeks. The women raised their eyes briefly and looked in my direction. One nodded slightly and said, "Welcome," in an unwelcome tone.

The other woman regarded me with unmistakable disdain, her mouth clamped tight. I tried to smile but felt myself grimace. Her mouth opened slightly and said, "Thornton was established for the finest young ladies of our community. Our responsibility is to instill further refinement." Her sharp English accent, and low tone, colored her words with foreboding. She stared straight ahead, as if looking at me was beneath her.

I swallowed. I was sure now that this was the woman I had seen outside before. She was truly intimidating. Sharp eyes, prominent cheekbones, dominating eyebrows. Maybe now would be a good time for me to retreat to my corner.

"So good to have met you," I choked. "I'll be going now."

"Yes. Splendid, Judith," said Mrs. Morgan, attempting to be cheery. "Bon Apetit!"

I tried to maintain my dignity and not rush away. As I walked carefully over, I was glad about the corner table. A salad on pretty china and a goblet of water beckoned. I was famished. Soup was waiting in a bowl for me. Exactly what I needed. I sat down. Although the soup was a strange shade of green, I ate it all, wondering until the last spoonful what it was.

A pretty girl appeared, honey hair and blue eyes and a sweet smile.

"I'm to ask if you wish another helping of consomme, otherwise known as soup, Miss Mintz."

She was holding a large platter of potatoes and chicken that smelled divine.

"Thank you, no. Although it was delicious, I'll pass. And your name is…?"

She set the platter down in the middle of the table. "I'm Pearl. It's my day to help serve."

"You're doing a good job. How old are you?"

"I'm fourteen and a half, ma'am. Old enough for kitchen duties." She smiled and dimples flashed on her pink-cheeked face.

I smiled back. She stood there fidgeting. "Do you know what kind of soup was served, Pearl?"

"Yes, it's Brussels sprouts soup. The cook's special recipe with summer squash and mushroom."

No wonder. I hardly knew what Brussels sprouts looked like, but I knew they were green. Pearl was looking at me expectantly, still fidgeting. "Is there something you want to tell me, Pearl?"

She blushed and said in a rush, "I love writing. I can't wait for your class." She smiled and did a mini-curtsy and hurried away.

I watched her go back to her seat. I looked at the whole group of girls. I had a good feeling about them.

I suddenly felt heat on my face and was shocked to find I was being stared at. Glared at. It was the intimidating teacher, Mrs. Mark or Mrs. Strassfeld, from the end of the long table. My innards clenched. I nodded to her and she stiffened and looked away. I reminded myself that it was just the first day, the first few hours, actually, and there was plenty to feel good about. I would do my job and try to stay out of Mrs. Mark's or Mrs. Strassfeld's way. I picked at my salad, finding some unknown vegetables among the ones known. I ate it all.

I reached for the potato platter and saw a smiling girl

standing there. She was tall and strongly built, with round apple cheeks and twinkly eyes. I found myself smiling.

"Hello, there. Did you come to visit me?"

She nodded. "I've already eaten my dinner."

"You're quick. What's your name?"

"I'm Henchie." She looked down at the platter I was holding and her eyes grew big.

"Did you enjoy your dinner, Henchie?"

"Yes, immensely. I would take a second helping but it would be impolite." She looked at my platter again.

"Would you like some of mine? I couldn't possibly eat all this."

Henchie's eyes lit up. "May I?"

"Please. I'd be happy to have you join me."

Henchie took the chair opposite me and happily took a portion from the platter. She reminded me of my brothers, eating with gusto. She patted her mouth with the cloth napkin. "I'm quite often very hungry."

"You must visit me often then. How old are you, Henchie?"

She swallowed. "I'm fifteen." She stood and tucked her chair in.

The clinking of a glass quieted the room. Mrs. Morgan stood and asked for attention, clinking her glass with a spoon.

"Thank you, Miss Mintz," said Henchie softly. "I'll be going now." She hurried to her seat.

"Welcome to our first dinner at Thornton," said Mrs. Morgan. "I am pleased to see all the girls returned from summer holiday, fresh and eager to begin. I know I speak for all of us in saying I look forward to a year of learning, of growth and working together..."

I listened with half an ear and guardedly observed the two teachers who had snubbed me. They both wore fierce expressions, especially the one who had made a statement. Their coloring and build was similar, dark and tall and broad-shouldered, though not heavy. They seemed so...irritated. It sent a shudder through me. What was bothering them? Was I really so different from them? From the girls?

They sat board-straight while Mrs. Morgan spoke, not moving an inch, their eyes dark and unsmiling. I admitted that in that sense, I was surely different than they were. Being spontaneous, my face usually broadcasted my feelings, and I was generally happy and liked everyone. If they could see me as unthreatening to the girls and to them, it would really help. But looking at them, I felt it would take a miracle to get through their impenetrable wall. I heard my name and snapped my attention back to Mrs. Morgan.

"...Mintz for consenting to cross the vast ocean on our behalf. The schedule for dining help will be posted on the stairwell board and you have your schedules for classes and lights out. Please remember to thank Paula and Vicky for their delicious culinary cuisine. Those who have kitchen duty, thank you for your service, the rest of you may return to your rooms. Miss Mintz, this way, please..."

Mrs. Morgan marched out.

I jumped up and quickly followed her.

CHAPTER 5

Mrs. Morgan was waiting for me in the corridor as I emerged. She promptly turned right and I followed her past the stairwell door and past two more doorways. "A classroom, a closet," Mrs. Morgan announced as she marched by at a fast clip, her heels tapping on the wooden floor. She turned into a dark alcove to the right, which led to a beautifully carved door. Mrs. Morgan unlocked the door and held it open for me.

I walked inside a small hushed room. Mrs. Morgan shut the door firmly and went to the chair behind the desk. "Please sit down, Judith."

I sat in a tightly upholstered chair in front of a mahogany desk and looked around. The room was without windows, an inner chamber. The walls, ceiling and floor were covered in rich paneling. A tapestry carpet adorned the space under the desk and chairs.

"Hardly any of Thornton's staff or students are ever invited here, but I felt it was the only way to speak to you, away from all eyes. It is my private sanctuary."

"I'm honored."

"Judith, I want to give you the girls' schedule from sunup to lights out." She withdrew a few sheets of paper from a neat pile and passed it to me. The heading read, *Thornton daily schedule 1950*. Quickly, I scanned the page. "Here is a compiled list of the girls and where they live and a brief family description. Yearly calendar." She passed two sheets of paper to me. "If questions arise, I am available for the answers. If you wish to post a letter, there is a box to the side of the main entry clearly marked 'Post'. Alfred takes the correspondence once a week and brings incoming correspondence to the table up front. Now that's squared away." She took a breath and folded her arms on the desk, leaning forward. "If you don't mind, may we be frank with one another?"

"Of course."

"Of course. Refraining from subtlety, two members of my staff showed intense disapproval towards you this evening."

"I couldn't help but notice."

"Right. Well, Mrs. Strassfeld and Mrs. Mark, although brilliant teachers, are your strongest opponents. The others, namely Mrs. Jacobson and Mrs. Werner, brilliant teachers as well, are milder by nature and not as vehemently opposed. They would approach you in a manner less... shall we say... less..?"

"Hostile?" I suggested.

She sniffed good-naturedly. "Strong word, but for lack of a better one, yes. In a less hostile manner."

"Question, Mrs. Morgan? Can you tell me which one is Mrs. Mark and which one is Mrs. Strassfeld?"

She laughed. "Good point. Pardon me for not introducing

you properly, only the tone of the conversation, or lack thereof, didn't quite allow for it."

It felt good to laugh. Mrs. Morgan was a gem. She reached for a picture book on her desk and opened it. "There," she turned the book so I could see and pointed to the woman who had disdainfully remarked that Thornton was only suitable for refined people. Meaning, not me. "That is Mrs. Strassfeld, brilliant woman, an outstanding teacher. The highest standards. Mrs. Mark is here. Another brilliant teacher." She pointed out the woman who had said 'welcome' without looking at me.

"Thank you, Mrs. Morgan. May I see Mrs. Werner and Mrs. Jacobson?" Good to know in advance who my adversaries were.

She showed me an intelligent, refined woman. "This is Mrs. Jacobson. And Mrs. Werner is right beside her, small and delicate but with great inner strength."

Neither one of these aristocratic-looking women had the fierceness of Mrs. Strassfeld. Or the aloofness of Mrs.Mark.

"Do you think I've gone through the worst of it, Mrs. Morgan?"

"I'm afraid not, my dear. Tell me, do you think you can withstand the onslaught that is bound to come?"

"I hope so. I plan to stay, no matter what. Is there any advice you can give me?"

"Yes. I would recommend that you keep a low profile. I will certainly do whatever I can. Know that I am behind you all the way, Judith. Please keep me informed and don't hesitate to consult with me, any time, day or night. And thank you for being so committed."

"Thank you Mrs. Morgan. If that's all, I think I'll go prepare tomorrow's lesson. I have lesson plans for each individual age group, but I need to rethink my plan to include the whole group."

"Very good, Judith. Don't forget to visit your class room, the sunroom." She beamed at me. "You'll adore it."

I stood and put out my hand. "I'm very glad I came."

She took my hand and covered it with her other hand. "Same here."

I exited Mrs. Morgan's study, proceeded to the hallway and then turned right. I passed a second narrow hallway off to the right, a doorway, another hallway and finally, a glass door.

I entered a room whose ceiling was completely glass. It was dark out and looking up, stars were everywhere. The room was bathed in starlight and moonlight. Mrs. Morgan was right. I adored it.

I could see couches, tables, chairs, armchairs and a portable blackboard. I mentally arranged the room, two long tables together end to end, the chairs and armchairs around them. I would do it tomorrow before class. I needed paper and pens. Did the school have secretaries? I would ask the girls.

The girls!!

I had forgotten that I told them I would inspect the room after dinner. I hurried back down the 'Sunshine Corridor' and found the stairwell.

I could hear shrieking as I went up.

I entered the main room. All sources of mayhem came to a halt. The room was a shambles. "I'm here to see what a good job you girls have done making the room orderly. I'm actually having trouble finding order." I looked around the room. Worse than before. I looked at the girls and saw faces tight with dread.

"It was tidy before we went to dinner," said a small, sincere girl. "Truly."

"Yes. Perfectly. Then…" another young girl said.

"You must believe us. We really did tidy everything. Before."

I remained silent, giving everyone a good moment to wallow in guilt. Now was a good time to lay down a few rules.

"I believe you," I said quietly. "And I don't mind that you play in the room. However." I looked at the girls' faces, one by one. "Only at specifically designated times. At all other times, the room stays tidy. In fifteen minutes, I will give you a detailed plan so it is perfectly clear what is expected of you. During those fifteen minutes, please return the room to its orderly state, like it was before dinner." I turned to go to my room.

"What if some of us didn't contribute to the disorder? Why must we work to correct a situation we didn't create?"

A strong, challenging voice. I studied the girls and found the speaker--a tall slim, brown-haired girl. I searched her face. She regarded me with bold eyes. "And you are?"

"What does it matter who I am as I'm merely one of the group who messes the room." Her chin came forward firmly. I detected a slight Slavic accent.

While I was thinking of a way to respond, I heard the girls trying to silence her, speaking her name.

"Well, Ruchama," I said. "Since you didn't contribute to the mess, I can hardly demand that you clean it up. But if you have a giving heart, you might offer to help." I waited for her response, but she looked away, impatiently. Was she trying to be difficult?

I looked around the room and found someone whose name I

knew, someone I could trust. "Ruthie? Please let me know when the room is ready for me."

"Yes, Miss Mintz."

I turned and headed to my room. What was going on with Ruchama? She was challenging me, outright. Not a good sign for the first day. I would need to learn more about her.

First things first.

In my room, I took out my notebook in which I had notated my lesson plans. I remembered sitting on the deck of the ship, Brittania, with plenty of time to dream and formulate ideas. Seemed like ages ago.

Now that I had met the girls, I wondered what changes I could make so my class would be suited for the combined ages. My mind began to churn.

I checked the schedule. Lights out at nine-thirty for the thirteen and fourteen-year-olds. And in the main room, ten o'clock. A note said that seventeen-year-olds could be granted an additional fifteen minutes. I quickly looked at the list of girls. There were three seventeen-year-olds. Ruthie, Miri and…Ruchama.

I looked at my watch. Nine o'clock.

The bureau caught my eye. I couldn't resist. I slid the drawer open. The frog was gone. Hmmm.

I sat down in the armchair and immersed myself in work.

Throat clearing caught my attention. Ruthie was standing in the doorway.

"The room is ready, Miss Mintz."

"Thank you, Ruthie. I'll be there in two minutes." She left.

I needed to think. They were good girls, I thought. Just a bit unruly, or 'spirited'. That was normal. I got up and asked myself what message I wanted to give them. They needed a firm hand and now was the time to put one in place. I set my notebook down on the frog-less bureau and headed back to the girls.

The room was orderly, I was pleased to see. The girls huddled in clusters. I walked around in silence, examining the edges and small spaces. I entered the adjoining bedroom. Eleven beds, their coverlets a bit crooked. Not perfect, but good enough for thirteen and fourteen-year-olds.

I returned to the main room, where the girls still huddled, looking apprehensive. I explored an alcove where I found two neatly made beds and a large, dust-free bureau. I glanced into the immense washroom. Clean. I returned to the main area and opened one of the cupboards lining the side wall. I peeked inside. No frogs. Just clean and neat. I opened another cupboard. Immaculate. I took a moment to glance out of one of the floor-to-ceiling windows that flanked the cupboards.

I turned to face the girls, keeping my face serious. "Well done."

A wave of relief washed over the room.

"Now," I said firmly, wanting to seize the moment. "Please gather around and listen well, as I generally don't like to repeat myself." There were twelve, well-spaced beds against the walls in the shape of an L. I chose the bed in the corner and sat down. I waved my hands to encourage the girls to come in close.

Hashem, help me make this good.

Tentatively, the girls came over. Only Ruchama hung back, contempt clearly on her face.

"To make our daily schedule perfectly clear, so there is no

question. One. Our day begins at seven. I expect each of you to rise, get dressed, make your bed and put away your night clothing, keeping your cupboards neat and the doors closed.

"Two. We leave at seven twenty-five for shacharis. Be on time. If you aren't well or you have a problem, please tell me right away. Follow your schedules for breakfast, morning classes, lunch break, afternoon classes, mincha and...tea. " I couldn't help smiling. It tickled me that tea was part of the schedule. "After all, everyone here is English."

"Not everyone," a sardonic voice said, from across the room. Ruchama, apparently commenting on my lack of English-ness. I ignored it.

"Three. Following tea, school work. You may use the sunroom or you may choose to work up here. But please. The room stays neat. If the day is warm and clear, you may go outdoors on the back patio or in the garden, but you must tell me first or there will be dire consequences. If you wish to discuss something with me, that would be an ideal time."

I looked around. The girls were with me.

"Four. We go to dinner as we did tonight at a quarter of seven. In pairs. After dinner, you may play a game or relax for forty-five minutes. Pillow Fight Day will be determined and granted...by your house mother." I paused and looked around. I pointed a finger at myself. I waited. They smiled.

"Five. The room must be tidied just as you did tonight before nine o'clock. I will come at nine to inspect it and I trust each night, it will look as good as it does now. After inspection... story time."

Murmuring ensued. Had I covered everything. "Questions?"

"What are we, children?" said a strong voice from afar. Ruchama again, flashing defiant eyes. "No thank you." She folded her arms.

I groaned inwardly.

I had my work cut out for me.

CHAPTER 6

"I love hearing a story, especially a good one," said a sparkly girl.

"Whether the stories are good or not will be entirely up to you," I told her.

"Up to me?"

"All of you."

"*We're* meant to read a story? Be dramatic?"

"I can be dramatic. I simply *adore* acting," said a small girl with enormous dark eyes. "Might we take turns reading?" Her eyes flashed dramatically.

I contained my smile. "Good idea, but not exactly what I had in mind," I said. "The stories will be about you."

"What?" said the button-face girl, whose name escaped me. "Story books about us?" She looked around, her face displaying mock dread. "Uh-oh." Her hand gripped her throat. Her face changed to a big smile. "Actually, mine would be funny."

"Girls," I said. "Every night, one of you will *tell* a story. Every person has a story. About yourselves, your families. Or something that happened to you. Please raise your hands if you sleep in the next room." Sparkly, Button-face, Drama Girl and seven others raised their hands.

"How about if we call you the 'Annex Girls'. Who from the Annex Girls would like to be the first to tell us a tale? Tell me your names first."

The dramatic girl immediately said, "I would. I'm Mindy. I tell great tales." Everyone laughed. "May I tell one now? I have many."

"We'll be here all night," said a sharp-looking girl with golden hair. She looked at me with keen eyes. "I'm Bychu. Annex."

I quickly glanced at my watch. Nine-twenty. "Sorry, Mindy, I see it's late and we won't have time for your story tonight. Annex girls, it's time for bed." Soft moans rose from the group. "Tell you what. Tonight I'll tell you a quick story about myself. And you'll have all day to think of something for tomorrow night. Please make yourselves comfortable."

The smaller girls settled on the bed in front of me while the older ones took space on the bed at my side. Ruchama was still in her chosen spot, leaning against the wall, her arms folded.

I lowered my voice. "I am a sandwich." Giggles erupted. "It's true. When I was born I wasn't a sandwich, but I became one after a few years."

"You're not really a sandwich..." said Mindy, her large eyes widening.

"Let her talk," a voice said.

"Oh yes, I am. Not just any sandwich." I leaned forward and deepened my voice. "A brother sandwich." More giggles. "You see, three brothers were born before me. Then I, a girl. Then three younger brothers after me. I am the girl in the middle of a

- 46 -

brother sandwich."

"How terribly awful for you not to have sisters and only brothers," wailed a girl.

"Au contraire, my dear girl, my parents showered me with clothing and outings and girly toys. My brothers were full of unstoppable energy and always at fault, no matter what happened. I actually learned a great deal from them." I smiled big, recalling the outrageous times. "It made me who I am."

"So being a sandwich was a good thing?"

"Oh, yes. It really was. Once, when I was ten, my father suggested that he take my brothers on an overnight trip, with tents and flashlights and picnic supper. It seemed so exciting and I wanted to go with them, although my mother didn't. I begged my father to let me come. He wasn't sure it would be a place for a girl. I convinced him that I would be like the boys and do whatever they did. I offered to make all the sandwiches and my brothers, who liked my sandwiches— I always put pickle slices inside— bombarded my father with unceasing begging until he let me come.

"We drove a long way to get to the mountains and found a nice clearing to make our camp and put up three tents. Then we hiked up a mountain and found a beautiful place to eat the delicious sandwiches I made. We were cleaning up and I went to retrieve a runaway bag when I saw a yellow and black striped thick rope sliding in front of me."

"Oh, no! Was it a snake?!" Mindy asked, her fingers on her lip, her eyes bulging.

"Yes. A rattlesnake. I saw the rattle. I was frozen with fear but my brothers were suddenly there. The older ones pulled me back and went in front of me. The younger ones stood behind me, holding my hands. We inched back together. The snake watched us and flicked its tongue. We kept backing up until we were at our picnic table and in a blink, we were scurrying back down the mountain to our campsite. My little brothers still held my hands. My older brothers talked non-stop about the snake the entire way down, telling my father how brave I had been."

"But you must have been so scared!"

"Believe me, I was very scared, and I looked for snakes each step of the way. I insisted that everyone examine my tent and sleeping blanket countless times before I would go in. Luckily, my father slept in the tent with me." The girls looked at me in a daze, lost in the story.

I stood up. "And that's my story. Right now, Annex Girls, please get into your night clothes quickly and I'll be in shortly to say goodnight."

The Annex Girls moaned halfheartedly, stood reluctantly, and then scampered to their room. I shut the adjoining doors and returned to the remaining group. "Your turn now. We have time for one or two stories until lights out. Who will be first?"

Feverish whispering amongst them didn't produce a volunteer. "While you're gathering your thoughts, I'll pop into the Annex and be back in a jiffy."

I entered The Annex and the girls were more or less getting into their night clothes, the room not too badly strewn with the cast-offs. Seeing me, there was a flurry of arms into nightshirts and a scramble into the beds. I couldn't help but smile. They were good girls.

All eleven of them. I remembered a few names...Mindy,

Blimale, Etty, other names on the tip of my tongue. Maybe Netty? "Good night, girls. I'll overlook it tonight but from now on, clothes go on the hanger or in the dirty laundry container. You do have one, don't you?"

"There's a chute," said a girl. Bychu, I remembered. "Inside that cupboard there." She pointed to to a two-door square at the side of the cupboards.

"I see. Girls, please use it. Everyone, say your prayers and lights out in five minutes. Who would like to be in charge of shutting the light tonight?"

"I'll do it," said Bychu.

"Thank you, Bychu. Girls, I look forward to seeing you tomorrow. Have a good night." I kissed my fingers and waved them.

Responses of 'good night' and 'good night, Miss Mintz' and one 'don't let the bugs bite' followed me out. I shut the double doors with a feeling of satisfaction.

One down, two to go.

What time was it? Nine thirty-five.

I returned to the corner bed and sat down. Many of the girls were now on the bed in front of me, their eyes on me. Some eyes were bright, some intense, some humorous, some serious, some sweet. "I must learn your names," I said, almost to myself. "Alright, who's first?"

"I volunteer," said a fair-haired girl with intelligent eyes. "I'm Brenda and I'm from London. I love to read and when faced with a lack of reading material, which happens quite often, I read the dictionary."

"What was your latest word?" I asked.

"Proboscis."

"Ah. That's a big word. Would you care to tell us anything else about yourself?"

"Yes. I love poetry and can recite by heart. May I?"

"Of course."

Brenda stood and cleared her throat and recited.

"If you can keep your head when all about you are losing theirs and blaming it on you,

If you can trust yourself when all men doubt you, but make allowance for their doubting too;

If you can wait and not be tired by waiting or being lied about, don't deal in lies,

Or being hated, don't give way to hating and yet don't look too good, nor talk too wise:

If you can dream—and not make dreams your master; if you can think—and not make thoughts your aim;

If you can meet with Triumph and Disaster and treat those two impostors just the same;

If you can fill the unforgiving minute with sixty seconds' worth of distance run,

Yours is the Earth and everything that's in it and—which is more—you'll be a Man, my son!"

Everyone clapped as Brenda sat down. She looked pleased. "Are you familiar with it, Miss Mintz?"

"I am. It's one of my favorite poems. 'If' by Rudyard Kipling. You shortened it a bit, didn't you?" How fitting that she had chosen this poem, apropos to what I was trying to do here.

"Yes. You do know it." She looked at me with approval.

I nodded. The left side of my head was beginning to ache, weariness creeping through my bones. "Would anyone else like to tell us something?" I asked.

"I would like to share one thing, Miss Mintz," said a petite, intelligent-looking girl with a contained smile. "I'm Becca."

"Yes, Becca, please go ahead."

"I'm from London. When the war broke out, I was a child and my whole life was before me with seemingly endless possibilities. The fighting didn't seem real. Bombs and running to shelters. Before the war, there wasn't a question about being protected, being safe, and I couldn't fathom any other life. My parents provided us with everything. But maybe that's not real. Maybe the difficult times are what's real. So whatever we're given, is a gift for which we are to be utterly grateful. Like having Thornton, a safe place to live and to learn. I just want to say how fortunate I think we are to be here."

My headache disappeared.

I noticed Ruchama standing closer, but still scowling.

"I agree," said a girl next to Becca.

"Yes. We're so very lucky," said a tall angelic girl.

I felt grateful myself. I said, "Yes, it is a gift. Thank you for reminding us." I nodded at Becca.

I revised my opinion. The girls were great.

"Girls," I said softly, not wanting to break the mood, "you made story time wonderful. Time for lights out. Please use your cupboards for your clothing or the laundry chute."

I stood. My neck was stiff. One last group and lights out for me.

"Ruthie, Miri and Ruchama, please come to the hallway for a few minutes," I said.

I waited for the three girls, holding onto the banister. Had

I sailed on a ship and traveled on a train just today? My eyes settled on a red, tightly upholstered bench nearby. I went and sat down.

The three girls appeared. Miri, a smiling, glowing angel of a girl, tall with a long dark ponytail. Ruchama, a scowling, belligerent girl with a story. And Ruthie, alert and refined, a model of maturity. What a threesome.

"You three are entitled to an additional fifteen minutes before lights out. If you don't mind, may I use this time to ask a few questions, this being my first day and I don't know my way around." My mouth wasn't working very well. "Maybe you could help me," I slurred.

"Of course," said Ruthie.

"Are there school supplies here, pens and paper?"

"Yes," said Miri, her voice soft and sweet. "In the front lobby, to the right of the front door, there is a supply room.

"The door adjacent to the office where Mr. Kohn works at times," said Ruthie. "Where Mrs. Braun does paperwork. She sees to the supplies."

"Very good," I said. "Would one of you like to volunteer to bring paper, at least 30 sheets, and the same number of pens to the writing room before class tomorrow?"

"I'll volunteer," said Ruthie.

"I'll volunteer with her," said Miri. They flashed each other smiles.

"Thank you. Would you also be able to help me put the sunroom in order right before class?"

"Yes, we'd love to," said Ruthie.

"One final thing, can I ask one of you to monitor the Annex Girls in the morning, see that they are up and getting dressed?"

Ruchama had been silent until now. "Why must you treat them like babies. They'll get up themselves. Or they won't," she snarled.

I was numb. I couldn't think about her now. Maybe tomorrow.

Ruthie said in a soft voice, "Yes, Miss Mintz. Miri and I will do it."

My brain was shutting down, my eyes closing. "Thank you. You have ten more minutes, but I'll bid you good night now. And," I looked at Ruthie and Miri, "thank you, girls, for your help."

"Good night, Miss Mintz."

I stood and wobbled to my room. I was exhausted. I sat down in my arm chair, taking my notebook onto my lap, thinking, just a few minutes to plan my notes and then lights out for me.

A thud and click woke me. I was in the arm chair, my lesson book sliding off my lap. I looked at my watch. One o'clock. I'd fallen asleep, no surprise. What had woken me? A thump. I stood and quickly looked around the room. Nothing. Maybe it had come from the girls' room. I went to the door and opened it and heard a clunk. I looked down. A covered jar lay on its side, right inside my door.

I lifted the jar and peered at it.

Caterpillars.

CHAPTER 7

I looked on in shock as a herd of elephants stampeded by. They stopped and flung branches and hay at each other using their trunks. One of them trumpeted. What in the world?? It was wearing a frilly nightshirt. They all were.

I sat up. I was in my bed at Thornton. The noise and thumping was coming from the next room. I squinted at my watch. Six o'clock. I groaned and threw on my robe and slippers. I rushed out, wondering what happened to "our day begins at seven"?

I stood in the doorway and heard and saw the elephants up close, having a pillow fight. And blanket fight. More girls than I could count at six a.m. The Annex doors were flung wide. High pitched war cries and sounds of triumphant shrieking assaulted my still- sleeping head. I closed my eyes. My voice never worked well before morning coffee.

"Girls. Girls. GIRLS!" That did it—silence. I took measured steps into the room. My throbbing head simmered down a notch. I stood in the center of the now-silent room. I closed my eyes. I breathed. In. Out. In. Out. A long breath in, slowly out. I opened my eyes. The girls were all in their beds with the blankets up. The Annex doors were shut.

I shook my head. There was nothing to say.

I went back to my room.

Six-fifteen. I looked again. Still six-fifteen.

I found the papers and scanned the list of girls. All girls lived either in London or Manchester. One girl in Gateshead. All lived at home. Good, stable homes. No. Not Ruchama. Her parents lived in Israel and she lived with an aunt and uncle outside of Manchester. This might be a clue, or not. A small note said 'Benefactor of Thornton'. Supporters of the school. Hmmm.

I looked down the list and wondered who would put a jar of caterpillars in my room in the middle of the night? A frog in my dresser drawer. No name leaped out. I didn't even know the names of most of the girls. I flung down the papers.

I got dressed, grumbling to myself. I wanted this. I came here to do the job. On a ship. On a train. They're good girls. So what if they woke up and went crazy in the room at six a.m.? So what if I laid down the rules in a firm tone just last night?

I stopped.

They hadn't actually violated any of the rules, now that I thought about it, none. They had just woken up early. I didn't have any rules for six a.m. But I did say no pillow fights, right? Not really. Just that pillow fights would be determined by me.

I looked in the mirror and straightened my shirt. "Judith," I said quietly to myself, "get to work".

I strode to the main room. The girls were in their beds, speaking quietly but abruptly silenced as I entered. I walked to the Annex doors and opened them wide.

"Good morning, dear ladies. I had an interesting dream this morning, just thirty minutes ago. A herd of elephants stampeded through the room. Trumpeting. Elephants wearing frilly nightshirts." I heard muffled giggles. "They lifted their straw pillows and blankets with their trunks and flung them wildly around the room." I paused. "It was a strange dream. But. I know I'll never have it again." I paused. I let the silence do my talking. My gaze touched on each girl.

Some of the girls averted their eyes. Some looked amused. Some neutral. Ruchama looked surly. "And now, since we're all very much awake, might as well rise and get the day started. Please tidy the room and since you have extra time, please make your beds with tucked in corners, tight."

A low voice said, "What if we didn't ask to wake early?" Ruchama. I reminded myself that she lived far from home with a rich aunt and uncle. Did that explain her rudeness? I ignored her.

"I will return in twenty minutes to see what a gorgeous job you did. Oh, and I wish to thank the ones who gave me nature gifts. I love them dearly." I looked. No one reacted. No matter.

I turned and went back to my room. As I organized my room, I decided I would change my lesson plan for the day. I went to the window. Ah, a beautiful day. I cranked the window open as far as it would go. I pinned my hair and turned to go but stopped to look at the jar of caterpillars on my dresser. *Who put you in my room at one o'clock in the morning?*

I shook my head. It was hard to believe.

I returned to the main room, happy to see most beds made, some with tight corners, and the girls dressed and neat. I glanced into the Annex, most beds were unmade and few of the girls were dressed or even half dressed. Ruthie and Miri were there, gently coaxing.

"Girls," I told them, "you have five minutes to finish getting dressed, tucked in and beds made." They shrieked.

I supposed it would take time to get the morning routine running smoothly. I returned to the main room while behind me, a scramble of high-pitched activity flurried.

"Girls, five minutes and then we go downstairs. Please get the room perfectly clean."

"It's clean," said a strong voice I had come to recognize. Ruchama.

I glanced at a few scattered objects on the floor. I waited. A blonde-haired girl scurried by and picked up a sock, a hair ribbon and shut a cupboard door.

It was done now. I noted the girl who had taken responsibility. "Thank you, now it's perfectly clean." A loud breath of air whooshed noisily nearby. I pressed my lips to keep from smiling.

I went to the banister and smirked there. It was seven-twenty. I announced, "Sixty seconds!!" There was a yelp from Annex. "Fifty seconds!" Running feet. "Forty seconds!" I gave a long pause. "Twenty seconds!!" Small squeaks. I was about to announce ten, when Ruthie and Miri appeared, regal and straight, leading the Annex Girls by twos. The older girls fell in line behind them.

I descended the stairs with my nerves intact.

I led the girls to the parlor for shacharis, right on time, a point I hoped my persecutors would note in my favor.

After shacharis, we filed into the dining room for breakfast. Paula and Vicky, jolly and pink, were placing bowls of fragrant rolls and scones on the table.

"Come in loves, get them while they're still warm," said Vicky.

"Hot porridge here," said Paula, setting bowls down on the table. "What you girls need to make you strong and smart."

Mrs. Morgan was seated at the head of the long, long table. At her side sat formidable Mrs. Strassfeld and next to her, Mrs. Mark. My insides clenched as I glanced at them. I forced myself to approach.

"Good Morning, Mrs. Morgan," I said. "Good morning Mrs. Strassfeld, Mrs. Mark." Nothing. Nothing but clamped lips and stony expressions.

"Judith, so good to see you!" said Mrs. Morgan. "I was pleased to see you brought the girls in good time this morning. I trust you had a good night's rest and are recovered from your journey." She nodded encouragingly.

"Yes, Mrs. Morgan, very much. As a matter of fact, I fell asleep fairly early last night and rose early."

"Splendid, Judith! Allow me to introduce Mrs. Werner and Mrs. Jacobson, our fine instructors of Historia and Dinim." She indicated the two women seated on her other side. I recognized them from the photographs.

The two women regarded me with intense interest. Their intelligent eyes quickly scrutinized my face, my hair, my clothing. Although I squirmed inwardly under their inspection, I noted their expressions were neutral enough to give me a sense of relief. I tried for a small smile.

"Welcome."

"Welcome."

"Thank you," I breathed. I could deal with this. Civil, if not warm. "So good to meet you," I said.

"And this is Mrs. Neufield, our Grammar and Science teacher." Mrs. Morgan indicated an energetic-looking woman wearing round glasses, seated next to Mrs. Werner.

She gushed at me. "Hello, Judith. Welcome to Thornton. We were eager to see the American who was bold enough to join us." She chuckled lightly. "My niece moved to America and you do remind me of her. Her hair is auburn, not quite as lively a color as yours, but all reds are of the same family, don't you think?" She extended her hand. "Delighted."

I was momentarily stunned. I took her hand and dared a quick glance at my antagonists. They looked like they had just eaten something foul. The other two, Mrs. Werner and Mrs. Jacobson, sat primly in their seats.

"It is an honor to meet Thornton's instructors," I said. Mrs. Neufield smiled broadly and released me.

"You'll meet the remaining three instructors at luncheon, Judith," said Mrs. Morgan.

"Looking forward to it," I said. If they were anything like Mrs. Neufield, I would be ecstatic. "I think I'll go to my table now." I bowed slightly, it seemed the right thing to do, and carefully retreated.

Vicky and Paula were still bustling about, urging the girls to take more helpings.

"I made sure, love," Paula said into my ear, "to put extra scones for you at your table. You could use a bit of fattening." She gave my arm a little squeeze.

I chuckled to myself. I found my table-for-one laden with

mounds of food. My safe haven. I sat down. A girl came by with a teapot in each hand.

"Tea, Miss Mintz? Coffee? Cream?"

"Coffee, please. No cream." She carefully poured coffee into my cup. "Thank you. What's your name?"

"I'm Tammy. In the main room."

"Of course. You're the one who picked up the odds and ends from the floor this morning, aren't you?" She nodded and left with the coffee.

I saw Henchie standing there. "Hello, Miss Mintz." She smiled as if I knew what she wanted.

I did. "Care to join me?"

"Love to. More food here than at our table. Mmm…still warm…" She sat down and helped herself.

"Henchie, are you shy to fill up your plate because the teachers are sitting there?"

"It does restrain one."

I darted my eyes to the end of the long table. I could see why.

"Here. Something for later." I wrapped a few scones and an apple in a cloth for her.

She gasped and looked at the package with awe. "Thank you." She got up, her package low and hidden.

Mrs. Morgan and the teachers stood and left the room in dignified form. Breakfast was over.

"Go on then or you'll be making your instructors cross," said Vicky, shooing everyone out.

"Right. Go on, learn something," said Paula.

Vicky and Paula, like doting grandmothers, stood together watching the girls leave, clucking and murmuring endearments.

"It was worth crossing the Atlantic if only to taste your delicious food," I told them as I came over.

"Ay, look who has the gift of gab," said Paula, her eyes wide.

"Must be your lovely red hair," Vicky said with a wink and a light elbow, "give you the flattering tongue.

I laughed. "Wish me luck, ladies. My first lesson is in…" I looked at my watch,"… ninety minutes."

"You survived lights out and morning madness by the looks of you," said Vicky. "I'd say you got the luck already!"

"I'll say!" said Paula. "Not for me!"

"Yes, you're right. I did survive. See you, ladies."

I dashed up the stairs, grabbed my lesson book and writing paper. I waved to the caterpillars and flew down the stairs. All was quiet. I exited the Sunshine Corridor through a glass door and crossed the enormous patio. I took note of a paved walkway that circled around the immense garden. The sun dappled lightly through the trees, the pretty poppies and primrose. Continuing around the side of the mansion, flowers and greenery begged to be admired. It gave me an idea.

I followed the path that Alfred had driven… was it just yesterday? I used my key for the gate and continued down the lane until I reached the corner. The entire area was absent of houses, only one small house across the road, set back. It held a quaint sign on the mailbox out front, Dressmaker for All Occasions. A dressmaker, way out here? I shrugged.

I crossed the lane to the park, small and pretty, and completely empty. I settled on a bench and wrote a letter to my parents.

With a start, I looked at my watch. Whoops! 10:40. Time to go.

I gathered my things and hurried back to Thornton. I entered the sunroom and looked around. A stack of papers and bunch of pens rested nicely on one of the tables. *Thank you, Ruthie and Miri. I could use your help right now.* I hoped they remembered. I began to pull one of the large tables, but it was solid and weighty. Suddenly, it moved on its own.

There they were.

"I hoped you two would appear right now."

Ruthie and Miri laughed. The three of us dragged two heavy tables, gathered twenty-five seats, some of them armchairs, and put them into position.

Not a moment too soon. The girls blew in like a swift breeze.

"Thank you, Ruthie and Miri." I raised my voice above the din. "Girls, take paper and pen and a seat."

This was it. My class. Twenty-five students ranging in age from thirteen to seventeen in a sun-washed corner of an English mansion. A challenge I had never faced before and probably never would again.

I was ready. I took a deep breath.

"Welcome to Written Expression."

CHAPTER 8

All eyes were on me.

Jump right in.

"What is writing? Writing is about you. About your senses and your personal experience. For example, when you see something, what details do you, as an individual, observe? Shapes, colors, size, small details. A greater vocabulary will produce greater expression, but your personal slant produces the most intrigue.

"In other words, what do you think when you see that which you see? How does it strike you? Does it remind you of something? Are you inspired or uplifted—or not? Is there a memory attached to it? What about when you see something or someone you know? Besides what you see on the surface, what are you 'seeing' with your inner eye? Our first lesson will focus on visual writing."

A girl's hand went up. I knew her. The dramatic Annex Girl with the dark eyes. What was her name? "Yes, you're…"

"Mindy. I like to look at everything, as if I'm in a story. And sometimes I write the stories and share them with my friends."

"Very good, Mindy. You're a writer. Any one else like to write?"

Five hands went up. "Beautiful. Six 'acknowledged' writers. The rest of you will discover that writing is a natural expression and you don't need to be afraid to put your words down on paper. Who can tell me what the senses are?"

A few hands went up. "Yes? Brenda." I pointed to the girl who had recited poetry last night.

"Senses are a faculty by which a person perceives an external stimulus."

I nodded. "Yes, very good definition."

Girls' hands went up again. I called on Ruthie.

"The senses are sight, smell, hearing, touch and taste."

"Very good, Ruthie. Yes, Henchie?"

"It's feeling things. Like being hungry." The girls laughed.

"Yes." I couldn't help smiling. "That's right. Girls, please take a paper and pen and pair up, form a line and follow me. We'll continue class outdoors."

A rush of excitement erupted. I motioned to Ruthie and Miri. "Would you mind following at the end of the line?"

"Not at all," said Ruthie.

I went to the doorway and watched the girls form pairs, Ruthie and Miri at the back. Ruchama stood behind them, looking disgusted.

We walked through the glass door and onto the large patio, the girls chattering animatedly. "Girls, pay attention to what your eyes see. Note textures, shapes, sizes, colors. Are you seeing something stationary or moving? How does it move? Let's follow the pathway around the garden. Keep your eyes open. Each of you will see things in your own unique way. This is similar to the idea of witnesses at the scene of an accident, when asked to describe what happened, each witness account is generally slightly different from the other. Our senses are fine-tuned differently. Stop here!"

We were in the middle of the garden, surrounded by foliage and flowers. "Please find a seat in this section of the garden and for the next ten minutes, no speaking. Choose one thing you see. It might be leaves, bark, clouds, sunshine, grass, flowers. Write a full page description of the one thing you choose. No need to punctuate or form correct sentences. You may write fragments or phrases. Fill the entire page and lucky you, if you need more space, use the back of the sheet. Begin now."

There was a bit of whimpering and scrambling for seats, as if we were playing musical chairs. Fortunately, there was a low wall around the flowering beds and many girls sat there. Other girls dragged garden chairs over.

Some girls took to the task immediately. Others looked lost and struggled to write. A few girls looked completely stumped. I was tempted to give them encouragement, more instruction, but I held myself back. Eventually, every girl was writing.

Except one.

Ruchama sat defiant, her chair apart from the others. Not writing.

After nine minutes I said, "Girls, you have one minute left. If you haven't written anything yet, do so now. If you don't write at all, you will need to suffer a literary consequence." I smirked to myself. Fifty tongue lashes.

"What is this?!" said Ruchama, her face contorted. "I don't

know how to write!"

"Of course you don't know how to write," I said evenly. "It's only the first day of writing. All you need to know is how to use your eyes. Simply write what you see."

Ruchama looked angry but to my relief, she scribbled on her paper for a few seconds.

"Girls, take your paper and pen and follow me."

I led the girls on the path. I stopped to admire a leaf.

"Look at these ruffles on the edges of this leaf, like a fan. And the maroon lines that divide the green are like an aerial view of streams and tributaries crisscrossing the land. Here, one side is smooth and glossy and the other, matte and embossed. The entire leaf possesses a graceful curve like a dancer's pose and the edges are its finger waiting for the dew. And look, this tree has begun to change its colors. How many colors do you see?"

Girls called out answers. I let them call out, nodding each time.

"Yes! And what of the rich green that enters our eyes and touches a corresponding place of rich strong green inside?" I looked at my watch. Time to return to the sunroom. "Girls, pair up and follow me!" I did a swift march back to the sunroom and went to the head of the table.

The girls were crackling with energy. I spoke above the din, "Girls, quickly sit down and please write your names on your papers. Your work for tomorrow is to read what you wrote on your papers. Choose two or more descriptions that you like best and write them down neatly on a clean sheet of paper. Please bring the two papers to class tomorrow. We will be reading them aloud. Questions?"

"Can we add to what we wrote?"

"Or change it?"

"Certainly," I said. "You may improve your words. Any other questions? No? Thank you ladies, you've done well." A clock on a side table showed twelve-fifteen, on the dot. "Class dismissed."

The girls didn't bolt. More than a few girls stood together and shared their writings with each other, exclaiming and giggling. Some girls were writing. I started for the door. "Girls, time for lunch." That did it. The girls headed for the door.

"Good class, Miss Mintz."

"I loved the garden."

"Are we going outside tomorrow?"

"What if I don't have two good writings?"

"I just love class outdoors."

I nodded at the comments as they passed. "Good. Yes. Maybe. Don't worry."

I exited the sunroom. I felt good. My first class had gone well. I stepped to the window and said a small 'thank you' for the sunny day and the beautiful garden.

A dark shadow clouded my window. I turned around. Mrs. Strassfeld was standing there, looking thunderous.

Involuntarily, I gulped.

"Am I to understand that you took the girls outdoors for class." It was a statement, not a question.

I felt fear. Her strong eyes bored holes into my brain. What was she angry about? Was there something wrong with going outdoors? I forced myself to stay calm and speak.

"Yes, Mrs. Strassfeld, I did. Thornton's garden was the

perfect setting for creative writing. Appreciating beautiful nature…" My legs were shaking. "Don't you agree?" Oh, Judith, don't whimper.

Her expression was grim, her mouth tight. "The classroom is the designated area where education is conducted. Inside four walls, there exists discipline and refined thought. The outdoors are reserved for unstructured time, for a relaxation of focus. Here at Thornton, we do not confuse education with relaxation. Nor exchange discipline with the casual. We certainly do not promote it. Perhaps in your country, you do. I trust you will model yourself on Thornton's standards. Miss Mintz."

She spoke my name as if it were a plague. I felt paralyzed.

Abruptly, she turned and walked away, her back ramrod-straight, her essence dominating the corridor completely. Helpless and weak I watched her, unable to take my eyes off her. She turned into the dining room and I realized I had been holding my breath. I held onto the window ledge and heaved.

I made my way carefully down the Sunshine Corridor, praying Mrs. Strassfeld would stay inside. I also hoped no one else would come out and see me in my pitiful state. No one emerged. Unsteadily, I made my way up the stairs to my room. I splashed water on my face. I brushed my hair. Think. Think!

Did I have to do what she wanted? Did she have a right to meddle in my class? Her intense disapproval intimidated me. Why? Did I need to be intimidated? Was she criticizing me simply because she didn't like Americans? Wasn't that small-minded? I was pretty sure my idea had been brilliant. Even Ruchama, the disdainful one, had written something. Okay, fine, maybe because I made a lighthearted threat. But she did write.

I had thought to take the girls outdoors again. Would I have to change my plans? Why should I have to? And why was Mrs. Strassfeld so condemning? Couldn't she speak to me in a civil manner? Was something going on that I was missing? I put down my brush. My head was stinging from my vigorous brushing.

I needed to speak to Mrs. Morgan.

I went downstairs and entered the dining room as unobtrusively as possible, sliding into my seat at my corner table. I was completely uninterested in food, my thoughts and feelings churning, and I nibbled halfheartedly on a piece of fruit. Henchie came and helped herself enthusiastically to a sandwich, feeling at home. I couldn't fathom how any of the girls could eat a meal while Mrs. Strassfeld sat nearby. I kept my thoughts to myself.

I peeked at Mrs. Strassfeld's place and…it was empty! Mrs. Mark and the other Limudei Kodesh teachers were absent as well. It seemed their day was over. Only Mrs. Neufield was there, animatedly interacting with the girls.

My appetite experienced a sudden improvement.

The atmosphere in the room, I now noticed, was light and airy. Vicky and Paula were their usual jovial selves and the girls were in high spirits. I found myself laughing with Henchie.

A girl appeared at my table. "Mrs. Morgan asked me to let you know she would be delighted if you could join her."

I stood. "Of course. Be happy to." Maybe now was a good time to gain a bit of clarity. "Henchie, duty calls. Please stay and keep my table company."

"Not sure what that means, but I'll stay. Gladly." Big smile.

I headed for Mrs. Morgan at the end of the long table.

"Judith!" Mrs. Morgan greeted me warmly. "Congratulations

on navigating your first lesson! I heard from the girls it was fresh and invigorating. Do sit down. The other teachers will be arriving soon and I wish to speak to you before then."

I sat and let a girl pour a cup of coffee for me.

"Well, here we are in need of a chat and only your first session of the year. Not one to waste a moment!"

"Mrs. Strassfeld spoke to you?"

"Pointedly. Objecting about your methods and insisting 'I told you so'. Very unpleasant."

"I know. She tore into me right after class."

"Judith, Judith. We spoke about keeping a low profile, did we not?"

"Yes. And I thought I was."

"You haven't a clue, do you?"

"It was an activity to benefit the girls."

"Clue getting colder." She was laughing at me.

"Mrs. Morgan, how does taking my class outside affect her?"

"Allow me to explain. Old school means protecting the old way. The way that is guarded. The way that is established. Traditional. Proper. Ultra refined. Class conducted outdoors, well, would you dare to define it as traditional? Proper?"

"No. I wouldn't. Fine, I understand. It was creative. Maybe unconventional. But is it wrong? Or *improper?*"

"You're missing the point. That is entirely irrelevant. It is not done. And if you ignore what is traditional, consider it breaking the mold. Understand?"

"Mrs. Morgan...!" I knew I was pleading. "I do understand. But I also understand that I need to reach all the girls. To stimulate their creative juices. All ages are together in my class. I need a vehicle and you're tying my hands!"

"Judith. For pity's sake! At least the first week, comply. Then we'll talk."

I nodded. "I hear. It's the first day. The first week, don't do anything different," I said, telling myself.

"Good girl. That's settled then." She breathed a deep breath.

I was glad Mrs. Morgan was relieved. I trusted her. Should I share my questions with her? Might as well, since it would be important for me to understand what was fueling Mrs. Strassfeld's fury. "Mrs. Morgan, is there something more going on? I mean, other than my being an American and having veered slightly from protocol?"

"Very good, Judith. Very perceptive. The answer you seek is not something I can share with you at the present time. Another day, perhaps. Now…" she stood "…you must meet our Limudei Chol instructors. I'm certain you will get along famously with them."

Entering the dining room was a trio of smiling women. They were Mrs. Davis, Mrs. Barnett and Mrs. Abbot. Warm and instantly accepting, presenting no challenges, we chatted amiably until lunchtime ended. I went back to the sunroom to finish my letter, nibbling my warm bundle of scones pleasantly forced upon me by Vicky.

After sealing my letter, I contemplated the sky through the skylight ceiling. I wondered about Mrs. Strassfeld and what she was protecting so fiercely. What about Ruchama? Something was eating away at her. Everyone had a story, I knew. A strong urge to get the answers overcame me.

Patience, Judith. The year has only just begun.

CHAPTER 9

It was time to find the 'mail box'. I wondered if there was a way to go directly from the sunroom to the front foyer where the 'mail box' was. I explored on my own down a dark narrow hallway immediately to the left of the sunroom. This hallway led to a door which opened onto a polished paneled corridor that angled leftward. Light was streaming in at the other end and I found myself at the back of the entry area of the mansion, exactly where I wanted to be! I located the mail box marked 'post' next to the front door and popped my letter into the box.

I turned around and my eyes drank in the lavish décor and the chandeliers. My fertile imagination conjured up bygone days reminiscent of a grand era. The dual staircases mesmerized me and I imagined people descending the stairs.

"Can you imagine," a woman's voice broke my reverie, "gowns of every color under the sun coming down these two staircases and here, where we stand, a twenty-piece orchestra playing the most beautiful waltzes?"

I turned to see a small elderly woman wearing a head scarf. Her face was etched with kindly lines, showing care and concern yet also good humor. "That's exactly what I was imagining," I told her. She had spoken with a strong accent, not British. "Are you Mrs. Braun?"

"Yes, shaifaleh, I am. And who am I speaking to, not a student, a teacher maybe?"

"I'm Judith Mintz, the house mother and writing teacher."

"Ah. Yehudis from America. I expected something more... I don't know."

"Uncivilized? I'm not too bad then?"

"Bad? *Chas Vechuleela*! You look like a good *Bas Yisruel*. You could come to my house for Shabbos whenever you want."

"Thank you, I would love to come to your house. Mrs. Braun, would it be permissible for me to take an entire stack of paper for my class? We'll be writing quite a bit."

"Of course, Yehudis. This is what it is for. Come."

I followed Mrs. Braun, whom I wanted to adopt as my Bubby.

"How did you come to work here, Mrs. Braun?"

"Mr. Kohn is my neighbor and he had rachmunis on me, since I am an almuneh and he gave me work. I moved to London from Eretz Yisroel to live near my son."

A sudden inspiration hit me. "Mrs. Braun, do you know Ruchama, she's from Eretz Yisroel."

She chuckled. "Eretz Yisruel is big but also small. Yah, I remember her family, the Fishmans. Ehrliche Polish people. But very very poor. It's a rachmunis they had to send their daughter away, so far and not to see her for so many years. Ach." She shook her head sadly.

"How many years has she been away?"

"Oy, it's a long time. Maybe four, five years, I don't know.

Before the war, they came to Eretz Yisruel from Poland with nothing. They couldn't even feed their children and they sent Ruchama here and I think I remember maybe a few children went to live by relatives. Maybe two or three children. Oy." She sighed. She clucked. "So hard."

"Ruchama seems…" I groped for an appropriate word, "… unhappy."

"Yes, she's tzibrochen. She lives with her very rich uncle and aunt and has everything a girl could want. Except a family." She handed me a large stack of paper. "Be matzliach, Yehudis. You're a good girl."

I thanked Mrs. Braun and returned to the sunroom. I mulled over what she had told me— that Ruchama had been away from home since she was around thirteen years old. She hadn't seen her parents since then… how awful. What about the aunt and uncle? I assumed they hadn't filled the needs of a young girl.

I deposited the papers on a side table and straightened the chairs. I collected pens and put them near the papers. Maybe I would get a cup for them, keep them organized. The afternoon light danced on the walls and I stood entranced for a few moments.

I picked up scraps from the floor and found a paper, dirty and crumpled. One of the girls must have dropped it. I smoothed it and saw that the writing was in Hebrew. With a jolt, I knew it was Ruchama's paper in my hands.

The handwriting was bold and strong.

I read, 'Haolam hi yaffa. Yesh ore vetzevah shemechaye et halev. Aval lo sheli.' *The world is beautiful. There is light and color that enlivens the heart. But not mine.*

She had written in Hebrew. Could this mean that she didn't know how to write in English? Her words came back to me, "I don't know how to write!" She had snarled. I had assumed she didn't want to write because she didn't know how, like many others in the class. But now thinking about it, maybe she didn't know how to write *English.*

I wondered if some of her other comments came across insolent because of her facial expression and tone, and really she meant something else entirely. Maybe she was merely stating the truth, in her own Hebrew way. Like last night when I had said that everyone here was English and she had said in a hostile tone, 'not everyone' maybe she meant that *she* wasn't English. I had thought she meant me. Oh, no.

An overpowering urge to speak to Ruchama took hold of me. I looked at my watch. Two-thirty. Afternoon classes would be over in an hour, then mincha and tea time. The girls were free after tea until dinner. I would look for an opportunity to speak to her then.

I took Ruchama's paper and folded it and decided I could sit in the garden. No one was around. I went out and sat down in the first armchair under a tree. It was very pleasant out. I wondered if I would actually have to drink tea. Or could I drink water? I didn't want to be the only one not drinking tea. I never drank tea before and had thought it was only for older people or for when one was sick. Maybe I would learn to drink tea… while in England, do as the English do. I watched the sun play on the leaves.

I woke to voices in the corridor. My watch said 3:40.

I scrambled up out of my chair and went inside, following

the girls to the parlor for mincha. After davening I drifted into the dining room eager to experience my first 'tea'.

The table was set up with tea pots, tea cups, milk, small sandwiches, finger cakes and biscuits-more like puffy crackers-on tiered servers. It seemed like a big deal for a regular afternoon and personally, I was inclined to take a few crackers and a drink, without the tea. I went to sit at my corner table but found no food there.

"No, no, love," Vicky's hands pulled me up by the arms towards the large table. "Everyone sits together for tea, what with most of the staff gone, so here you go, dearie, just plunk yourself down wherever you fancy."

Girls were milling about and only two teachers, Mrs. Barnett and Mrs. Abbot were present. I was surprised to see that Mrs. Morgan wasn't there.

"I see that attendance for tea is optional, Vicky."

"Don't say that," she puffed herself up and looked indignant. "Tea is a tradition and every inch of cucumber sandwich and biscuit was made just so. Isn't that right, Paula?"

"You can say that again. Been working for hours, both of us, a labor of love for you young lovelies."

I looked at the perfectly made delicacies. It was a lot of work just for tea. "Everything couldn't be more perfect," I told them. "I'll just admire for a while."

Paula elbowed Vicky. "She's a charming one. Do eat, love, abundantly. You'll need your strength so you can fight the good fight." She looked at me meaningfully, her eyes bulging. Vicky mimicked her look, nodding. "If you know what I mean."

I laughed. They knew what I was dealing with. "With both

of you here feeding me, I'll be strong as an ox."

I looked for Ruchama and saw her seated, secluded in her world of one. There was an empty seat right beside her.

"The last time I drank tea, I had the flu," I told her as I sat down, "but I'm open to trying it the English way- in good health. Everything here is a new experience for me. You probably remember what that's like, from when you first came here. A whole new world, wasn't it?"

Dead silence. *That went well,* I thought. I reached for the three-tiered server, eyeing its display. "Never seen a sandwich like this before. What's inside these, cucumber?" I certainly didn't want to wash and *bentch.* Maybe just a plain cookie and lukewarm tea. "What do you recommend?" I glanced her way, hoping for a response.

"I recommend going home." Her teeth were clenched.

I knew her story, so I knew she didn't mean me. But I still flinched and was taken aback by the force of her comment. I struggled to keep my gaze steady. "Because you don't like it here?"

"Why would I like it? Nothing makes sense."

"Is that why you wrote this?" I pulled out her paper and unfolded it.

She looked at the paper. Her cheeks flushed and her lips pressed together. "It doesn't matter. Because I didn't plan to read it to anyone."

"Why? Because you wrote in Hebrew?"

"What do you think? I told you I don't know how to write."

"What about in your other classes? Surely you must write something."

"I don't write. What does it matter?"

"You don't do any of the work?"

She glared at me. "I told you, no."

My breath caught in my throat. I was at a loss for a moment. Could she be illiterate? "Ruchama. You can write in Hebrew, didn't anyone teach you to write in English?"

"They gave up and anyway why would I want to learn? I came here only temporarily." She snorted derisively. "Well, it's five years and I'm still here." Her mouth turned down, bitter.

"What do your teachers say? Don't they want you to do the assignments?"

"My teachers?! They hate me. I am the bad girl who is an imbecile."

It was overwhelming. So much pain in this girl... She looked at me with heavy eyes.

"This situation is unacceptable," I said quietly. "Ruchama, I read what you wrote. It was powerful, poetic even. You're a writer. And I think it would be a terrible thing to waste. I can help you learn to write in English."

"How? I'm almost eighteen years old and this is my last year in school."

"I'll find a way. As long as you're willing to learn."

She looked at me with mournful eyes. "You promise?"

I took a sip of tea and almost burned my tongue. Could I make her a promise? I took a deep breath. "We can do it together, I'm sure," I gasped. "But you need to be with me. All the way."

"You're meant to put milk in." She reached over and poured milk into my teacup. "The English way."

"You show me how to drink tea and I'll show you how to write."

A brief light sparkled in her eye. She stared at me for a long moment, as if deciding if she could trust me. "We'll see."

I took that as a yes, since she hadn't said no. I had a sudden compulsion to get spelling books and readers. "I must go now," I said. "We can get started today, if you like." She looked at me steadily and I saw a future beyond the walls she had built around herself. "Meet me in the sunroom in thirty minutes." I waited for her to nod. Nothing.

My mother always told me that once an idea was in my head there was no stopping me. My father always said that there was fire inside me to match my red hair. Whatever it was, it propelled me with a burn. I stood and went over to Mrs. Abbot, who I remembered was the English teacher. Her eyes lit up when she saw me.

"Judith, how nice."

"Mrs. Abbot, hello, you're just the person I need. May I ask you for help?"

"Why, certainly, Judith. How can I help you?"

"Would you possibly be able to give me basic books on vocabulary and grammar? And basic reading books? We're starting off slowly and it would help some of the girls in my writing class." I didn't want her to guess who it was for.

"Of course, Judith, with the greatest of pleasure. I have books at home that I can bring tomorrow. I must say…" she lowered her voice and came in close to me, "…I heard about your interesting lesson. Personally, I thought it was brilliant."

"You don't know how much that means to me. Mrs. Abbot, is there a library here at Thornton?"

"Well, not an actual library but I recall seeing one or two

education books in the parlor. You might have a look in the built-in shelves in the corner of the room." She smiled broadly at me. "You are a breath of fresh air, you know."

I smiled back. "Some people might think it a bit too fresh."

She gave me a knowing look.

I hurried to the parlor and found the shelves in the corner. A small needle-sized opening had materialized for me and I didn't want to lose the opportunity. Would I be able to teach Ruchama and perhaps repair some of the damage?

I saw seforim. I saw siddurim. Aha! English lettering. A dictionary. I searched again, but nothing else useful materialized.

I took the dictionary.

CHAPTER 10

Dictionary in hand, I stepped into the sunroom. Ruchama was standing there, stiff as a board. I said a silent prayer.

"Let's sit down, Ruchama." I went to the table, laid her paper down and pulled up a chair. She seated herself next to me. "Let's begin by translating what you wrote into English. Begin with the first sentence."

She looked at the paper and read without expression. "Haolam hi yaffa. The world is beautiful."

I jumped in. "To spell 'the', although a common word, is the first challenge because this small basic word is difficult to spell. The combination of 't' and 'h' form the sound 'th'." I got up and brought back paper and pen. Please write that rule on your paper. 'T-h' for *the* and *that* and *think* and *those*— "

"The words 'the' and 'think' are different sounds, but have the same t-h?"

"Correct. That's one of the convoluted rules of English. Many different sounds are spelled the same and many like sounds are spelled differently. Not like Hebrew."

"I told you nothing makes sense."

"Yes, you did. And you're right."

"I'm not an imbecile, then."

"Far from it." I looked at her carefully. "English is a matter of learning a few rules and memorizing the rest. Those who read and write often, store the words in their brain. It's the only way." Ruchama's gaze was expressionless and unblinking. Was I getting through to her?

Painstakingly, she and I wrote notes on her paper and eventually eked out the spelling of her three sentences. She was bright and learned quickly. I showed her how to use the dictionary to learn the spelling of words.

"Now read what you wrote, Ruchama."

Slowly, haltingly she read, "The world is beautiful. There is light and color that enlivens the heart. But not mine." She frowned.

"That was very good. Why the frown?"

"I want to change the last sentence."

My heart leaped, excited. "It's yours to change. Perhaps try to work on it yourself."

I looked at the clock. Six-thirty! Time had flown. Time to round up the girls for supper. I stood. "I'll be glad to help you later, if you wish. Right now, I must run upstairs and get everyone ready for dinner."

I felt a rush of accomplishment. Ruchama sprang up and opened the door for me, surprising me.

"Miss Mintz… thank you," she said, quietly.

Her eyes were intense with an inscrutable expression. What a complicated girl.

I nodded. "We'll continue tomorrow."

I scurried down the Sunshine Corridor in as ladylike a fashion as I could muster. Ruchama strode alongside me.

"Can I borrow the dictionary? To study?" she asked.

"Of course," I said. "Good idea. Bring it with you tomorrow." I handed it to her, dashed up the stairs and entered the main room. Girls were milling about.

"Girls," I said, "tuck in and pair up. I'll be back in four minutes and we'll go directly to dinner. Ruthie? Miri?"

"We're here, Miss Mintz," Ruthie said, appearing before me with Miri.

"I knew you were. Same routine as last night?"

"Yes, of course," said Ruthie.

I hurried to my room. I felt good. Early morning mayhem had given way to a smooth few hours and our outdoor writing exercise, although dampened by Mrs. Strassfeld's rebuke, had been exciting. Meeting Mrs. Braun had been a blessing and because she had shed light on Ruchama's story, we achieved so much in a mere few hours.

I peered into the caterpillar jar on top of my bureau. I thought I had seen four black ones before. Was there a fifth one, a little reddish tinged?

I blinked and shook my head. Did someone add another caterpillar?

I headed back to the staircase and saw Ruthie and Miri, serene and ready, the Annex girls behind them. Ruchama was further down behind the older girls.

"Good job, girls."

I pivoted, my spirits high, and we marched down the stairs and entered the dining room. Mrs. Morgan was seated at the end of the long, long table and seated next to her—oh, my heart clenched—was Mrs. Strassfeld and Mrs. Mark, rigid and stony as ever. Would they be here for supper every night? I sighed and slid into my seat at the corner table.

The table was laden with salads and crackers and bread. I realized I was starved. A girl came over carrying a soup tureen. Soup was definitely calling to me.

"Hello, Miss Mintz," she said. "I just adored the writing assignment. Would you care for soup?"

"I would love soup, if you tell me your name first."

"Esther." She ladled soup carefully into my bowl.

The soup was orange tonight, not green. Sweet potato? "Thank you, Esther. It looks and smells delicious." I tasted it. Not sweet potato. Something else, but close. "What kind of soup is it tonight?"

"It's butternut squash and parsnip. Tata."

Vicky and Paula certainly knew how to cook. My soup and I communed quietly.

Another girl came to my table carrying a mouth-watering platter of glazed salmon surrounded by colorful, steaming vegetables. "Hello Miss Mintz. I loved the class today." She placed the platter gently on the table.

"Thank you. What's your name?"

"I'm Hindy."

"Thank you, Hindy." I tried to make a mental note of all the names and faces but it was overwhelming.

Henchie came and sat down. "Hello, Miss Mintz. I did the assignment. I think it affected my brain because I'm beginning to look at things oddly."

"Oddly?" I helped myself to vegetables and fish, then passed it to Henchie.

"Yes," she said, helping herself. "I find myself looking at objects and people and noticing the most peculiar details."

"Really? That's marvelous."

"You think so? It's driving me batty. I'll be in the midst of a word and notice a small dot in the person's eye…"

"Henchie, you've just given me an idea for a visual writing exercise."

"I did?"

"You definitely did." From the corner of my eye, I saw Mrs. Morgan rise. Mrs. Strassfeld and Mrs. Stern stood and headed towards the door. "Please tell Vicky and Paula that the meal really hit the spot." I saw Henchie's baffled expression.

"I don't know what that means," she said, looking up at me.

"It's American for the meal was perfect."

Henchie's apple cheeks went up.

Mrs. Strassfeld and Mrs. Mark exited the room, their heads stiffly held. I waited for them to pass and approached Mrs. Morgan, who was slowly making her way out, chatting and smiling with the girls.

"Mrs. Morgan, hello. May I please have a word with you?"

"Yes, Judith. How did your first day transpire? You look well enough."

"Very good. Very gratifying. Mrs. Morgan, would it be permissible to have the girls bake something in the kitchen, perhaps a babka?"

"A babka? What on earth, Judith?! Your duties at Thornton do not embrace the culinary arts!" She laughed.

"I know this may sound strange, but it's an element of a writing exercise." It sounded strange even to my ears.

Mrs. Morgan's mouth puckered as if she had eaten a lemon. I almost burst out laughing. "Don't tell me you'll be writing with dough!"

"No," a tiny giggle escaped, "actually it would be an exercise exploring the tactile sense. We're writing about the senses. Their hands will knead and shape the dough…"

"Aha. For a moment there I wasn't certain your request was of a civilized nature, but now I understand how dough fits with your writing. I grant you permission. You certainly are creative, Judith." She gave me a pointed look.

"Thank you, Mrs. Morgan. Can we try it tomorrow?"

"Have a talk with Vicky and Paula and coordinate with them. Let them know what you need."

"I will, Mrs. Morgan."

"And Judith? Please bear in mind that there are eyes watching you." Her eyes were full of concern.

"I understand. I'll do my best to be unobtrusive."

Mrs. Morgan nodded and said, "Yes, please do." She left the room, shaking her head.

Vicky and Paula weren't in the dining room so I made my way to the kitchen. Somebody was singing an opera. Loudly.

I stepped inside the swinging door and was assaulted by good smells, happy singing and clanging pots and pans. Both women were washing at the large sinks and bellowing a sort of classical duet. I couldn't help laughing and although I didn't know the song, I found myself singing along.

Paula turned and saw me and produced a bellow that may have been part of the song. Then she pranced over, wiping her wet hands on her apron, grabbed me by the arms and twirled me around, vigorously. Vicky ran over and joined in and we did an impromptu jig that left me breathless.

"You're alright, Judith Mintz," Vicky said and clapped me firmly on the back.

"We never had a threesome before you came along. Much more delightful," said Paula, heaving.

"Do you sing and dance every night?" I asked.

"Most nights," they both said together.

"I'm tempted to come and join you, even if it's just for a few minutes," I said, wondering if this would be considered unobtrusive.

"Oh, love, do come!" said Paula. "You'll be my redheaded partner!"

"And what am I?" complained Vicky. "Cast me aside like some worn washrag?"

"No, no, my dear Vicky, you know you're the harmony in our song, our duet can never be split asunder." They both laughed heartily.

I couldn't help laughing along. "Before I forget, the soup was scrumptious and revived me, body and soul. And the fish was delish."

Vicky and Paula linked arms and flew around in a circle with one hand held high, chanting, "The fish was delish!" Over and over, while twirling, coordinating spontaneously.

They suddenly stopped, clutching their hearts and blowing out air.

"So, dearie, did you come here just to dispense gracious compliments?"

"Or did you come for food?" asked Paula, looking greedy.

"Well, actually, aside from wanting to thank you, I also wanted to ask if the girls may come to your homey kitchen to make something, mostly to knead and roll and shape dough." I motioned with my hands.

Vicky and Paula both went into a thinking pose, gazing off at the corners of the ceiling with their arms folded.

"You want the girls to knead and roll…? What time of day?" asked Vicky.

"A little bit after eleven."

"Well, it is in the realm of possibility to have lunch prepared before then. Maybe if the girls help with set-up…"

"And clean up after said activity…"

"Yes, that too," said Vicky. "It could be quite jolly, you know."

"Really? You're the best! And good ladies, do you have a recipe they could follow?"

"I don't give out recipes," said Vicky stiffly, with a huff.

"No," said Paula, her eyes serious. "Because then we'd have to lock you all up forever—possibly in a tower—so as not to divulge our secrets."

Hm. Maybe I could ask Mrs. Morgan for a recipe.

"How's about Vicky and I mix up a nice cinnamon yeast cake dough ourselves and the girls knead it and roll it and sprinkle it and then we bake it?" suggested Paula.

"Perfect!" I said. "Did I mention that you two are the best?"

"You did. But it's nice to hear it again," said Paula.

"Same here," said Vicky.

"You're the best! So may we do it tomorrow?" I asked.

"Short notice, but don't see why not. You, Paula?"

"I'm game."

I gave each one of them a hug and they squeezed the breath out of me.

"See you!" I hurried out to the hallway and ran up the steps with a happy heart.

Eight-forty. Almost time for room inspection.

I entered the main room. It didn't look too bad. "Hello, girls. The room looks fairly presentable. Ready for me to inspect? Annex Girls?"

"We're nearly done," called a voice from The Annex.

"Good. I'll be back in two and a half minutes," I said.

I went to my room and found my notebook. I usually liked to make a note of what worked and what didn't. I penned in *Outdoor class successful. No further outdoor lessons this week- Mrs. Strassfeld objects.* I looked at tomorrow's lesson and put a line through it. In its place I wrote *Tactile lesson in the kitchen.* I closed my notebook.

Time for a story.

I returned to the main room. "Ready?"

There was a small scuffle in the Annex, then many high pitched voices shouted, "Ready!!"

The Annex Girls marched in, in synch, and chanted, "We hid our stuff, with a huff and puff, so please please say, it's clean enough!"

I clapped my hands together. "I'll look and see, with faith in thee, that all was cleaned up perfectly." I saw smiles, which was more than I could hope for my spontaneous rhyme.

I quickly examined the rooms, knowing instinctively that the girls had really cleaned. Indeed, it looked very fine and I was quite proud of them.

"Well done," I said, smiling at them. "Story time, everyone."

I settled myself on the corner bed like last night and the girls arranged themselves on the beds nearby. Ruchama stood, but not far.

"Now then, who will be first to tell us a story? One of the Annex Girls."

The dark-eyed, dramatic girl, Mindy I think, had her hands clasped together and her eyes huge, "Oh, please may I tell my tale? I've been waiting the entire night and entire day for this!"

"Mindy, right?" She nodded. "I think you waited long enough. You're first tonight."

She sat up perfectly straight and smoothed her skirt. "Well, my friends already know that I have many sisters, six to be precise. And all my sisters, and also my mother, simply looove to dance. When we're home, we create steps and the most beautiful dances *ever seen*. We perform our dances almost every night, in our kitchen. Sometimes we ask my brothers to be our audience, but for some odd reason, they always decline. I miss the dancing so much! If you like, I could show you one of the dances and then imagine my sisters and mother dancing together with me again."

I wondered how long Mindy had been away from home.

I didn't want to break the momentum. "A wonderful idea, Mindy," I said. "Any other girls like to dance?"

Many girls said they did. "Then, shall we dance?"

I stood and went to the center of the room with Mindy and most of the girls followed. Mindy began to teach us her dance with confidence and clear instructions. Her energy was infectious and more girls joined. I looked for Ruchama and caught her watching at the side, standing with two other girls. A tiny improvement.

We pivoted and stepped and twirled. And counted.

"…walk front, two, three and turn, side step, three, and twirl, clap, slide, together…"

We had the steps and the rhythm. Suddenly the girls stopped cold in their tracks.

"What is it?" I asked. Had a girl been hurt?

The girls stood frozen. An icy hand clutched my heart as I looked toward the door. Mrs. Strassfeld stood in the doorway, still as a statue.

CHAPTER 11

I had no idea what to do. How could I explain? How could I defend myself?

I couldn't move or speak.

My inner voices spoke to me, though. *Great, Judith. You were supposed to be unobtrusive. Yes, but we were upstairs, in the privacy of our sleeping quarters. Yes, but it looked like you were instigating a wild activity. It wasn't wild, just dancing, and I didn't instigate. You're the adult, think about how it looked to her. She shouldn't have come up here and it was just dancing. Not proper. Not refined. What's not refined!?*

The decision was taken out of my hands. Mrs. Strassfeld turned and left. Without a word.

I finally found my voice, though my heart was still pounding. I spoke quietly. "The rest of Mindy's dance will need to take place on a different night." I looked at my watch and saw it was long past nine-thirty. The girls whimpered with disappointment.

"So marvelous…"

"I love the dance."

"We were just getting it."

"I wish we didn't have to stop."

"Girls," I said. "I didn't realize how late it was. Time flies when we're having fun. Annex Girls, please get ready for bed. I'll be there in three and a half minutes." More moans and soft complaining, but the girls drifted over to The Annex.

"We have time for one story," I told the main room girls.

"Miss Mintz, isn't it odd that Mrs. Strassfeld came upstairs?" asked Tammy, as we walked to the corner bed.

"She's never done that before," said Henchie. "I nearly fainted."

The girls tittered. I wished I could laugh.

"I hardly know her," I said, "so I don't know. You say she's never done this before?"

"Never." The girls shook their heads, looking dumbfounded.

I fought the feeling of dread in my stomach. I was sure that tomorrow I would hear how I had failed. How I had acted improperly.

"I'll be back soon," I said. I went to The Annex.

I found Mindy. "Mindy, thank you for sharing your dance with us. I really enjoyed it."

She flashed her dramatic eyes. "You know it really was nearly like dancing with my sisters." She sighed and fluttered her eyes heavenward. "Maybe even better."

I smiled at her. She was a gem. "Goodnight." I gave her a hug. She hugged back. It had been worth it.

The girls jumped into their beds and called goodnight to me. "Sleep tight," I said and turned to leave. "Girls, I sincerely hope you'll stay quiet in your beds until seven o'clock tomorrow morning. I know you can do it. Make me proud. Bychu, don't forget to remember to shut the light."

"I won't. I mean, I will."

As I went out, from behind me I heard more good-night calls. I began to shut the double doors.

"Don't let the bugs bite."

"Don't let the caterpillars out."

I paused, my hands on the knobs, the doors almost completely closed, and wondered who had said that. It was too hard to tell from where that small voice had come. I didn't want to make an issue. I closed the doors with a gentle click. The caterpillar culprit was inside.

I went to my spot on the bed in the corner. The girls were gathered around.

A sudden thought occurred to me. "Girls, before we start, maybe you can tell me… last year's house mother, what was she like?" I asked.

"We hardly saw her," said Tammy.

"She was pale and tired…" said Becca.

"And very timid," a tall girl said. "She didn't come out much…"

"…or tell us what to do," said Henchie. "Mrs. Morgan scolded us sometimes."

"What happened to her?" I asked. "Why didn't she come back?"

"We don't know," said Ruthie. "She didn't return after Pesach holidays."

"Mrs. Morgan slept up here the rest of the year," said Henchie, making a face.

"Oh my," I said. This was too complicated to delve into right now. "Girls, let's have a story. Who wants to tell us a tale?"

Henchie raised her hand. "I have a story. May I?"

I nodded, glad to hear from Henchie.

"My younger brother is quite interesting. When he was eight years old, he begged my parents to let him learn to play the violin. He had heard a young violinist playing at a wedding and became inspired. My parents decided to let him have a try. Well, aside from the wailing he produced, sounding much like a wounded animal, he developed a huge blister on his chin, where it rested on the chin cup. My mother put a huge gauze pad over the wound but it kept growing bigger. Soon he had three gauze pads covering his chin. That, and the fact that my father always fled the house holding his ears whenever my brother played, ended his short career as a violinist. The end."

The girls were engulfed with laughter, but in an English way. Some had their hands over their mouths. Some had their heads down, chins tucked in, shaking but not producing very much sound.

"Good story, Henchie. I think I speak for everyone, that if we see a boy with a red chin, we'll know it's your brother. Now it's time for bed. And girls, may I remind you to please do me a kindness and stay quietly in your beds until seven o'clock tomorrow morning? Actually tomorrow, we'll be doing something special in writing class. So if you can bring a smock or an apron, it would be useful. Have a good night's sleep, everyone." I gave a small finger wave. "Ruthie, Miri and Ruchama, join me outside for a few moments?"

I went to the hallway and went directly to the bench and sat down. It had been quite a day. I looked at the three girls as they came over. Ruthie and Miri were outstanding girls and had been invaluable help for me. Ruchama was a different story. Although things had progressed a smidgen, we had a long way to go.

"I was just wondering," I said to them, "did something happen to the house mother?"

"She never did seem well," said Ruthie, looking disturbed.

"Yes," said Miri. "She didn't come to the dining room with us. Or to our room much."

"She was Mrs. Strassfeld's niece," said Ruchama. "I overheard my aunt saying so."

Mrs. Strassfeld's niece. The implications hung heavily between us for a few moments. I wondered if this was the source of the hostile feelings. It certainly had potential to be.

"Girls, is there anything you want to talk about? This is your time."

"You will stay the entire year, Miss Mintz," said Ruthie, "won't you?"

"It was quite sad when Miss Abrams didn't return," Miri said.

"Girls, I may be a little tired right now, but one thing about me— there's always plenty of strength left and I plan on staying the entire year. Those who know me know that I don't give up, ever. My parents call it a stubborn streak but…" I smiled at them, "…I like to call it determination."

"Determination," said Ruthie nodding. "It's what sees everything through."

"You seem to know," I said.

"I hope so. I'm determined to help my family," said Ruthie.

"It's something that's often on my mind especially since they're there and I'm here."

"Do they need your help?"

"They don't request it of me, but... well... I know there is support that's needed."

"Maybe we help our families by being here," said Miri softly.

"Maybe," said Ruthie.

"Yes," I said. "Your family wouldn't have sent you here if they needed your help at home, would they?" Ruthie and Miri nodded. I looked at Ruchama. Was she listening? She was staring at me. "Ruchama?"

"I worked on my writing," she said. "Can you look at it?"

I flinched slightly at her abrupt manner. "Yes, of course. Ruthie and Miri, you still have free time before lights out."

They understood. They turned to leave. "Good night, Miss Mintz."

I watched them go. Good girls. "Good night."

Ruchama withdrew her paper from her skirt pocket and unfolded it. I stood up and looked at it. She had changed her last sentence to *Just look and see it*. It was a positive ending. *The world is beautiful. There is light and color that enlivens the heart. Just look and see it.*

"Beautiful, Ruchama. And spelled perfectly correct." Her eyes were down and she stood very still. "You used the dictionary completely on your own, that's quite an accomplishment." Her eyes were still down. "You worked hard."

She looked up. "I know." Her eyes narrowed.

I hesitated. Better not to prolong the conversation. "I'll say goodnight now."

Her eyes burned into mine. "So many years wasted."

Her bitterness pierced my heart. I had to agree with her about the waste, but now was not the time for pity or else we would be stuck here forever.

"Everything has its time," I said gently. Her mouth tightened. "It seems your time is now. Don't waste it." Strong silence. "Good night, Ruchama."

"Good night."

I went to my room and looked at the caterpillar jar. I counted. There were five caterpillars. A girl in The Annex had done this. Was the frog girl also the caterpillar girl?

I moved closer. "Hello there, caterpillars. Do you want to hear my problem? You do. Well, there's a teacher who's out to get me. She came upstairs tonight to check up on me. It was horrifying. She saw us dancing. She thinks I'm an American lunatic. Frankly, with her watching, it did feel wrong. You hear?"

One of them faced me. I continued talking to that one. "Now I find out her niece, who apparently is ill, had my job last year and quit or got sick in the middle of the year. So maybe her aunt is angry at me for taking her place. Maybe she's angry that not only do I take her place, but the girls are enjoying themselves, or in her eyes, being improper. Maybe every time she sees me, I remind her of her niece who's sick. Or maybe because I'm not one of her 'old school' people, I shouldn't be the one to replace her. Does any of this make sense? What do you think? Tell me, how do I break through a stone? Any ideas?"

I looked. They were unmoving. I think they were sleeping. "Didn't think so." I shook my head. I was talking to caterpillars.

I got ready for bed, brooding about what to do. Was there a way to change things? I pondered and wondered and thought. Ideas came and went until my mind was numb and my eyes grew very very heavy…

Happy chattering and giggling invaded my senses. Huh? I bolted up and looked at my watch. Seven-ten. Oh, no. I had overslept. I jumped up in a panic and quickly washed and got dressed. I rushed to the main room and announced, "Girls, we go down in ten minutes. Please make sure the room is neat."

I rushed back to my room and quickly brushed my hair. I looked at my dresser. Something was wrong.

The caterpillar jar— it was gone! I stared at the empty spot, uncomprehending. A girl from The Annex had come into my room while I was asleep. Very naughty.

I hurried back to the main room and saw girls tidying the room, happily. I glanced into The Annex where Ruthie and Miri were helping the girls finish up. I breathed. Things were rolling along quite nicely. I looked at the Annex Girls wondering who was bold enough to come into my room without permission while I was asleep? Nobody leaped out yelling, "It's ME!"

"Girls, good job. Very nice. I'll wait for you at the head of the stairs. We leave in three and a half minutes."

The girls arrived on time. "Girls, this morning you were perfect, on time and organized. I'm proud of you."

Glowing faces descended the stairs and entered the parlor, neat and civilized. At breakfast, I got a private elbow in the ribs from Paula and a quick wink from Vicky. Their friendship gave me strength for what I was about to do.

I made my way over to Mrs. Morgan. Mrs. Strassfeld and

Mrs. Mark were seated in their usual places at her side.

"Good morning, Mrs. Morgan," I said. "Good morning Mrs. Strassfeld, Mrs. Mark." Not a muscle moved.

Mrs. Morgan smiled up at me. "A very good morning to you, Judith. I trust you had a good night's rest?"

"Excellent, thank you, Mrs. Morgan. The girls are very well behaved. Though I must tell you that one of the girls was a bit homesick last night and..." I leaned down and forward slightly so Mrs. Strassfeld wouldn't miss what I was saying, "...she asked if we could participate in a dance that she and her sisters and her mother did at home. It was something she missed. Of course, I allowed her to show us her dance and we all participated with her. It helped her equilibrium. Do you agree that was the right thing to do, Mrs. Morgan?"

"Yes, yes, I do agree. I think under the circumstances, you did precisely the correct thing." Mrs. Morgan glanced quickly at Mrs. Strassfeld, whose mouth was a thin line, her eyes like hot coals. Mrs. Morgan looked back at me, her expression approving. "Very commendable, Judith. Thank you for informing me." She nodded like the incident was closed and behind us.

I turned and held my breath all the way to my corner. I sat down and let my breath out. I felt weak. I had cleared myself but I knew it wasn't the end.

A girl came and poured coffee. I think I thanked her. Henchie came over and made herself at home. I wrapped a few scones for her and reminded myself that in the very near future there would be an enjoyable tactile class with the girls.

"Henchie, these are for you. And please do me a favor and remind the girls to bring smocks or aprons to writing class."

She sniffed her package. "I will. I can't wait." I wasn't sure if she meant the class or the extra scones.

I left the dining room after breakfast and got writing paper and pen from my room. I went downstairs and out the glass door. It was a glorious day and as I headed towards the front of the mansion, I soaked up the fresh air, the trees, the flowers, and felt better. I let myself out of the gate.

A shiny black long car drove slowly up Thornton's driveway and stopped right beside me. The back passenger window opened and a woman I didn't know pointed her finger at me.

CHAPTER 12

"Young lady," the woman said, pointing her manicured nail at me, "are you by chance a member of staff here?" Her wrist glittered with a bracelet of imposing diamonds.

She was completely British, upper class and apparently very wealthy. I ducked my head a bit to see her better and saw fair skin, high cheekbones, light brown coiffed hair, a diamond necklace and earrings. A fur collar, oh my. Who was she?

"Yes," I said, feeling intimidated by the apparent high society. "I am the writing instructor and house mother here." Did I dare ask who she was?

"May I trouble you to give this to Ruchama Fishman?" She withdrew her finger and extended a small, cream-colored box with a gold ribbon, out her window. "You do know her?" She withdrew the package a fraction of an inch.

"Yes, of course. She's my student...I can give it to her."

"Very well." She extended the box towards me again.

I took the package. "Um...who shall I say it's from?"

"Her aunt. It's her birthday today," she said casually. "Carry on, William," the woman said to her driver and the car backed up.

Her aunt? Her birthday?! I was stunned. Didn't 'her aunt' want to come in and give it to Ruchama herself? Or send a personal message, at least?

"Thank you, dear," she murmured, not looking at me, as the car drove off.

I felt cold.

I continued my walk to the park, holding Ruchama's birthday gift and brooding, a bad taste in my mouth. My mind conjured up a pristine, perfectly decorated mansion where no one ever spoke to each other and expensive gifts were left on the dust-free mantelpiece. Maybe a name would be engraved on a note so its recipient would know to take it. The home I pictured could make Ruchama very angry, could make anyone very angry.

I sat down on my bench and wrote to my parents. I didn't want to burden them about my challenges with Mrs. Strassfeld because I knew they would worry. I wrote briefly that one of the teachers was 'old school' and liked things a certain way. I smirked at my understatement. I wrote humorously about the situation. I didn't need to try to be humorous as I wrote about the girls and chuckled to myself, writing about Henchie and Mindy and the phantom caterpillar girl.

I looked at my watch. Time to go. I was eager for today's class, not only because of what it held for the girls but because Vicky and Paula were a joy to be with. I hurried back.

I had ten minutes to spare so I popped into the kitchen where scents danced to the accompaniment of singing and beating of huge bowls.

"Hello, Vicky and Paula," I shouted. Vicky and Paula said, "What?" to each other.

"Over here!" I yelled.

Paula located me and screamed. "Ahhh!! We're not ready yet!"

"Never rush the batter!" said Vicky, pointing her wooden spoon aggressively, one hand on her hip.

"It's just me," I said, holding up my hands. "I'm alone and I come in peace. Just confirming that I can bring the girls in twenty minutes."

"Twenty minutes it is. The batter and we shall be ready!" said Vicky. She twirled her wooden spoon in the air.

I saluted them and left for the sunroom. I placed Ruchama's birthday present out of the way on a side table and made a mental note to give it to her later. How would she receive a gift so coldly delivered?

A rush of excitement announced the girls' arrival.

I turned to greet them. "Girls, please be seated quickly and place your visual writing in front of you on the table."

The girls scurried and found seats. I saw Ruchama take a seat at the far end of the table, a scowl on her face. Ruthie and Miri sat together nearby.

"Girls, to review yesterday's lesson, I asked you to describe in minute detail what you saw in the garden, what your observations evoked— either a memory or a sensation or a feeling. You should have two or more visual writings on your page. Who would like to share theirs first?"

Hands went up. I chose an adorable, perky-looking Annex Girl. "Please remind me, what's your name?"

"I'm Blimale."

"We're ready to hear you, Blimale."

Blimale took her paper in hand and stood up. She read, "The

leaf I hold is cheerful and green, decorated with pretty ruffles at the edge. It divides in two, right side and left, a sort of road-way with lanes for travel and the one traveler is a cream-colored inchworm, inching itself carefully on a grooved reddish path." She looked up.

"Very visual, Blimale. Excellent!" I was impressed and excited that she had written so well so soon. "I could really see your leaf. Girls, this is a good example of visual writing. Blimale wrote how she saw her leaf in her mind's eye. It is exactly what I wanted. Thank you, Blimale, you may sit down now." She was beaming and stood eager to read more, but sank into her chair.

The girls' hands flew up, some waving fingers to get my attention. "Girls, I know you want to share your writing and you will get a chance to present them… tonight." Hands descended accompanied by moans and murmurs of "tonight?" I was secretly satisfied they were moaning because to me it meant they liked the assignment.

"Yes, tonight. Leave your papers exactly where they are on the table because after dinner tonight we will continue this writing lesson. Because…? Remember I asked you to bring your smocks? Please bring them and make your way to the door for today's lesson."

Without waiting, I went to the door and opened it. There was a buzz in the room as the girls stood up, donned smocks and made their way to the door. Miri and Ruthie stood at the back of the group gently herding the girls. Ruchama was expressionless and stood nearby Ruthie. The girls were clamoring with questions.

"Where are we going?"

"Why do we need a smock?"

"Are we to go outdoors again?"

"I never wear a smock when I go outdoors."

"Probably we'll paint."

"With what, earth?"

"No, silly, with... we're going the wrong way."

"What? Where are we going?"

I led the confused but excited girls on a half-minute's walk through the hallway and on through the swinging door of the kitchen. Vicky and Paula stood ready and I announced, "Good ladies, the girls of Thornton have arrived."

Vicky and Paula were planted at the side, puffy hats on, standing at attention, and indicating with an outstretched arm the sink where the girls must wash their hands. "Go on," they ordered.

The girls understood, although they looked bewildered, and washed up. Then Vicky and Paula stood stiffly and pointed to the counter that had been scoured and made gleaming.

"Girls, Vicky and Paula prepared a sparkling clean surface for our use. Thank you, Vicky and Paula." The girls murmured thanks, still completely baffled. "Please find a spot for yourselves, shoulder to shoulder alongside the counter and I will put an end to your puzzlement and confusion."

Ruchama stood aside with her arms folded, refusing to comply.

"Ruchama?" I said, indicating the counter, encouraging her to join the others. Her mouth was tight and she snarled, "I don't have a smock and I don't care to cook or bake."

I addressed the room and announced, "For those of you who think we are here to bake, you're mistaken. We are here to write."

Hmm...that grabbed them. Also, the acoustics in the room

were excellent. No wonder Vicky and Paula sang here.

"WRITE??!"

"Yes, I said write. Vicky and Paula will distribute a small amount of their carefully crafted concoction which you will take into your hands and wait for my instructions." I whispered to Paula to get the dough ready.

She placed a puffy palm-sized ball of dough before each girl.

I motioned to Ruchama to get to the counter. She looked disgruntled, but edged her way there.

"Now," I said. "Close your eyes. Everyone. No peeking. Take the dough in your hands and think how it feels. Pass it from one hand to the other. What words come to mind? Its weight, texture, its temperature. Give it a few good squeezes, maybe ten squeezes and then shape it into a ball."

The girls were squeezing.

"Now place your dough on the counter and flatten it with your palm. Press down hard. Keep your eyes closed and make sure your dough is even and thin."

No one spoke. That was a first. I gave them a few minutes and could feel the concentration. I checked on Ruchama. Ah, she was working her dough.

"Now Paula will coat your material. No peeking. Just spread the coating and note the feeling."

"It's slimy," piped one of the girls.

"Mine too."

"Mine's slippery."

"You'll have plenty of time to tell us after. Now Vicky will bring a second coating. Distribute the coating evenly and feel its textures. When you've done that, you may open your eyes."

Watching them, I smiled to myself. "Good. Now roll your dough jelly roll fashion and come and wash your hands."

The girls quickly washed and were bursting with comments and exuberance.

"Squeezy and warm."

"Soft and cool."

"Like squishing a baby."

"Like squeezing mud."

"Smoothing a pillow."

"Slippery and greasy."

"Slimy."

"Gooey and scratchy."

"Rough."

"Like gravel."

Most comments had come from the Annex Girls in a rush.

"Good tactile words, girls," I said. "What did your sensations make you feel like inside?"

"Relaxing."

"Gentle."

"Soft."

"Like a massage."

"Like Shabbos at home."

These last words came from the older girls. I was glad there had been something for everyone. I looked at Ruchama. She had not spoken and stood a bit separate from the others, but she was there.

"Very good," I said.

A mellow mood took hold.

"The rest of our tactile lesson is to clean up here and then set up for lunch. Vicky and Paula will tell you what to do. While you work, pay attention to your tactile sensations and later on, write everything you experienced in sentence form. Please bring your sentences to class tomorrow."

Paula and Vicky bustled about, loudly showing the girls how to place the dough seam side down on the baking sheets. They enthusiastically doled out wash rags to the 'angels' 'lovies' and 'beauties' and with great vim and vigor, encouraged every girl to clean and shine. Afterward, Vicky and Paula gave the girls linens, plates, cutlery and glassware and the girls trooped out to the dining room to set up. As they left, I heard comments of a tactile nature.

"So cold."

"So smooth."

"Slippery."

"It's heavy."

Things had gone well. "Good session," I said. Paula patted my arm. I looked at Vicky, who was wiping the mixing bowls. "You're good with the girls."

Vicky walked over, put down her dish towel, smoothed her apron and put her hands together and batted her eyes. "I'd like to join your class, Miss Mintz," she said it in the sweetest voice, making me laugh. "Well," she said in her regular brassy voice, "my school never had such teachings when I was a girl."

"Oh, go on with you," said Paula. "You never went to high school."

"And why is that important? I still wish to be in her class."

"Forget about you," Paula said lowering her voice, "she has her hands full with that one." Paula pointed her chin. "A lost girl."

I saw Ruchama leaning against the wall in a corner of the

kitchen. What had happened to her? A moment ago she had looked almost happy.

An image of the woman draped with diamonds inside a long black car entered my head. "You know what?" I said softly. "I'll bet nobody knows it's her birthday today. She must be lonely. Could you possibly whip up a cake for tonight, for dinner dessert? If it's not too much trouble? Maybe it'll help her feel loved."

"Dream on, dearie," she whispered. "She'll need lots more than birthday cake to feel loved. But we've got plenty of time to make a 'carefully crafted birthday concoction', especially with all the extra help today. Right, Paula?"

"Right." She gave me a toothy smile.

They both spontaneously burst into song and I contained myself with great difficulty while the girls who entered the kitchen gaped in surprise.

"You two are... I don't know. There are no words to describe it."

I went over to Ruchama.

"Ruchama, please come with me to the classroom. I need to show you something."

I thought now would be a good time to give her the gift. It was nearly lunch time and the lesson was finished. I led the way to the sunroom, Ruchama following, and headed straight for the package. I held it out to her.

"Your aunt came by today and asked me to give this to you. She told me it's your birthday. Happy Birthday, Ruchama." I smiled at her, hoping she would smile.

Her face turned red and she grabbed the package and hurled it across the room.

CHAPTER 13

I went still.

I looked at the wall where the package had struck, still hearing the thwack.

I slowly looked at Ruchama. Her face was a mask of fury, her anger burning without words. I was unfamiliar with such rage. Wild eyes, red face and deep heaving as if she had run a marathon. I felt my own pulse hammering and tried to slow my breath and calm down.

It took a few minutes until her face color became more normal and her breathing quieted. I pulled out two chairs and sat down in one of them. "Please, Ruchama, sit down," I said quietly. I tried to imagine what she was feeling but I had never gone through what she had. My parents were the fabric of my life, always caring and thinking about me. It wasn't possible to put myself in her shoes.

But I could listen.

"You're upset," I said softly. "Sit down and tell me what it is."

She took the chair and slowly sat at the edge. She stared at the floor, her face devoid of life. "I hate them."

"Your aunt and uncle?"

She nodded. "I am treated like a piece of furniture. Dusted by the maid. Straightened and placed and fed by the maid. I am a task with a check mark beside it on a list. Not human, not alive, just an errand to be dealt with. Ruchama, birthday gift, check." She slashed a check mark through the air with her hand, her expression bitter.

She looked at me with fierce eyes. "Five years, I've been invisible. I am nothing. I have no family. No one cares whether I laugh or cry. Whether I have friends or not or whether I do well in school or not. Only to make sure I get my birthday gift. Check." She motioned again, another angry slice through the air.

I had no words to respond to her. Her raw emotions, her abandoned existence, receiving everything money could buy. Except love.

I looked at her. "I hear what you're saying," I said. "It must be awful."

Her face suddenly showed anguish. "Why did my parents do this to me? Why did they send me to this uncaring place? Why didn't they write or visit me? Or bring me home for Pesach? Once a year? Am I so despicable that they don't care to see me? Well, I don't want to see them either. I hate everyone." She looked forlorn, like she was about to cry, then she quickly caught herself, anger dominating her expression once again.

But I had seen the pain beneath the angry façade and now knew the reason for her toughness. Every person had a story.

"Ruchama. I don't know. I don't know your parents or your aunt and uncle. I only know you and I know you're not despicable. Look at me."

She slowly glanced up.

"You matter."

She looked so angry, I flinched. "You're the only one in a very long time that has treated me like a person. The majority rules."

"I beg to differ."

Out of the corner of my eye, I saw movement at the glass door. My skin crawled when I saw it was Mrs. Strassfeld and Mrs. Mark standing there, glaring at us.

The door opened. "Miss Fishman," said Mrs. Mark in clipped tones, "you're meant to be at luncheon now." Both women's mouths were tight with disapproval.

Oh, groan. What terrible timing. Ruchama gathered herself together and stalked out.

Mrs. Mark followed her. Mrs. Strassfeld stayed.

I willed her to leave.

It didn't work.

"It would be advantageous for you to spend your free time encouraging the good girls." Mrs. Strassfeld spoke through clenched teeth. She paused, overbearing and apparently waiting for my consent.

"I think she is a good girl," I said. Whoops. I had meant to say *they are all good girls.*

Her expression became hostile. "She doesn't belong here and, in fact, would not be here if not for certain circumstances. You are to engage the girls who are meant to be here. The others." Her tone had become outright demanding. This was not a good move because I felt my stubborn streak rising.

"I think my job is to engage everyone."

"Your job is to encourage refinement and proper values at Thornton. She is a negative influence and is best kept at a distance." She enunciated each word separately.

The unfairness of her judgment riled me. "In what way is she a bad influence?"

"You, an American who dances with the girls, would not ever understand. It is not necessary for you to understand. You are here to do whatever is in Thornton's best interest."

She looked down at me as if I was disgusting. Since I couldn't agree with her or pretend to comply, I exercised my right to remain silent.

"If you wish to remain here, do as I say," she said, glaring at me, one final shriveling moment, and then turned and left.

I almost wilted. She certainly had power.

But I found myself in one piece, and my redheaded self began to huff. What nerve! She threatened me. Why? What was she worried about? She apparently didn't know anything about Ruchama or what she was going through. Was this still about her niece? It seemed like something else. There was more to this than a sick niece, I was sure.

In the meanwhile, I knew I couldn't do what she asked. Not when Ruchama's survival was at stake. If anything, I was even more determined to help Ruchama now that I knew her story.

I remembered the gift box. I walked over to the wall and found it on the floor, surprisingly unscathed. I slipped off the ribbon and opened the box.

Nestled inside was a golden 'R' completely covered with diamonds. I gasped. I carefully lifted it out and saw that it was a necklace. It must have cost a fortune. And Ruchama didn't want it. Now what?

My stomach growled.

I decided to go to lunch.

I put the necklace back in its box and hid it in the deep pocket of my skirt. I made my way to the dining room and slipped into my chair. I took a cloth napkin and quickly wrapped the gift down under the tablecloth.

Henchie appeared. "You're here at last, Miss Mintz. May I?"

"Of course." I put the wrapped gift into my skirt pocket and helped myself to fruit and crackers and cheese and vegetables.

Henchie did the same. "I loved the lesson, Miss Mintz," she said between bites. "All the girls did. Might we perhaps have another go and eat our lesson immediately afterwards?"

"Hmm, it's a thought," I said. "You'll be happy to know that today's 'lesson' is probably in the oven as we speak and will surely be on the table at tea time."

"Mmmm, we could have a 'taste' lesson at tea."

"You inspire me with ideas, Henchie."

"I think one day I'd like to be a cook or baker. Imagine being able to have all you can eat all day." Her eyes turned heavenward and she sighed.

I smiled.

Blimale rushed over. "Mrs. Morgan says to invite you to her table when you have a chance and I loved squashing the dough." She fled.

I patted my mouth and stood. "I think after working with food for a while, Henchie, you might not be as interested in eating it," I told her. "Might even destroy your good appetite."

She looked stricken. "That would be awful. But I've never

seen a thin cook or thin baker, have you?

"You have a point there. It bears contemplation. Henchie, duty calls. Carry on as best as you can without me."

"I'll do my best."

I made my way over to Mrs. Morgan. Had Mrs. Strassfeld spoken to her? Neither Mrs. Strassfeld nor Mrs. Mark were there, and I remembered that they weren't at lunch yesterday either. Mrs. Morgan looked up at me as I sat down in the chair beside her.

"Oh my word, Judith Mintz, the girl everyone wants to be with! You've created quite a stir and just your second day! I heard all about your culinary tactile class. Marvelous idea!" She smiled and nodded, then sipped from her tea cup.

"I'm glad the girls enjoyed." I lowered my voice. "Even Ruchama participated."

Mrs. Morgan spoke quietly. "Yes. Ruchama. Such a pity. What do you make of it?"

"Well, today she told me she's miserable at her aunt and uncle's, painfully lonely, and it's been that way for years."

"Such a shame. I don't know what's to become of her. It's her last year here and we've not progressed at all."

"Mrs. Morgan, do you think she's a negative influence on the girls?"

"Heavens no, Judith. She has no influence other than to evoke pity. The girls don't relate to her in the least. What makes you ask that?"

"Because today Mrs. Strassfeld told me she was a bad influence and she shouldn't be here, and that if I wanted to remain here I was to keep away from her."

Mrs. Morgan shook her head and clicked her tongue. "This is a problem." She shook her head again. "What can I say? Mrs. Strassfeld is an outstanding teacher, par excellence, and her standards are the highest. But there are powerful forces at play here. Mrs. Strassfeld has wanted to expel Ruchama many times over the years. There is more to the story and deep issues, troublesome ones." She shook her head again. "Nothing concerning you, my dear."

"I thought so," I said. "I'd like to try to help Ruchama."

"Yes. You can do that, Judith. You're different, a fresh start, a new approach…" She looked at me carefully. "I would like you to."

I nodded. I understood she was giving me permission.

"Mrs. Morgan, I must show you this." I removed the wrapped package from my skirt pocket and turned my back to shield it from all eyes. "Ruchama's aunt drove up and caught me outside this morning. She gave me this package to give to Ruchama, a birthday gift. Today is her birthday." I looked at Mrs. Morgan who raised her eyebrows. She hadn't known.

Mrs. Morgan watched as I opened the box. She glanced inside without expression, just a small tightening of the corners of her mouth and a raised eyebrow. "She cares nothing about this," she said. "The gift she needs, money can't buy."

"Ruchama threw the box away without even opening it. What should I do with it?"

Mrs. Morgan sighed again. "Hold onto it for now and wait for an opportune moment to give it to her." She looked at me. "Keep trying. You're her last hope, Judith." She patted my hand. "I'm glad you're here. You might just move mountains."

I was taken aback by her embracing support. She was relying on me to help Ruchama, even if it meant standing up to Mrs. Strassfeld. "Thank you Mrs. Morgan. I'll do my best."

I replaced the cover, rewrapped the box and slipped it into my pocket. "Mrs. Morgan, one more thing. What happened to last year's house mother?"

"Miss Abrams? She developed a condition and needed dry air, most unfortunate. Her family took her to the hills of Switzerland to recuperate."

"And did she recover?"

"Oh, yes. And got married and moved to Belgium."

There went the 'sick niece' theory. I stood and spotted Mrs. Abbot, the English teacher. "Thank you, Mrs. Morgan."

I made my way to Mrs. Abbot.

"Why, Judith, I didn't forget," Mrs. Abbot said warmly. "I fetched the grammar books and readers for you. They're in my classroom on my desk. You're welcome to use them."

"Thank you, Mrs. Abbot, much appreciated. I'll go now. Which one is your classroom?"

"It's the third door down the corridor. I'm going there straightaway. Shall we walk together? Oh, and Judith..." she gave me an impish look, "...outstanding tactile for the girls." Her eyes were bright. "Such marvelous ideas."

"Thanks," I said, feeling slightly overwhelmed by the conflicting emotions of the past hour. We were at the dining room doorway and I realized I wanted to remind Ruchama to meet me in the sunroom after tea time.

She wasn't there. There were clusters of girls milling about the dining room but she wasn't one of them. Did she come to lunch today? I actually hadn't noticed her in the room before.

I experienced a sinking feeling.

Ruchama and I were cut off in the middle of our intense conversation by Mrs. Strassfeld and Mrs. Mark. I hadn't had a chance to bring the conversation to a satisfying close. Mrs. Mark had followed Ruchama down the corridor. I wondered, had she spoken harshly to her?

Mrs. Abbot and I walked briskly to her classroom while my thoughts churned. I had a thought…maybe Ruchama was in the classroom.

"Mrs. Abbot, do you teach the older group now?"

"Yes, it's their time. Here we are."

Mrs. Abbot went into the classroom and I peeked. I saw Ruthie and Miri, but not Ruchama. My heart tightened. Mrs. Abbot came and handed me three books.

"Thank you so much," I said, grateful for the books but feeling a compelling urge to run.

I scurried through the corridor and up the stairs and looked into the main room. Not there. I looked into The Annex. Not there. I flew down the stairs and across the length of the corridor, looked into the sunroom. Empty. I looked out the corridor windows towards the garden.

Someone was out there. Collapsed on the stones.

I ran across the corridor, flung open the door and ran.

CHAPTER 14

It was Ruchama.

She was crumpled at a low wall, her arms folded in, her body doubled over, hyperventilating. Fear flooded me.

"Ruchama." I sat down next to her on the stones. I touched her arm. "You're not well."

She hunched her shoulders and continued to struggle with great heaves, her hand on her heart. I wondered briefly if I should run inside and call for help. But I didn't want to leave her.

"What is it? Tell me so I can help you."

"I can't breathe." She rasped as if a hand squeezed her throat.

Fear gripped me. What could I do to help her?

I put my hand on her back, trying to steady and calm her heaving. "Take it slow, try to calm down... slow down... let the air in slowly... nice and easy... be calm... nice and slow..."

I repeated my words over and over, silently begging her to breathe, willing her to breathe. I found myself breathing hard from terror, my heart pounding. After many minutes, her gasping slowed. Then in a little while, it became quieter.

I kept my hand on her back, murmuring my words.

Her breathing became less ragged. I stayed silent and let her take her time.

She sighed deeply. Her hands dropped into her lap.

She sat quietly for a long time, just breathing. I did the same. My heartbeat quieted.

"I'm alright now," she said in a low voice, speaking to her hands.

I was relieved to hear her talk.

"What is it? Asthma?"

"Yes."

"Does this happen often?"

"No." She didn't look up. "I don't cry. Ever. Just can't breathe."

"Did Mrs. Mark say something upsetting to you?"

She was silent. I had guessed right.

She sighed again deeply and shuddered. She put her hand on her heart.

Oh, please, no. I was afraid of another attack. "Keep breathing," I said softly. "Go slow."

She breathed and nodded. Her eyes and head stayed down.

After a while she said, in a barely audible voice, "She said I should be grateful Mrs. Morgan lets me stay here." She slowly turned her head and glanced at me. Her face was deathly pale, her eyes haunted. "She said money paves the way only up to a certain point." She looked back down at her lap.

I stayed quiet. There was so much I could say but I didn't feel it was the right time. "Would you come inside, Ruchama? I don't want anyone to see us."

She nodded.

We stood. She wobbled a bit. I caught her arm. Then she walked, slowly, carefully. I paced myself, ready to catch her.

We entered the building. "Let's go upstairs."

We went up the stairs, one slow step at a time. I let her go first, in case she became weak. She made it to the top.

"Let's go to my room."

I led the way and showed her the armchair and she sank into it. I put Mrs. Abbot's English books onto the dresser top. I blinked. What? The caterpillar jar was there, back on top of my dresser, full of leaves.

I peered into the jar. I saw one caterpillar, but it was hard to tell if it was alone. There could be one or a hundred of them behind the leaves. I shook my head. Not now.

I poured a cup of water for Ruchama from a water jug I kept in my room. She sipped a drop.

"Do you have asthma medication?" I asked her.

"No."

"Have you been to a doctor?"

"Yes. In Israel."

Five years ago. "Your parents took you?"

She nodded.

"That was a long time ago. Did they get medicine for you?"

She shook her head. "I was leaving to England the next day."

"Didn't you get medicine here?"

"No. No one knows."

It was shocking. A girl with a medical condition no one knew about.

"Why haven't you told anyone?"

"I have no one to tell."

I couldn't believe the situation.

"Why didn't you tell Mrs. Morgan?"

"I don't know."

"Do you know what triggers it?"

"When I'm overwhelmed with upset and can't cry."

"How often does it happen?"

"Not often. A few times a year."

I sat there digesting it. She was like an orphan, without anyone.

With asthma.

"Ruchama. I'm not a doctor but I'm certain you need to see one and get medicine for your attacks. Please agree to go to a doctor, and I'll ask Mrs. Morgan to make an appointment for you."

I looked at her steadily until she met my gaze. "Please," I said.

She shrugged one shoulder and averted her gaze.

"I'll go with you," I said.

She went still. I waited.

"Why would you?"

"Ruchama. I told you, you matter."

She stared at her lap for a long while.

"I care that you're ill," I said. "It hurts me to see you unwell."

"Fine," she finally said. "I'll go if you come with me."

I closed my eyes. *Thank you.*

"And if you promise not to tell my aunt and uncle."

The depth of her estrangement from her family was disturbing. But she needed medical attention and unless I made this promise to her, she wouldn't go. I had no choice.

"Yes. I promise. I'll speak to Mrs. Morgan. In the meanwhile, I want to tell you something confidential. Mrs. Morgan, who cares about you, said we could work together, even if Mrs. Strassfeld doesn't approve. Mrs. Morgan also hinted at a grudge Mrs. Strassfeld harbors—not against you personally, but somehow linked to you."

Ruchama's mouth tightened. "I never did anything to her. She's hated me from the moment I stepped foot into the school. And Mrs. Mark, as well."

"More reason to understand that it's nothing about you since it makes no sense."

Ruchama's face turned pink and she glared at me. "So I'm to be the punching bag for her sorrows?"

She had a good point. I chose my words carefully. "I agree it's unfair and wrong. But I'm telling you so you can to see it for what it is. I know how terrible and debilitating it is because I'm also treated with condemnation for no other reason beside that I'm an uncouth American who's here to poison the girls. Or maybe I remind her of her ill niece, the house mother of last year. Maybe when she sees me, she sees her ill niece and gets furious. But what's clear is her antagonism toward me and anything I do."

I looked at Ruchama. She looked disgusted. "So you know what it's like to be hated. For no reason."

"I do. I was earmarked for persecution before I ever stepped foot in Thornton. There's something eating away at Mrs. Strassfeld and it's not me. And it's not you."

She looked at me fiercely. "You're able to withstand it because you're a teacher. You can come and do as you please.

I'm a student, subservient to her. Her treatment defines my existence."

I heard her. She was at a bigger disadvantage than I was. I thought for a moment. "I see what you mean. What if you and I can redefine our existence?"

Her face lost its fierceness. "Redefine it? How?"

"Let's become stronger ourselves." I thought quickly. "What we are. What our goals are and what our focus is." I looked at her and smiled. "I'm thinking out loud. You and me, we can survive together. As friends." I put out my hand.

She looked at my hand, uncomprehending. Then her eyes met mine, searching.

"Friends?" She looked at me with disbelief.

"You're not that much younger than I am, you know."

Her entire face changed, as if a light had turned on inside her. I let the thought sink in.

The tiniest smile touched the corner of her mouth. I imagined it was a long time since she had a friend. I gave her time to let the thought sink in and went to the dresser. I looked at the English books and flipped through the pages. One of the books was perfect.

"Would you be interested in working on English now?"

She looked up at me, her eyes intense. "Yes."

We worked until it was time for mincha.

"Shall we continue after tea?" I asked.

"Yes, I'd like to. Before we go, I have a question."

"Yes?"

Her eyes narrowed. I braced myself.

"Why do you keep a jar of leaves on your dresser?"

I burst out laughing. All the tension of the day flew right out of me.

"I'll tell you on the way down." I gathered the books and stood to leave.

We descended the stairs completely different than how we had come up.

"There's a girl who shares her caterpillars with me," I said. "At the moment, I have no idea who she is. All I know is she's an Annex Girl."

"A girl with caterpillars? Isn't that revolting?"

When I was seven years old, I collected two caterpillars in a jar, wanting to watch them become butterflies. They both died.

"To most girls, yes. And a frog in my dresser drawer as a welcome gift on my first day. The frog disappeared. Then the caterpillars appeared and then disappeared for a day and now they're back. With leaves."

Ruchama laughed, a quick snort. We were in the corridor.

I looked at her. "I'm so curious who she is, just to know. Want to help me figure it out?"

She smiled. Her whole face changed. She had green eyes, I realized. I couldn't stop looking at her.

"Perhaps."

There was a commotion in the corridor as girls came out of the classrooms. I quickly headed to the sunroom to put the English books there for later and hurried to the parlor for mincha. I was grateful the difficult afternoon had ended well.

It was time for tea, my favorite time of the day, although I didn't really care for tea. Or cucumber sandwiches.

It was the relaxed atmosphere, like yesterday, with only two teachers, Mrs. Barnett and Mrs. Abbot. The table was absolutely gorgeous and the room smelled heavenly.

Vicky and Paula were milling about, proudly placing tiered plates of goodies on the table, like tea was their masterpiece moment.

"Are any of these luscious-looking and delicious-smelling delicacies from our tactile exercise?" I asked them.

"Just look, love, over there. Fresh as the morning," said Paula.

"And they came out just fine," said Vicky. "I was a bit surprised, with their eyes closed and all."

I saw the white-dusted cinnamon rolls. "I must try one," I said.

"I hope you take much more than one," said Paula sternly.

"You're right. I will."

I took a few cinnamon rolls. They were still slightly warm. I sat down next to Ruchama and put two on her plate.

"These are the end results of our lesson today."

I bit into mine and nodded at Ruchama. "Mmm. Pretty good."

I held up the other half of my cinnamon roll and called out to the girls nearby. "Girls, the cinnamon rolls you made are scrumptious!"

"They are??"

This launched a flurried rush for cinnamon rolls followed by squeals of delight.

I passed a few pastries to Mrs. Abbot and Mrs. Barnett, who became instantly enthused.

Ruchama chewed hers slowly. She nodded at me gravely.

I poured tea into my cup and Ruchama added milk.

"The English way," she said. "Now stir."

Was it only my second day here?

I took a sip. Not my cup of tea. "Ruchama, I'll meet you in the sunroom in fifteen minutes."

I got up and went to Vicky and Paula. "I love tea time. It's a little bit of heaven." They beamed at each other. "Would you good ladies mind if I borrowed a few smells from your kitchen?"

They glared at me.

"Borrow a smell? Have you gone daft?" said Vicky, her face contorted.

"As I hear you say it, it does sound odd," I said. "I meant onion, banana, lemon… spices like pepper or cinnamon…"

Vicky and Paula made eye contact. "Ohhhh."

"Come along, love," said Paula. "Let's get your smells."

She propelled me by the shoulders ahead of her through the open door to the hallway and through the kitchen's swinging door.

Vicky and Paula bustled about noisily opening cabinet doors and refrigerators, muttering loudly to each other. Every so often, they dumped two or three "smells" into my arms until I was laden to my chin.

"Methinks she needs a basket," said Vicky.

Paula brought me a basket and I settled my load inside.

"Thanks." I made my way out the door.

"And we shan't forget the birthday cake!" called Vicky, as the swinging door shut behind me.

I leaned in for a split second. "Thanks!"

I went to the sunroom, carrying my basket, smiling to myself.

Ruchama was at the table, working. She had taken pen and paper and was writing intently, using the dictionary.

I put the "smells" basket on one of the side tables and came around to peek at her work. It was her tactile assignment. I experienced a moment of satisfaction.

"Nice. I'll be here if you need my help," I said to her. She nodded without a pause in her work.

I looked through the basket and planned tomorrow's lesson.

The package in my pocket, Ruchama's pendant, kept banging against the table leg. I reminded myself that I needed to give it to Ruchama. If I took a gamble and gave it to her, would I lose the tenuous thread of trust I had achieved today?

I couldn't risk losing her…

CHAPTER 15

We worked.

Ruchama was intensely focused, toiling without letting up. She completed her tactile writing, struggling to master spelling and composition, and then added more writing to her previous visual assignment.

All the while, an internal dialogue chattered in my head. *Give her the present. Don't give her the present. Give it to her. Don't. You have to give it to her.* On and on.

I decided I wouldn't. Not now.

My watch said it was almost time for supper. "Good work, Ruchama. We'll stop now and I'll be going to get the girls. It's six-thirty."

She looked bewildered, as if surprised by the passage of time. She had been completely absorbed.

She blinked and gathered her papers.

"Leave your visual paper here, Ruchama. We'll be coming back after supper to finish the rest of the lesson."

She placed her papers on the table and looked up at me. "I never knew I could do this."

"You write beautifully. Would you read your piece to the girls?"

"I think not."

"Maybe some other time." It was too soon. She wasn't comfortable in the group. "Ruthie and Miri are good girls. Couldn't they be your friends?"

She frowned and shook her head. "We have nothing in common."

It was a shame. I understood why she felt that way but still, it was a shame. "I'll be going upstairs. Coming?"

She went to the door and held it open for me. We strode down the corridor.

"I'm not accustomed to anyone give me so much time," Ruchama said, her head down. "And caring. I don't know how to thank you."

"Maybe with your newfound writing ability, you could write me a note."

"Possible."

I ran up the stairs and found the girls frolicking about. "Hello, girls. Ten minutes until line up. Ruthie, are you here?"

She materialized in front of me. "Ruthie, hello. Please come to my room for a quick minute?"

Ruthie followed me to my room. I shut the door.

"Ruthie, it's Ruchama's birthday today," I said quietly. She gasped softly. "I found out this morning and didn't get a chance to tell anyone. Vicky and Paula are making a cake for dessert. What I was hoping to get your help with, if you agree, is to have the girls make a birthday card, to go with the cake. What do you say?"

"I would love to, with the greatest pleasure, only there isn't much time, is there?"

"Right. I thought maybe you and I could create the text and put it onto paper and then perhaps you can have all the girls sign it. What do you say?"

She gave me a pointed look. "And not have Ruchama see us."

"Right." I hadn't factored that in. "Is it feasible?"

"With determination..." she said with a big smile, "...anything's feasible."

"Beautiful. Let's quickly write..."

We dashed off a happy ditty and I penned it on my stationary paper in pretty lettering. Ruthie rushed out with the note and pen.

Ruthie was a solid girl, capable and willing, intelligent yet understated. I was curious to know her better. Was she the oldest in the family? She had mentioned wanting to help at home. Was there post-war work that her family needed her help with? Maybe we would talk tonight.

I returned to the main room and found the girls ready. We made our way down.

During supper, I shot meaningful eye contact towards Vicky and Paula, who shot meaningful eye contact back at me. I made eye contact with Ruthie and she gave me a grin and a nod.

Everything was in place.

I whispered to Vicky, "Wait until after the teachers leave."

I silently begged. *Let Ruchama accept our gifts with an open heart.*

The moment arrived. Mrs. Strassfeld and Mrs. Mark marched out. Mrs. Morgan exited soon after. Ruchama was lost in thought. The girls were giving each other eyes, like 'now?'

The door opened with a bang and Vicky and Paula paraded in, bearing a dazzling tall white iced cake with red piping, and luscious strawberries around the edges. I lifted my arms and the room burst into enthusiastic 'Happy Birthday' song. The cake was gently placed in front of Ruchama, Vicky and Paula bellowing the song directly into her face.

Ruchama looked utterly shocked, her mouth and eyes wide.

The singing came to a crescendo as Ruthie placed the birthday card near the cake. I came over for a better view and admired the lovely 'card' that was bordered with flowers and leaves, the signatures of all twenty-five girls among the leaves, embellishing the border. The text in the middle read,

> On this special day
> Our heartfelt wishes, we send your way
> For a year chock full of good cheer
> Happy Birthday, Ruchama, from all of us here
> At Thornton, in the year 1950

Ruthie cleared her throat and said, "Ruchama, in the name of all the girls of Thornton, may we wish you a very happy birthday and many happy more."

The girls applauded.

I caught Ruthie's eye and silently thanked her. She nodded.

I watched Ruchama. She was still stunned, her face frozen, eyes flitting from the cake to the card to the girls, and then back to the card again. She glanced my way and blinked multiple times, clearly disbelieving.

"Let's get on with this," said Vicky. "The cake's for eating, not for staring at. Here you go, dearie, cut the first slice." She held out a large serrated knife.

In a dream-like daze, Ruchama took the offered knife and slowly sliced through the tall cake. She cut a piece and struggled to get it out.

"Here, love, let me help you," said Paula. "The first one's always stubborn."

Ruchama was served first and the girls lined up. It was strawberry shortcake, one of my favorites, and it was delicious. The girls dug in. I glanced up and saw Ruchama sitting, not eating, staring at her piece of cake.

"Girls," I said. "After the cake, no running out tonight. We'll be going straight to the sunroom."

I got up and approached Vicky and Paula who were standing together, fondly watching the girls eat. I whispered to them, "Simply stupendous." They beamed.

I made for the door and called, "Girls, I'll be in the sunroom. Don't make me wait too long."

The sunroom was aglow in starlight and moonlight. Perfect.

After a few minutes, girls began to drift in.

"It's dark in here."

"I can't see."

"I can see."

"Shall we turn on the light?"

"Girls," I said, "please find your seat where your visual paper is. If you allow yourself a moment, your eyes will adjust to the dim light." After a short while, all the girls had arrived and were seated, including Ruchama.

"Girls, make yourselves comfortable and look up through the glass ceiling." I waited until they were all gazing upward.

"Just look. In absolute silence, please note what you see."

I let the night sky due its job. I heard hushed gasps and wondrous tones.

Keeping my voice low, I began. "What do you see? Colors, shapes, luminescence... How does it make you feel? Are you big...or small? Are you part of it or separate? What does it make you think of? Now float up...right into the starlight. What surrounds you? How is it different than being on the ground? Are you different up there?"

I watched the girls transporting themselves to another realm and let them dwell there. I was pleased to note that no one was speaking. Not even Mindy. I looked up and got lost in the stars.

It was time to write.

"Henchie," I said, "will you please turn the lights on?"

With the lights on and the girls blinking, I gave them their assignment. "Girls, for the next five minutes, your work is to recreate the visuals you found in the sky, plus the sensations and thoughts evoked by the visuals. Just write whatever is in your mind's eye."

Heads went down and intense writing ensued.

I looked at Ruchama. She was writing something. I couldn't have hoped for more. I wondered how she had felt being the object of attention and being given simple gifts of friendship. I hoped she had taken our good intentions to heart.

"Five minutes are up, girls," I said. "Write your name and place your papers here in a pile." I pointed to a spot in the center of the table and the girls passed their papers. "Now, let's hear a few visuals from down on earth, from our excursion in the garden."

Girls raised their hands. Ruchama's hand went up. My heart stopped. Did she change her mind about reading in front of the group?

I called on her.

She stood up slowly. She looked down at the table and fingered her paper. She stood silent, her brow furrowing, as if grappling with something. The girls waited. I waited. The air in the room began to get thick.

She cleared her throat. She darted a glance at me. I nodded to her. *Go ahead.*

She licked her lips and began to read. "A perfect pink flower resides in the shadows until touched by the sun, new shades of color emerging with the light. Nearby, leaves on a tree wave me closer, inviting me to bask under its cool green cloak. Yet I must have passed this way for years without ever knowing, ever seeing it. The world is beautiful. There is light and color that enlivens the heart. Just look. Only then will you see it."

Ruchama looked up from her paper, her features tense. There was a collective intake of breath, followed by murmurs of admiration. They hadn't known. Her eyes met mine. I was proud of her. She licked her lips again. She wasn't done.

"I... want to thank... all of you," she said, while staring at me. "For the cake. And... the card. I think... I mean... it meant... a great deal to me." She paused. She looked at the girls around the table. She pressed her lips together. She looked down at her paper. "Todah," she said quietly.

She sat down, rigid, taut. I knew it had been a great effort for her. A small applause broke out, I think it was Ruthie and

Miri. The girls became excited and began raising their hands, asking to read their visuals. The next twenty minutes passed in a blur. I called on girls, and they shared their writings. I enjoyed every one.

It was time to go. I dismissed the class and reminded the girls that I'd be coming upstairs soon for room inspection. I asked Ruchama to stay.

It was time.

I withdrew the package from my skirt pocket. "Ruchama, this is yours."

She looked at the box with disdain. "I have four identical boxes in my cupboard at my aunt's house." Her lip curled. "Untouched."

"Please take it. You don't have to wear it but someday, you might change your mind. Or maybe you'll give it to your daughter one day." I held it out to her. I held my breath, afraid of losing her.

She looked at the package, clearly disgusted. "It's an exorbitantly expensive piece of jewelry that I will never wear. What do I need it for?" She glared at me with hard green eyes for a full minute and then, I almost fainted as she gave me a slight smile. "Maybe you're right. Maybe I'll give it to my daughter one day." She took the package.

I watched her leave and heaved a great sigh. What a day!

I needed to see Mrs. Morgan right away. I jumped up, gathered the girls' papers and shut off the lights. I made my way down the corridor to Mrs. Morgan's private office. I knocked and the door opened. Mrs. Strassfeld stood in the doorway.

"What an interesting coincidence, Miss Mintz," she said with the disdainful tone and unmoving mouth that made my skin crawl.

"Oh..." I blubbered unintelligently. "I was looking for Mrs. Morgan..."

She moved past me, an imposing pillar of concrete. I sucked my breath in and flattened myself against the door until she was gone and my muscle capability returned.

Mrs. Morgan was sitting behind her desk. "Ah, Judith Mintz, come in, if you can."

I peeled myself off the door and stepped carefully into the room, trying to remember why I had come.

Mrs. Morgan chuckled. "You must have a sixth sense, my dear. We were just having a discussion about you..."

CHAPTER 16

I remembered there was something urgent I needed tell Mrs. Morgan.

"Mrs. Morgan, there's a girl that needs immediate medical attention."

Mrs. Morgan leaned forward. "What is it, Judith? Is one of the girls ill?"

"Yes. Very much so. Ruchama had an asthma attack today and fortunately I found her and stayed with her until she recovered. She clearly needs medicine and she's been keeping her illness a secret, hiding it. We need to take her to the doctor as soon as possible."

"Oh my. This is serious. You did say 'we'". I consider this a matter for her family, don't you?"

"No, Mrs. Morgan. We can't tell them. I promised. Ruchama will only allow you and me to know, and only because I insisted that I ask you to find a doctor. And more than that, she only agrees to see a doctor if I take her. No one else."

"Oh, my word, Judith. You have become important to her. I must consult with Mr. Kohn whether or not we may circumvent the family and take her medical condition into our own hands." She clucked her tongue. "Such a sad situation. How long has she been ill?"

"Since the day before she left Israel to come here, five years ago. She's had a number of attacks each year and believe me, Mrs. Morgan, it's beyond frightening. I must go to the girls now, but if you can inquire about the doctor for her, I don't think we can let time go by."

"Yes, Judith, I agree. I'll take care of it. It's good you told me straightaway."

"Thank you, I'll go now... time for lights out." I headed for the door.

"Before you go, just so you know, Judith, Mrs. Strassfeld perceives your influence on the girls as an intrusion. She detects a certain presentation of, shall we say, excessive happiness, or as she refers to it 'lightheadedness' from the girls, some of whom are in her class immediately before yours. Just thought you might like to know, the girls apparently appear happy and are eager for your writing class." She smiled at me. "Carry on, Judith Mintz."

I hurried down the empty corridor and up the stairs, with a light heart. The girls were happy. Ruchama would be taken care of. Mrs. Morgan and I would work on it together. Mrs. Morgan was behind me.

"Here I am, everyone," I said, arriving at the main room. "Time to inspect the dust and must, and find nothing to sneeze at." I was in a good mood.

The girls were ready, the rooms and cupboards clean and neat. I made a quick inspection and was done in a wink. I told them I was very pleased and headed for the corner bed.

The girls gathered around and a girl, Netty, told us her story.

"My older sister, at thirteen, was granted a summer away from home at camp, where she promptly became homesick and returned home after two weeks of complaining. My parents offered me the same option this past summer and I would have gone but I'm petrified of insects— they're in camp everywhere, even indoors." She whispered the last words and rolled her eyes in horror. "Instead my parents sent me to Thornton for the year. If I promised I wouldn't be homesick."

I made quick eye contact with Ruchama, who glanced at me impassively. Nettie wasn't our caterpillar fiend. "And are you fulfilling your promise?" I asked her.

"So far, I think magnificently! Well, it's been only three days and we've been so busy and having so much fun, I haven't actually thought about home much."

Good, I thought. An idea struck me. "Girls, just as a survey, with a show of hands, is anyone here homesick?"

No one raised their hands. Only Mindy raised a finger. "Not really," she said. "The dancing is even better here."

"Is anyone afraid of insects?" I asked, probing for clues.

Many girls raised their hands. It was hard to keep track.

"Is anyone *not* afraid of insects?" A few girls raised their hands, Annex girls and main room girls. I glanced at their faces, mostly familiar but what were their names? I wasn't sure and couldn't ask now. I glanced at Ruchama, who had an amused glint in her eye. Maybe she knew.

"How many of you are finding writing enjoyable?"

I was immediately bombarded by enthusiastic hand raising.

Everyone. Even Ruchama held a finger up.

So it was true.

"I'm very glad," I said. "We've been here three whole days and you've done very well. In just three days, you'll be going home for Shabbos, which reminds me, girls, if any of you can't go home, please let me know so I can place you."

A mishmash of voices began at once, voices telling me that they were going home, or they couldn't go home, or they were going to friends or relatives, or they didn't have a place to go. It was too complicated to sort out at the moment. Besides, it was late.

"Tomorrow," I said, raising my hand to stem the din, "whoever needs arrangements for Shabbos, please come to me at tea time and we'll make plans then. Now it's lights out for Annex, so off you go and I'll be coming in five minutes to admire you in your beds."

I watched them leave and said to the main room girls, "We may talk about anything that's going on, a difficulty with a teacher or school work or you may tell us something about yourself. A talent or hobby you have that you can share with us. Choose among yourselves and I'll be back in three and a half minutes."

I went into The Annex thinking that one day soon I would know all their names, including the caterpillar girl, whose mystery would be uncovered bit by bit, it seemed.

"Marvelous. The room is neat and you're all in your night clothes," I told them. "See you tomorrow, not before seven a.m. please. Good night, girls."

I made my way to the door.

"Are we going to do anything special tomorrow?"

"Of course we will," I said without turning around.

"Will we go outside?"

"Not tomorrow but possibly another day." *I promised to stay inside this week.*

I shut the lights.

"Good night, Miss Mintz."

"Good night, girls, sweet dreams."

I began to pull the doors shut. No comments about caterpillars. The doors gave a satisfying click and I heard a tiny voice from within say, "Sweet dreams, caterpillars."

Hm.

I went to settle myself on the corner bed.

"Now, then, who's first?"

"I would like to start, Miss Mintz. I'm Tammy and I'd like to say that Thornton is changed this year for the better. I think I speak for everyone, not just for myself."

"Can you tell me how?"

"Many of us, including me, came here because our parents were rebuilding their businesses, the war had caused them to shut down. The same thing occurred with our regular schooling and many sad tidings robbed us of our regular childhood." She paused and looked down at her hands.

"It must have been hard for your parents to let you go away," I said.

"Yes," she said, looking up, "theirs was a selfless act. I'm the oldest in the family and the sole reason my parents sent me here is so I could focus on school and friendships and nothing else…to enjoy a happy childhood. Last year at Thornton, I often felt the serious overtones that had prevailed at home, a certain intensity that was a bit restricting. But this year, mainly because writing class is so very full of discovery, the world feels open, like it's mine to experience along with my friends, like before the war."

I felt my throat tighten. It's what I had come here for. What I had told my parents was the reason I wanted to travel all the way across the ocean.

I saw other girls nodding.

"I'm so glad, Tammy. Your childhood is your time, like a flower bud just beginning to bloom. Would anyone else like to add something?"

"Might we sing?" asked a refined, pretty girl.

"I would love it," I said. "Softly, please."

She began a song in a gentle sweet voice and the others joined in. It was lovely and I could have listened all night.

I sang along and we melded together on the waves of song. After a while I raised my voice slightly and sang, "It's time to say goodnight, my friends, we'll see you all tomorrow again..."

The girls laughed.

"Lovely," I said. "We must sing again soon. I bid you good night now with a reminder to please remember to *not* get up before seven A.M. and to have sweet dreams." I stood. "Ruthie, Miri and Ruchama?"

The girls called out 'good night' as I made my way to the hallway bench. I made a mental note to organize today's details in my notebook, but first, three great girls were standing in front of me, offering a chance to talk.

I spotted another bench at end of the guest area. "See that red uncomfortable bench? Would you girls please bring it here?"

All three girls went to get it and I was pleased to see Ruchama helping.

I instructed them to place the bench opposite me and suggested they sit down.

"Ruthie and Miri, were you here last year?"

"Yes," said Ruthie. "I was here."

"I was here as well," said Miri.

"Ruthie, would you tell me what made you come here?"

"Yes, of course. We're six children, I'm the oldest and during the war, we moved out of London to the suburbs where my aunt has a summer home. It was safer for us and better for my mother's health... she... My mother felt very strongly that I finish my schooling and my aunt sponsored my schooling at Thornton. I feel very grateful because my father would never be able to manage the tuition... my mother, she's not well... and the medical costs are exorbitant... it's difficult for my father.."

"Is that what you meant when you said you wanted to help at home?" I asked gently.

"Yes. My mother needs expensive treatment and in the very near future, requires a surgical procedure. My father is reluctant to ask my aunt for more money, as she's already been so generous...and he can't afford the operation... his business is just starting to get back on track... I thought if I could go to work, I could earn money and help my father pay for my mother's operation..."

She clenched her hands in her lap. Miri covered Ruthie's hand with hers.

My heart went out to her. Such a good girl and laden with

enormous burdens.

Ruchama had turned her head to stare at Ruthie, her expression clearly disturbed.

"Ruthie," I said. "I would think your father wants you to be here, to finish your schooling. I'm sure he wouldn't want you to leave to go to work, would he?"

She shook her head. "No. He wouldn't. That's my dilemma. I, too, wish to finish my schooling. It's my last year...I want to make the most of it. But I'm quite torn about not being able to help."

"I hear what you're saying. Let me think about it. Sometimes I get ideas-as you probably noticed in class- maybe an inspiration will strike me and a concrete solution may materialize, something you can do while you're here." Ruthie looked at me with bright eyes and I thought how brave she was. "Just know that I'm here to listen. And I'll be thinking."

"I'm here, too," said Miri.

Ruchama was silent, a fierce look flushing her face. What was agitating her?

"I'll bid you good night now," I said, "and if you can write down your mother's name for me, Ruthie, I'll have her in mind when I daven."

"Yes, I'll give it to you. Thank you, Miss Mintz." She stood and turned to leave with Miri at her side.

"Ruthie, would you want the other girls at school to daven?"

She turned back and smiled. "Thank you, but no. I prefer to keep my mother's illness private for now."

"I understand. Good night."

She left with Miri.

Ruchama was standing with hands clenched and fire burning in her eyes, glaring at me. Was it something we said? We were just talking about Ruthie's situation. What happened?

"Is something bothering you, Ruchama?" I asked, bracing myself for I-didn't-know-what.

Through gritted teeth, she spat, "Does nothing make sense?! It's completely intolerable!"

CHAPTER 17

I was at a complete loss to understand her.

"Can you tell me what you're upset about?" I asked.

"Ruthie's mother is very ill." Ruchama said, through gritted teeth. "You heard her. They can't afford the surgery her mother needs. While I live in a mansion, surrounded by wasteful wealth nobody makes use of. One of the painted untouchable urns that sits upon a side table is worth more than enough to cover the cost."

I was reeling from the force of her resentment. The girl was so complex.

"I understand," I said gently. "You see the world isn't perfectly balanced. Some have so little and some have so much. But it's not our decision who gets what...and it's not ours to say what's fair or not. It's what's meant to be."

Her mouth clamped tight. She didn't care for my explanation.

"Ruchama, please, there is only one thing possible in all of this. Ruthie is in trouble and we need to think how we can help her. That's all we can do."

She lowered her gaze. "Yes. I must help her."

"Then you'll think. I'll think. We'll think of something."

She looked at me and I saw her eyes turn from dark to clear green.

She nodded, "Yes. Yes, I will. Good night."

Just like that, it was over. "Good night."

I made my way to my room, breathing my fifth sigh of relief of the day. Was it only Tuesday night? Time seemed compressed here. A month's worth of experiences compacted itself into one day at Thornton. I looked at my dresser. The jar of leaves was there, bits of leaf missing. Eaten. I saw two caterpillars. They looked full and fat.

"You don't know what you're missing, being in here all day," I said to them. "Out there we have asthma attacks, lonely birthdays, and glowering teachers. We have golden girls with sick parents and troubled girls who detest pricey presents and expensive urns." My brain began to hum with a kernel of an idea. "You're probably better off in here." The idea began to turn into words. I looked at the caterpillars in a new light. "Thanks. The two of you helped me think of something worth exploring."

Maybe we could somehow link Ruchama's aunt and uncle to Ruthie's family. It was a bit vague and probably farfetched, but maybe something concrete would materialize.

I looked down at my hand and realized that all this time I had been clutching the girls' papers from our session in the sunroom.

I took my notebook and pen and sank into the armchair. I looked through the papers until I found Ruchama's.

I read.

Mahls frum urth evreething is peesful and serene. Gentil myuzik plays.

I am a brite stah and sher my lite and wormth with the uther stahs, Safe. Neva alone or lonelee for I flote alongside my felo stahs.

Al urthly things ahr far— pane, soro, hurt. The blu blanket of heaven obzorbs evree nuonce of sufring and cushons me in totil tranquility.

She was a writer, no doubt about it. Although not yet a speller. I looked through the papers and found Ruthie's. I read.

The deep blue swirling vastness envelops me, drawing me up, up high, inside. I have no fear. I am here among the stars, dreamy, bright, floating on a blue cushiony bed. My companion stars wink at me and warm me, communicating beauty. Wholeness and peace. I bask in their glow. All is well.

Beautiful.

I felt myself sigh. The writing of the two girls expressed their inners selves so magnificently in ways that ordinary life could only hint at. I read the rest of the papers. Just gorgeous.

I took my notebook and added notes, including the details of the day.

While cutting cards for tomorrow's lesson, I thought about Ruthie and her willingness to shoulder her family's burdens and what she had written. *All is well.* I prepared the scarves for tomorrow and thought about Ruchama's blue blanket of heaven to float in, where there was no suffering. It gave me much to think about.

I went to the window and looked up at the stars.

Hashem, help me help Ruchama and Ruthie.

I decided to say tehillim for Ruthie's mother, even though I didn't know her name. I prepared for bed and got cozy.

* * *

I sat up. Thumps invaded my brain. They were coming from the room next door. No voices cried out.

I looked at my watch. Six forty-five in the morning. Time to get up anyway.

I got dressed and entered the main room at precisely seven o'clock.

Mindy and many other girls were doing the Mindy dance from Monday night, whispering the dance steps, trying to prance as silently as possible.

In stocking feet. Thump, thump.

"This must be the silent version of Mindy's family dance," I told them.

All thumps came to a standstill. "We were trying to be quiet," said Mindy, sheepishly.

"Sounds like the silent hippo dance to me," said Henchie from her bed.

I agreed, but I let it be. I cleared my throat. "Good morning, wonderful young ladies of Thornton. It is seven-oh-one, all rise and all shine."

They rose and shone and we descended the stairs in a timely manner. Later, I watched the girls head off to class and couldn't deny a deep sense of satisfaction. Here it was just a few days since school began and our routine was basically in place.

I got my stationary and gate key and headed for the park.

I had so much to tell my parents that I was bursting at the seams. I sat down on my bench and noted again that the park was empty. I felt inspired to bring the girls here for class one day and looked around for other benches. There were a few, not very close together, but if we squeezed everyone together tightly or… I remembered there was a waterway beyond the park.

I walked across the park and found a small creek, in front of which was a row of benches. This would do nicely. I sat down on one of the benches and enjoyed an hour of complete tranquility writing my letter, facing the water.

"You're industrious," a woman's voice said. "The only person I ever saw here was an unsuccessful fisherman, who was dozing."

I looked up. A woman with a bright kerchief and a broad smile stood a few feet away. I hadn't heard her approach. I looked down at her shoes. She was wearing soft slippers.

"Same here," I said. "You're the first person I've ever seen and it's my third time here," I said.

"Ah. It's usually deserted. A good place to get away. You belong to the school behind the trees, correct?" She spoke with a slight accent, not British.

"Yes. That's right."

"I live in the house diagonally across from the park."

"Are you the dressmaker?"

"Yes, you saw my sign. You are probably one of the only ones to see it. There are not many people around here."

I wanted to ask her why she lived here, with no one around, but I sensed it was time to go. I looked at my watch. Yes, it was time. "I have to go to class now. In case I need a dress made, I'll know where to find you. Nice meeting you."

"Likewise."

I hurried back, got the scarves and cards from my room and hurried to the sunroom with only a few minutes to spare. I prepared the room.

The girls blew in.

"What are we doing today, Miss Mintz?"

"Come in, girls, and bring your chairs over to these two round tables, as close as you can." The girls began to drag their chairs over. "When you are seated, each of you take a scarf or piece of material, which you'll find on the table. Sit down and... blindfold yourselves."

There was a collective gasp, followed by a barrage of questions.

"Yes, yes," I told them. "I did say blindfold." I held in a private chuckle, knowing I'd surprised them.

Once the girls were ready and blindfolded, I said, "I will be asking you to identify a scent, a smell. Listen carefully. You are not to call out your answer. You will write your answer on the card I give you. Any questions?" None.

I gave each girl a card and a pen. A girl raised her hand. "Yes?"

"How are we meant to write if we can't see?"

"Good question. You will feel the card with your sense of touch and direct your pen with your fingers. Let's begin."

I took the lemon from the "smells" basket and waved it in front of their noses. "Silently, girls."

The girls wrote. I proceeded to delicately wave all the "smells" in this manner, one by one. A banana, cinnamon, strawberry. They inhaled, somewhat noisily, and wrote.

"Those were the easy ones," I said. "Please turn your card over and we'll do the challenging ones." The girls gasped, whispering the word "challenging" with dread.

The challenging ones were a piece of strong Swiss cheese, an onion, from which they flinched and wrinkled their noses, then vanilla, cucumber, basil and orange, all which evoked grimaces. And skepticism.

"I don't know what I'm smelling," said one of the girls.

"Me neither."

"A description is fine," I said, noticing more than a few girls sitting baffled and discouraged. "Girls, it needn't be correct, you may guess if you don't know. More important is how you describe it." That helped get the girls going.

"Last one," I said, offering a piece of chocolate. The girls inhaled deeply and exhaled in delight.

"Mmm, that one is easy," said Henchie.

"Girls, you may remove your blindfolds now. Look at your card and check the basket to see what your nose knows." I brought the basket over to the tables and heard the girls giggling at their contorted handwriting and their delight at having guessed right.

I assigned homework and glanced at Ruchama. She wasn't scowling, so we were doing well. "Bring it tomorrow along with your tactile writing. Class dismissed."

The girls jumped up, excited, talking at once, showing off their handwriting samples. They took their time drifting out. I lingered in the sunroom a few minutes, relishing a feeling of contentment. I realized that my ideas were just that—ideas. Until it actually happened, I didn't know how the girls would take to it.

As I headed to lunch, I remembered that I would need to get the girls settled with their Shabbos plans. I got paper and pen. My own plans were up in the air, although I had invitations from Mrs. Morgan, Mrs. Braun and Mrs. Weiss, from the train.

I learned that the majority of girls were going home. Four girls needed to be placed. Henchie, Blimale, Bychu and Shaivy. Shaivy and Bychu merely needed supervised rides to London, but Blimale and my friend, Henchie, had more complicated needs.

"So, what's your story?" I asked Henchie.

"I live in Gateshead and no one, save me, travels there," she said. "It's far."

"Do you want to go to a friend?" I asked her.

"Where are you going, Miss Mintz?"

"Well, I don't know yet."

"I'll go where you go," she looked at me with a smile, "if you don't mind."

It seems we really were friends. "I'll let you know if it's possible."

Blimale showed up. She was a cheerful, happy Annex Girl. "Have you nowhere to go?"

"My parents told me I could go wherever I wanted."

That was interesting. "Where do you want to go, Blimale?"

"I like to go to new places that I've never been. A place with many trees would be nice."

"How about going to a friend's house? Or a relative? Do you have brothers and sisters?"

"Yes, but they don't want me. And my friends invited me, but I don't want to go there...Where are you going?"

Hmm, another friend. "I'm not sure. I haven't decided yet."

"Maybe I could go with you...?"

"I'll work on it, Blimale."

Where would I go? Where would I go with Henchie and Blimale?

The girls went to afternoon classes and I took my letter to the 'mailbox' in the front lobby. I felt an urge to go out front. I stepped outside and walked across the front veranda. It was so lovely, quiet except for sounds of birds chirping and someone clipping hedges at the far end of the property. I sat down on one of the wicker benches and envisioned an unbelievable writing session here.

One day.

I planned tomorrow's class, tossing ideas around.

I wondered where I could go for Shabbos with two 'homeless' girls.

At tea, I sat next to Ruchama and told her about Henchie and Blimale request for a place to go, with me, and with a possibility of trees.

She poured milk into my tea. "There are plenty of unused rooms, to put it mildly, at my relatives. They have an immense garden that no one sits in. With plenty of trees. The girls can come."

"That's very generous, Ruchama. Would your aunt and uncle mind?"

"I don't know what they mind or don't mind. They don't usually speak to me. Most likely they won't know the difference."

"It's a thought. The girls seem to want to go together with me." Maybe this might be an opportunity for me to see how things were at Ruchama's relatives. "Would you like me to come for Shabbos?"

She looked at me with unblinking, direct eyes. "You said we might be friends."

"Yes. And I meant it."

"Then as a friend, will you come?" Again the unblinking look.

I thought about the wealthy woman, draped in diamonds, in the car. Not very inviting.

"Yes," I said. "I will. As a friend."

CHAPTER 18

We sat in back of the roomy limousine, Ruchama, Henchie, Blimale and I. A mismatched foursome, with William at the wheel.

I had asked Mrs. Morgan's opinion about going, and although slightly disappointed that I wouldn't be joining her for Shabbos, she was delighted with the idea and offered to make arrangements with the Abramsons, Ruchama's aunt and uncle. She warned me that I owed her a Shabbos at the soonest convenience. She also hinted that Blimale belonged to an unusual family.

I had been granted the opportunity to give the writing class I had dreamed of, after dinner Wednesday night. Mrs. Morgan, bless her, gave me permission to take the girls onto the front veranda, saying with a quick wink that Mrs. Strassfeld wouldn't be there to see us.

Arranged on inviting chairs, we closed our eyes and listened to the night sounds, sharing stories and singing. It was cozy, like family, and difficult to pull ourselves away to head inside.

The next day the girls spent class time putting all they had heard down on paper. I was quite busy that morning and afternoon, compiling all the girls' writings into a large notebook. I entitled it *'Using Your Sense'* and brought it upstairs. Ruchama had consented to submitting her writing only after painstakingly perfecting her compositions to her satisfaction.

To celebrate the end of our first week, instead of story time that night I announced, "Pillow fight time!" I was immediately rewarded with cheers and pillows flung at me, which I thought necessary to promptly fling back. It was a fitting end to a wonderful week.

Friday morning began like all other days but as soon as breakfast was over, a feverish frenzy began. Clothing selection and packing plus coordinating departures, created a frenetic hullabaloo. I insisted that the rooms be spotless before leave-taking and this jumpstarted another round of whirlwind activity.

Then hurried good-byes.

And here we were.

I had never ridden in a luxury car before and apparently, neither had Henchie or Blimale. They were not silent about it.

It wasn't a very long trip and through it all Henchie and Blimale kept up a constant chatter. Ruchama did not utter a word the entire way. We entered a very exclusive neighborhood, the houses a good distance from one another and far from the road, behind stone walls.

"What neighborhood is this?" I asked Ruchama.

"Prestwich," she said in a surly tone, facing forward.

"We're here together this time, Ruchama."

She turned to me and her eyes lightened. She nodded. "Yes. I forgot."

The wrought iron gates were opened by an attendant, to

whom Blimale cheerfully waved. We continued up a fairly long brick path flanked by miles of grassy fields and what appeared to be a small bridge in the distance, off to the right.

"I see a bridge! Surely there is water under it! Oh, this is marvelous!" squealed Bimale. "Maybe there'll be fish! Maybe frogs!"

Ruchama struggled to hide a small smile.

William drove carefully around a fountain and stopped in front of a three-story, Tudor-style home that sprawled elegantly to each side. William got out and opened the passenger door. Blimale and Henchie scrambled out. We took our bags, set down by William at the foot of the front steps, and followed Ruchama up to king-size front doors. A man emerged from one of the doors, tightly tucked in, a bowtie clamped at the top of his throat. Everything about him was stiff, his upper lip and the curved moustache attached to it. His lower lip dropped and he said, "Welcome, Mistress Ruchama. The rooms are prepared."

Ruchama ignored him and went inside. I followed Ruchama, Henchie and Blimale followed me.

The front foyer was overwhelmingly enormous and decorated with delicate, expensive-looking objects. Works of art and ornate mirrors hung on the walls and priceless pieces of interest were precisely set upon decorative tables.

"Come up," said Ruchama, her tone flat. She ascended a wide softly-carpeted spiral staircase and I followed, the whispers of Blimale and Henchie at my ear. Framed ancestors glared at us from the walls, accusing us of being common and I wondered briefly why wealth made people so arrogant.

"Here is a guest room for two," said Ruchama, as we made our way down the wide hallway, indicating a huge lavender room with canopied beds. "The Lavender Room," she said with contempt.

"Here is another guest room for two or twenty," she waved her hand dismissively at an immense peach-colored room with a sleeping area, sitting area, bookshelves, a piano, a small kitchen and an outdoor terrace. There was a cart laden with pastries, fruit and pitchers of drink. "The Peach Room."

"My entire house is this size," said Blimale cheerfully.

"Do you have guests here regularly?" I asked Ruchama.

"Rarely. Dignitaries and other important people on occasion." She walked down the hall. "This is where I stay. The Rose Room."

She led us to a rose-colored room with a huge canopied bed and few other furnishings besides a secretary desk and three rose-colored armchairs. There was nothing personal to indicate that Ruchama lived here.

"Is that your bed?" asked Henchie.

"You must be a princess," said Blimale.

Layers of rose-colored gauzy material draped from the ceiling, the wall and from a frame surrounding the bed.

"I'm not. I don't use the bed. I sleep in the armchair or on the carpeting. Down that hall is a green room."

"It's not called 'The Green Room' by any chance?" asked Henchie.

"How did you know?" Ruchama said, looking amused. "Now then, what color room do you fancy?"

"How about if Blimale and Henchie stay in the lavender room and I stay in the peach room?" I said, thinking we could use my room for getting together. The girls nodded in agreement. "Do your aunt and uncle have quarters up here?"

"No, they have a wing on the ground floor."

"Well, let's put our things away and meet back here in a few minutes and then maybe you can show us around."

Henchie and Blimale dashed off.

I unpacked my clothing and went onto the terrace. I looked down on the spacious grounds and found it beautiful but impersonal, not like a private home, more like a country club or vacation resort. Something was missing. There was certainly no homey atmosphere, no warm inviting hostess, no lived-in comfortable feeling. I wondered for a moment what Shabbos would be like.

I heard a commotion behind me and saw Blimale and Henchie standing at the doorway to my room with big smiles.

"Might we have something to eat?" asked Henchie.

Cookies in hand we explored, with Ruchama unenthusiastically giving us a tour. The downstairs featured an entire wing for three separate kitchens-dairy, meat and Pesach. One large section in the dairy kitchen was assigned for baking. Uniformed kitchen staff bustled about in the meat kitchen preparing what was apparently our Shabbos food.

We walked through a grand ballroom completely bare of furniture that Ruchama referred to as a "simcha room" that she told us was never used. A lavish and grand dining room was prepared with six table settings on a lacey tablecloth covering a mile-long table. We peeked into an opulent living room and then into a large library with floor-to-ceiling bookshelves.

"Might we go outside now and see the bridge?" asked Blimale.

"You mean you're not interested in seeing the rest of the house?" Ruchama asked.

"To be honest, it's not very interesting," Blimale said. "No offense."

Ruchama looked at her, blinking, and then broke into her beautiful smile.

"I don't find it interesting either," she said, smirking. "To be honest."

Outside, I walked alongside Ruchama while Blimale and Henchie ran ahead on the grassy fields. I wondered if it was sad for the Abramsons to have all this bounty and not have any children to share it with. I wondered where Mr. and Mrs. Abramson were hiding.

"Are your aunt and uncle home?" I asked Ruchama.

"It's difficult to know."

"Look!" Henchie came running over to us, holding something in her skirt folds. "I found a baby frog!"

Ruchama and I exchanged glances. Blimale scooped a miniature green frog from Henchie's skirt and held it in her palm for us to see.

"Better not bring that inside," said Ruchama.

"Do you have a jar for it?"

"I'll see if I can find one."

Ruchama went back inside with Henchie at her heels and I watched Blimale explore and catch things. Could she possibly be our caterpillar girl?

A jar was found and frogs and other crawly things were eagerly yet gently placed inside, but left outside. We returned to our rooms to get ready for Shabbos. Once bathed and dressed, the girls visited my room again for quick refreshments, after which Ruchama led us downstairs to the dining room where

Mrs. Abramson was lighting Shabbos candles.

She was startling in gold and ivory, wearing some sort of caftan, a golden scarf streaming down her back. She sparkled everywhere with jewels.

She turned her prominent cheekbones our way. "Ah. The girls from Thornton. Welcome to Brellenson, our home. Ruchama will show you to the parlor until Mr. Abramson arrives from prayers."

We were being dismissed.

"Good Shabbos, Mrs. Abramson. Thank you for having us," I said.

She blinked at me, seeing me for the first time. "You're quite welcome."

"Would you care to join us in the parlor?"

She raised a perfect eyebrow at me, looking at me as if I was completely deranged. "That would be unseemly." She turned and floated away.

What a strange woman. Didn't she want to talk to us? She didn't show an interest to talk to Ruchama, either. I was sure she didn't have work to do.

"Don't bother to be friendly to her. It won't help," said Ruchama quietly, as she led us to the parlor. "I know. I tried."

"What does Brellenson mean?" asked Henchie.

"They named the house after themselves. Brendon and Ellen Abramson. "

Henchie burst out laughing and said, "When I have a house, maybe I'll name it Henchiewhateverhisnameis house."

"I'll name mine The Blimale Garden Pavillion."

We sank into deep cushiony couches. Henchie and Blimale continued to conjure up possible names for their future homes.

I found a corner and davened.

A maid entered and said, "Master Abramson has arrived."

Ruchama stood and said, "That means we go to the dining room."

I followed Ruchama. Henchie and Blimale clung to my sides.

"Is your uncle scary like your aunt?" asked Henchie.

"No, but he doesn't speak much, just warning you."

"Will we be able to eat?"

"Yes. But you mustn't take yourself. Tell the server what you want." She gave Henchie a pointed look. "Eat quietly."

"Yes, but— " Henchie began, but fell silent as we approached the dining room. She retreated behind me. So did Blimale.

A trim clean-shaven man in a grey suit stood at the head of the table. He glanced up at us as we entered and gave a small nod. "Good Shabbos, Ruchama," he said gravely.

Ruchama murmured a response. We followed her to four chairs on one side of the table and stood at awkward attention, Ruchama first, then myself, then Henchie, then Blimale. Mrs. Abramson stood poised regally on the opposite side, near her husband, in her own private world.

Kiddush was quiet and without embellishment. We followed Ruchama to a washing station, built into the wall of the dining room. The Abramsons washed in a second built-in station. The challah, fish, soup, water and main course was cut, spooned, ladled and poured entirely by the server, in silence. Mr. and Mrs. Abramson indicated without speaking their choice of meat, cutlet, vegetables and potato tarts.We did as they did, although I felt Henchie's agitation at my side.

"I saw Hannah today," said Mrs. Abramson to Mr.

Abramson, patting her mouth delicately.

He continued to eat. "Mmmhm?"

"She told me her family is doing well."

"Good to hear," said Mr. Abramson, without raising his eyes.

The silence yawned. I racked my brains for a neutral topic of conversation.

"I want to give cook notice," said Mrs. Abramson. "She's become erratic of late."

"Mmhmmm," said Mr. Abramson.

The silence deepened as we ate. I had never focused this much attention solely on food, which was presented elegantly, but was actually quite bland. Must be why Mrs. Abramson was letting the cook go.

Mr. Abramson laid his cutlery down and mumbled from a siddur a while, presumably zmiros. While this was going on, the server presented us with a choice of pastries. I saw him turn towards me after placing a pastry on Henchie's plate, but she pointed to another two pastries. The server pressed his lips together in disapproval but complied. I pressed my own lips together so I wouldn't laugh.

Each of us was formally presented with a small bentching booklet on an individual silver platter. Afterwards, Mr. Abramson patted his mouth, stood, nodded to no one in particular and left. Mrs. Abramson did the same, without nodding.

I looked at Ruchama. She turned slowly to look at me. She raised her eyebrow.

"Inspiring, wasn't it?" She said, her tone dead.

"They seem on the quiet side, your aunt and uncle," Henchie said.

I burst out laughing. "Do you ever make conversation at the table, what we, in America, call shmoozing?" I asked.

Ruchama looked revolted. "Rarely. And not to me."

"Let's do something," said Blimale. "I can't sit any longer."

"Same for me," said Henchie, standing up. "At home, I hardly ever sit."

"What do you usually do after the meal, Ruchama?" I asked.

"I go to the rooftop terrace. I look at the stars."

"Yes!" said Blimale. "I would adore looking at the stars!"

"Maybe we can walk somewhere first, stretch our legs a bit?" I asked.

"Out back there is a walkway along the perimeter of the trees."

"Lead the way," I said.

Henchie and Blimale were eager and excited, exclaiming about everything they saw on our way out. We entered a domed glass atrium that opened onto a patio garden.

I grappled with my feelings of unease. I'd never known hosts who didn't speak to their guests or try to put them at ease. I wondered why they didn't speak to Ruchama, ask her about school and such. What was going on with Mr. and Mrs. Abramson?

CHAPTER 19

The patio was astonishingly beautiful.

Flowers and miniature trees, fountains, ponds and graceful lighting beckoned us forward. We went through a wide trellis archway adorned in trailing flowers and followed a softly-lit walkway edged with layers of blooms and flowering trees, fronds and English ivy. I felt myself relax and inhaled the soft air and the comforting night sky.

"Lots of tactile here, Miss Mintz," said Henchie.

"Lots," I said. "I'm tempted to bring the class here. You come here often, Ruchama?"

"No." She gave me a sardonic look. "It's my first time."

Henchie, Blimale and I gasped in unison.

"No point going alone," Ruchama said without expression.

"My family always strolls after Shabbos meals," said Henchie. "My mother cooks mountains of food and we eat it all, then we stroll for ages and meet other people strolling."

"My parents are too old to stroll," said Blimale.

"Are you the youngest in your family?" I asked.

"Oh, yes! Very much so. Some of my siblings are old enough to be my parents."

That would explain a bit about Blimale's parents encouraging her to go elsewhere instead of home. Wouldn't it?

"Aren't your parents lonely without you?" I asked.

"Oh, no! They learn and read and sleep and say tehillim the whole Shabbos through."

"Ruchama, what about your aunt and uncle, do they ever go out?"

"Not to my knowledge."

Strange. My mind couldn't grasp the dynamics. Maybe they spent their Shabbos the same way Blimale's parents did, in their private wing. I thought again how beautiful this place was and what a shame it was that more people didn't use it.

We had come full circle and Blimale and Henchie pranced through a second flower archway and up onto the patio. We congregated around the fountain and Blimale peered inside, searching in the dark for fish.

"Shall we go up to the rooftop now?" I asked.

Blimale let out a whoop. "Yes!"

"Might we take treats with us?" asked Henchie, her hands folded together.

"We can have a look in the pantry," said Ruchama.

We followed Ruchama into the house to the kitchen with the huge walk-in pantry. There was an entire cabinet labeled "Confection".

"This looks like it might have something," said Ruchama, opening the doors.

"Have you never taken treats from here before?" asked Henchie.

"No. Never. They leave a tray of refreshments for me in my room."

"You're lucky that food is brought to your room," said Blimale.

"Yes. Very," she said, flatly.

Henchie seemed to have a good nose for finding sweets. She discovered bins with chocolates, cookies and candies and dug out fistfuls of it and emptied them into a bowl that Ruchama had unearthed.

With plenty of goodies we ascended another staircase, the servants' stairs, up past the second and third floors.

"More guest rooms on this floor," said Ruchama as we climbed past the third floor.

"Who sleeps up here?" asked Henchie.

"No one," said Ruchama. "It's just there."

A short staircase led to a door which opened onto a huge concrete deck.

Chairs and lounges and small round tables were positioned as if they expected a party. I didn't ask whether anyone came up here or not. I knew they didn't.

I understood completely why Ruchama was disdainful about the house not being used and why she couldn't tolerate being here. I wondered what the story was, why her aunt and uncle had taken her in.

We made ourselves comfortable and gazed at the stars. Henchie and Blimale munched on goodies to their heart's content.

"It's different with all of you here," Ruchama said to me.

"How so?" I asked.

"It's sharing…not escaping."

"Friendship does that," I said.

She looked up at the stars. "Yes."

We ate chocolate. We talked. We sang songs. It seemed we couldn't possibly get any more mellow, so we dragged ourselves downstairs to our rooms.

I sunk into the peach-colored canopy bed.

* * *

I didn't grasp where I was for a few moments. My bed was bathed in sunlight. I blinked for a while, accepting that it was morning and decided I would daven on my private terrace.

Afterwards, I passed the girls' rooms and saw them still sleeping, so I ventured downstairs. I peeked into the dining room and saw no one. I peeked into the parlor. Empty. I tried to find the atrium, but got lost. I wandered around and found myself in the library, the kind of place I loved.

I browsed the shelves and realized how much I missed reading. Jewish books mingled with English classics, atlases and encyclopedias. I pulled an encyclopedia off the shelf and flipped through the pages. *Ruchama might like this,* I thought.

"Are you a reader?"

I jumped. Mrs. Abramson's voice had startled me. She was sitting in a corner at the far end of the room, a book in her lap.

"Yes…I am," I said, recovering my composure.

"Books are my constant companions," she said.

Was this where she retreated every time, to the library in order to read? "What sort of books?"

"All fine writing... classics... anything well-written."

"Are you reading one now?"

"Yes. A marvelous book. *The Secret Garden* by Francis Hodgson Burnett. Familiar with it?"

"Yes. I read it and loved it. How do you like it?"

It was hard to believe. I was having a conversation about a shared interest with an aloof dismissive woman who couldn't even make conversation at the Shabbos table.

She had much to say.

"I was looking at the encyclopedias," I said, "and thought Ruchama might enjoy reading them," I said.

"Ruchama? Read? Sorry, my dear, but she can't. They did try to teach her, but found that unfortunately she is not able to learn."

"Mrs. Abramson, that may have been true in the past, but this week she and I have been working on her reading and writing and she's made astonishing progress. She's an excellent writer."

Her mouth opened. "I find that difficult to believe. I was given the impression that she is learning disabled."

"Mrs. Abramson, that couldn't be true, after all, she reads and writes in Hebrew. She's actually quite bright." Mrs. Abramson was so taken aback, she actually flinched. "What gave you the impression that she was disabled?"

"One of the teachers informed me, after numerous attempts to teach her to read and write English, years ago when she first arrived, said she was hopeless. Deficient."

I wondered who had decreed this fatal verdict.

"That's simply not true. This past week, I learned there is more to Ruchama's story, Mrs. Abramson, reasons why she couldn't learn back then. Whoever decided it was because of poor mental ability was sorely mistaken."

Mrs. Abramson looked at me in shock, blinking her eyes rapidly. She shook her head and looked out the window.

"I hope I'm not out of line, but I was curious if you could share with me what made you bring Ruchama to live with you?"

She stared out the window, lost. I must have tread on sensitive ground. I formulated an apology and a change of subject, yet... something told me to wait.

"It's complicated..." she said after a long while. "My sister and I had come to England at the onset of the war... on the Kindertransport. We were placed with a wealthy family, Jewish... and we became part of the family. I married their son. My sister married a man she met and they relocated to America. My brother, Ruchama's father, had emigrated to Israel before the war. He became ill and debilitated and turned to me to take his three children... he couldn't support them." She closed her eyes for a moment and sighed.

"You sent for Ruchama then?"

"Yes. I had the means and told my brother I would try with one, the eldest. If I managed well with her then I would send for the other two children." She sighed again and looked at the book in her lap.

"It must have been difficult."

Her eyes lifted and her face became tight. "A thirteen-year-old homesick girl. She didn't take to me. She didn't take to anyone. She couldn't learn, learning disabled they called her. I had hoped... I... had never had children of my own..."

I was silent. The complexity of her story hit me. I spoke quietly, "Did you think to send Ruchama back home?'

She pressed her lips together. She nodded. "Only it was not possible. There was no home to return to. My brother unfortunately suffered a complete collapse and his wife became bedridden. I never told Ruchama. I didn't wish to hurt her."

"Is that why they haven't written to Ruchama or tried to see her?"

Voices in the hallway brought our conversation to an abrupt halt.

I went to the doorway and called out, "Good Shabbos, girls, I'm in the library."

Three girls appeared, two of them bright-eyed and beaming. Ruchama, alert but expressionless. As I looked at her, I felt the weight of the full story that was unknown to her.

I beckoned them inside.

"Come in, girls," I said. "This library is marvelous." The girls came in and began browsing. "Look at this set of encyclopedias…" I pulled three encyclopedias off the shelf and handed one to each girl. They opened the books and perused the pages. "I was just having a chat with Mrs. Abramson about some of her favorite books."

I saw Ruchama stiffen and search the room. She saw her aunt and then looked back at me, her eyes sharp, accusing.

"Your aunt is an avid reader," I told her. Ruchama flinched. "Yes," I said softly, "we had a nice chat."

A maid announced, "Master Abramson has arrived from prayers."

"Oh, good," said Henchie. "I'm famished."

Mrs. Abramson hadn't risen from her chair. She seemed lost again, in her own world.

"I'll be along shortly," she said.

As we headed to the dining room, Ruchama hissed, "She actually spoke to you?"

"Yes, she actually did. She's not so bad," I whispered.

"What did you talk about?" She hissed in agitation.

"About books. About you…"

She immediately turned fierce and gritted her teeth. "Me?! You're meant to be my friend!" She glared at me. "How could you speak to someone like her about me?"

"She had important things to tell me, things you need to know. There's more to the story… history that explains things…"

"Does she explain and give you history why she's so cold and ungiving?"

Henchie and Blimale had stopped walking. We were near the doorway to the dining room. We approached, Ruchama stewing, steam rising from her.

"Yes."

"You'll tell me everything later?" She looked murderous.

"Yes."

We peered into the dining room. There stood Mr. Abramson in his grey suit. I wondered why he kept so silent. I took the lead and entered the dining room.

"Good Shabbos, Mr. Abramson." I felt the girls behind me. "Your home is so beautiful. We're enjoying it immensely. Thank you so much for having us."

He nodded. "Good Shabbos, my pleasure," he said quietly, making brief eye contact with me.

What could I talk to him about? "Just curious, is the shul far from here?"

He looked at me and said, "Yes. A bit."

"How far?"

"And you are…?"

"Judith Mintz, from America. I'm the house mother and writing instructor at Thornton."

"Ah. Pleased to meet you." His tone was soft, as if he didn't use his voice much. "Well, it's a bit more than a half hour's walk."

The server came in from the side door and murmured into Mr. Abramson's ear. "Excuse me a moment," said Mr. Abramson. He went through the serving door, the server him.

"Probably a skirmish in the kitchen," said Ruchama. "The cook has a volatile temper."

"What does she do?" asked Henchie. "Bang pots and pans together?"

"More likely bang the kitchen staff together," said Ruchama.

Ruchama had just made a joke, I realized. I guessed she was happy, despite my talk with her aunt.

"Does that mean we won't have the meal?" asked Henchie, looking nervous.

Mr. Abramson came back through the serving door shaking his head. Mrs. Abramson came in the through the hallway door.

"What is it, Brendon?" asked Mrs. Abramson.

"Sophie threatened the help again, wielding a carving knife this time."

"Oh!" Mrs. Abramson's hand went to her throat.

"I took care of it," he said, going to his place at the head of the table.

"We must do something about her," said Mrs. Abramson, taking her place.

"Yes. I just did. I gave her notice," Mr. Abramson said quietly.

Was the cook the only thing they spoke about to each other? As Mr. Abramson said a subdued Kiddush and we washed, I went through my mental index for a topic of conversation I could introduce.

The silence deepened.

I tried to bring up the parsha. It got no reaction. I tried to bring up school. No interest. The server brought in the meal, sometimes bending to whisper into Mr. Abramson's ear, which stirred mild interest between Mr. and Mrs. Abramson for a few moments. I ate my meal, wondering if the cook was stable enough to put the correct ingredients into the food. Ruchama gave me a sidelong glance and a meaningful look.

"Would you mind recommending a book for me to read, Mrs. Abramson?" I asked.

Mrs. Abramson looked at me as if I was standing on a distant planet. She then smiled slightly. "With pleasure, uh...what did you say your name was?"

I didn't say, since you didn't ask. "It's Judith. Judith Mintz." I felt a great need to laugh, but held myself in.

"Yes, Judith, I would be delighted. Perhaps later on in the day. In the library."

"Yes, I'll be there, thank you."

Dessert was an assortment of small tarts, causing Henchie to repeat her behavior of last night which brought the same disdainful reaction from the server. Mr. and Mrs. Abramson declined dessert and began bentching from the fancy individual trays. They retreated.

Henchie and Blimale popped up out of their chairs.

"I'm leaving," said Blimale. "Going outdoors with Henchie."

"Fine," I said.

"Only we don't know how to get out," said Henchie.

"I'll show you," said Ruchama. She looked at me. "Coming, Miss Mintz?"

"Absolutely."

We trooped after Ruchama through the maze of rooms, through the atrium and out. The patio was beautiful by day, as well. I settled myself in a lounge chair. Blimale and Henchie ran off. Ruchama stayed.

Time to talk. How upset would Ruchama be to hear about her parents' illness? What about the teacher who had labeled her learning disabled? I was sure that would make her furious. Did I need to tell her everything? I closed my eyes.

"Tell me," Ruchama said.

CHAPTER 20

She pulled over a chair and sat down at my side.

"As your friend, I say brace yourself," I said.

She took a deep breath. So did I.

I told her that her parents had become severely ill, to the point of being completely incapacitated. Tears filled her eyes.

"It's why you couldn't go home and why your parents haven't written or sent for you."

Ruchama put her head in her hands. I let her cry.

I felt the shock of the news with her. The parents she wanted to go back home to were in essence, no more. The home she dreamed of, gone.

She looked up at me, her face wet and pale, and asked, "Why did my aunt treat me so coldly? Why didn't she tell me?"

"Your misery was intimidating. Your aunt was at a loss how to communicate with you. She left you alone in your misery, while she was in her own misery, feeling a deep sense of failure. She was afraid to tell you about your parents, afraid she would make you more upset. She had originally planned to have your siblings come here, but never sent for them because she felt she had failed with you."

Ruchama roughly pushed a few straggly hairs off her face. She sighed deeply, blowing her breath out. She covered her face with her hands and leaned on the chair nearby, gazing out towards the field, seeing nothing, sometimes wiping her cheek. In the distance, Blimale and Henchie were chasing each other and giggling.

I debated whether to tell Ruchama about the teacher. It was difficult enough for her to deal with the news of her parents' illness and her aunt's abandoned hopes. I would tell her a different time. Or never.

"You're saying my aunt wished to be close with me but didn't know how?" She shook her head. "It's too much..."

"She said she didn't have experience, not having had children of her own. She had wished you would be her child."

We sat for a while, looking across the field at Blimale and Henchie, not talking. I knew it wasn't a simple task, reconstructing perceptions of the mind. I could feel the wheels in Ruchama's head turning, filling in the missing parts of the story, painting an entirely different picture.

The afternoon passed in silence. Ruchama brooded. I closed my eyes.

Voices invaded my consciousness. Giggles. Panting, as if from running.

"Might we go for refreshments now, Miss Mintz?" More panting.

Henchie, I thought.

I opened one eye. Yes, it was Henchie.

I opened the other eye. Blimale, grinning.

"You girls finished out here?" I croaked. I must have fallen asleep.

"Not really," said Blimale. "Henchie became hungry."

Where was Ruchama? I saw her near the pond gazing at the water, her expression neutral. Perhaps she had come to terms with her new story.

I peeled myself from my chair. "How about if Ruchama takes you to explore the refreshments while I go to the library for a book?"

Ruchama looked our way, gave a small nod and said, "Let's go."

She seemed recovered.

The girls bounced along next to Ruchama and I followed. When we were at the kitchen door, Ruchama gave me directions to the library.

As I made my way over, I wondered if Mrs. Abramson would be there.

She was.

She was tucked into the same armchair in the corner, a soft throw covering her lap.

She looked up from her book. "I wondered if you'd come," she said.

I walked toward her, but didn't get too close. She seemed to have a glass wall around her, a sort of protection against anything that might pierce her carefully constructed facade.

"I was looking forward to it," I said. I looked around at the shelves. "Your library is quite extensive."

"Yes, and current." She laid her book on the side table and stood. She walked toward the book shelves.

I found myself drawn to a photograph on the shelf. It was a beautiful, smiling Ruchama, radiant and confident. I'd never seen her look so happy. "Is this— "

"My sister," Mrs. Abramson said, quickly looking away. "Before she got married. Have you read Laura Ingles Wilder? She's American and quite good. Come have a look on this shelf." She touched the spine of a book. "*Little House in the Big Woods, Farmer Boy, Little House on the Prairie, On the Banks of Plum Creek*, four more here..."

I began to drool at the sight of the collection.

She turned to look at me. "They're marvelous. Have you read them?"

"I read *Little House on the Prairie* and loved it. You have all her books..." I trailed off, overwhelmed to be this close to so many good books.

"Yes, you may read them. All of them." She pulled them off the shelf one by one and handed them to me. I had seven books piled in my arms. "And look here..." she seemed excited. "The Black Stallion books, if you don't mind the horse. And," she pointed, "for younger readers, *The Boxcar Children, Surprise Island*. I had purchased them for Ruchama, hoping she would enjoy reading them..."

"I would enjoy reading them, Aunt Ellen," said Ruchama, coming in through the door.

Mrs. Abramson's hand froze in mid-selection. "Ruchama, I...didn't know... Miss Mintz told me... you... you're able... I have so many books meant for… they're here for you…" She pulled the two books off the shelf and then moved to another bookshelf and took out a book. "The Little Prince… I purchased it for you…"

She seemed uncomfortable and pleased at the same time, while holding the three books out to Ruchama. Ruchama came forward and reached out for the books. They made eye contact and their fingers touched. It was a very moving moment, probably the most connection ever, in all the years.

Henchie and Blimale entered and were excited about the books. They made quick selections and plunked themselves onto the couch, reading together, smiling and looking content.

I went to the couch opposite them and set my load down on the cushions. Ruchama had brought her books and settled at the other end, placing her books near mine in the middle.

A serene segment of time passed, all of us reading. Sometimes Ruchama showed me a word and I helped her read it, with barely a whisper. The sun drooped lower, casting shadows in the room.

"Master Abramson has arrived for dinner," a maid announced.

Mrs. Abramson rose, walked towards us and said, "I'm so pleased to see all of you enjoying the books."

Blimale stood and showed Mrs. Abramson the cover of her book. "*Pippi Longstockings*," said Blimale. "She's funny."

"Yes, isn't she? Shall we proceed to the dining hall?"

Mrs. Abramson led the way to the dining room where approximately ten domed silver trays lined the center section of the dining table.

I was curious what one could possibly hide under silver covers for *shalos seudos*. The silent process of washing and partaking of individual rolls gave way to the silent process of the server arriving and ceremoniously presenting each tray, removing the dome with a flourish. I peeked at Henchie and Blimale and saw their mouths gaping.

Salmon, I think, with grass and leaves and flowers adorning it, was the first unveiling. Then salad greens and vegetable slices. Rolled flounder, I think, was next. Melon slices. Then berries artfully arranged in a pie shell. Scones. Apple pudding. Cinnamon rolls. Fruit soup. Other biscuits and cookies.

"Brendon," said Mrs. Abramson, who had declined to choose any of the food, "I had company in the library today. The girls came to read. Isn't that marvelous?"

"The girls?" He looked up from his plate and blinked, as if he had forgotten we were there.

"Yes. Ruchama, as well. She can read."

"Ruchama? But I thought you said... that is, we were given to believe..." His glance darted to Ruchama and then back to Mrs. Abramson.

He was speaking carefully. I prayed with all my might he wouldn't use the word "disabled" or say that a teacher pronounced her unable to learn.

"Yes, Brendon," said Mrs. Abramson quickly. "It seems it was all a misunderstanding. She can read." Mrs. Abramson's cheery expression looked somewhat awkward. "Isn't that simply marvelous?"

I felt Ruchama stiffen.

"Well, yes." Mr. Abramson seemed flustered. "Delighted to

hear." He looked at Ruchama with smiling eyes. "Congratulations, Ruchama."

"Thank you," Ruchama murmured, here eyes on her plate.

Did she catch that last connotation? That someone had been involved in leading them to believe she was not able to learn? I sighed. Judging from the silent daggers I felt stabbing at my side, I assumed she did.

"This has been a most pleasant Shabbos," Mrs. Abramson said to me. "You must come again. Will you?" Her eyes caught mine directly.

"Thank you. That's very gracious of you, Mrs. Abramson. We certainly would love to. I need to speak to Mrs. Morgan and allow her to decide, but I'm sure the girls would love to, as well." I was blubbering.

I actually wasn't sure whether we would come again. Of one thing I was sure—Ruchama absolutely needed someone to accompany her whenever she went home.

The rest of the evening passed quickly. Blimale and Henchie wanted to check on the frog and we followed them outdoors. We were summoned inside for *havdalah* and afterwards, we packed our things. Mrs. Morgan had been vehement, insisting that we return to Thornton in time for *shacharis.*

* * *

Mrs. Abramson came out in the early morning in a magnificent dressing gown. She gave each of us a book to take with us. "Bring it back next week," she said meaningfully.

We thanked her. She watched us depart.

As we rode in the long car, Henchie and Blimale chattered about their books and about the car and anything else that entered their heads. I watched the countryside and couldn't help feeling sorry for Mrs. Abramson. What did very wealthy people do with their time? No chores, no cleaning, no cooking... nothing to actually take care of. They didn't even slice their own challah. How boring. And lonely.

"My first good Shabbos since I arrived five years ago," Ruchama muttered to me. "Friends. It makes the difference."

I nodded. It had been a strain. I imagined how tortuous it had been for Ruchama all the years. Enough silence to make one go mad.

I looked out the window. William had turned onto the small lane that led to Thornton. I gazed at my park as we passed. *See you later.*

"You need to bring a friend or two along every time," I said to Ruchama, quietly. "For your sanity. You know, Ruchama, your aunt isn't so bad, once you find common ground. Books seem to rate high with her."

I thought I heard her snort.

The gates were wide open and we drove up to the mansion. Other cars were discharging passengers and girls stood holding their overnight bags. Mrs. Morgan was outside greeting the arriving girls as we pulled up. I was glad to see her.

"This was the first time I actually saw her act human," said Ruchama into my ear. The car stopped in front of the steps. "You coaxed it from her somehow," she said and slid from her seat to climb out after Blimale and Henchie.

"Welcome home girls!!" Mrs. Morgan said, as William opened our doors.

"Welcome Judith," said Mrs. Morgan, giving me a hand and

a significant glance. She pulled me close. "How was your visit?"

What could I say? "Interesting."

Her eyes shifted to Ruchama and her eyebrows lifted. "An interesting experience for all, it seems," she murmured to me.

I looked at Ruchama. Was there a perceptible change?

"Straight to *shacharis*, girls," Mrs. Morgan announced, her arms wide, indicating the doors.

As we went up the steps with our bags, Ruchama said to me, "Later you'll tell me the rest of what you coaxed out of Aunt Ellen. I know there's more."

Smart girl.

* * *

I was glad to see the sunroom. I arranged the tables and chairs, papers and pens, thinking of the chaotic yet pleasant morning and how good it was to be back in class. The girls arrived.

"Welcome girls. Please take a seat. I'd love to hear about your Shabbos and to share mine with you…" I found Henchie, Blimale and Ruchama and gave them each a small smile, "…but we'll hear those stories tonight. Today, we are moving on from the tactile exercises to a place of thought." I saw expressions of consternation. "Your observations."

"Please take paper and pen and write three things you appreciated about the Shabbos, wherever you were. For example, the beautiful Shabbos table or the special Shabbos food and please don't use the examples I just gave you." The girls laughed. "Or…you may write how you would add your own extra special touches. Once you list these three things, please write a good-sized paragraph for each, using tactile writing wherever possible. First think, then write. You may begin."

Ruchama looked at me pointedly, her expression troubled. I opened my palm slightly. *What is it?* She lowered her head and glared, clearly in discomfort. Her anguished eyes found mine again.

I had no choice. I motioned for her to come to the corner of the room.

"What is it?"

"I can't do it," she whispered fiercely. "I can't do it. I don't know what I like or don't like. It's just a jumble. My entire life has just been turned upside down. I need time…!"

CHAPTER 21

I hadn't been thinking.

"You're right. A lot happened on Shabbos." I nodded. "Just leave it be. When you're ready, we'll work on it together."

She looked relieved and returned to her seat.

I collected the papers and made a mental note to proceed with care. In essence, Ruchama had just lost her parents and her dreams of returning home had completely shattered. Besides that, forming a new perspective of her aunt must have been terribly confusing, to say the least.

I tried to put myself in Ruchama's shoes, to imagine what she was going through. It was daunting.

That afternoon Ruchama came to the sunroom and said, "I will never have this opportunity again, to learn to write. Even if it's painful, I'd like to try." She looked at me and a small smirk touched her lips. "Isn't that what writing is? Pain?"

I smiled back, wondering if I could be so brave. "Often, it is."

It took a few days of grunting and sweating for her to identify and write the three things I asked for. All three things were from this past Shabbos. Apparently there were no memories before this week, worth mentioning.

"You did say you would tell me about your conversation with my aunt," Ruchama said, when we were done.

I had hoped she'd forgotten. "There's not much more to tell, Ruchama, other than your aunt was given the impression that you couldn't read."

"From whom?"

"She didn't say. But she was beyond pleased that it wasn't true."

"Another reason to treat me like a leper?"

"Another reason she felt lost. She was at a loss to understand anything about you. How to approach you. Try to see it from her perspective."

She looked at me bleakly. "I'll try."

* * *

I brought the girls' papers to the corner bed at story time. I read them without revealing the author. The girls jumped in with enthusiasm, telling countless tales until I forced them to go to bed. We did this every night for the next few nights.

Each night, I retired to my room, tired but fulfilled. One night I found a frog in a jar plus a number of strange colorful insects, on the floor inside my door. There was a note inside.

Thanks for always sharing your food with me.

Henchie? Was she the caterpillar girl?

I had been sure it was Blimale. What about the goodnight comments from The Annex? I went to sleep pondering sweet mysteries.

I woke up refreshed and looked forward to a great day. Mrs.

Morgan had granted me permission to use the front veranda for class. She said I had behaved admirably and that Mrs. Strassfeld had not complained about me at all that week. And here it was, already Wednesday.

I was ecstatic. Maybe now I could consider myself officially proper and refined. An American who could behave well enough to satisfy Mrs. Strassfeld. I patted myself on the back, proud that I had passed the rigorous test.

I formulated an idea for class. Each girl was to depict in pantomime a strong emotion, such as fear or excitement, while the rest of the class called out descriptive words, guessing what she portrayed. The correct word would win.

The veranda was perfect for it, seats along the back and plenty of room to perform. I ushered the girls out and they performed wholeheartedly. Afterwards, I made my way down the corridor to lunch, feeling good.

Uh-oh.

I saw Mrs. Strassfeld at the end of the corridor, armed to the teeth, ready for battle. My stomach clenched. Was she gunning for me? It sure looked like it from they way she glared my way. No turning back now. I walked cautiously, trying to act natural, as if there were no daggers aimed straight at my heart.

I kept my eyes fixed on the doorway, and told myself, *keep walking, you're almost there.* I approached and nonchalantly said, "Good day."

"I hope you are satisfied," she growled. I dared to look. Her teeth were clamped, her eyes deadly. "You chose to ignore the proper path, and may I remind you I gave you full warning.

Encouraging that sort of girl. Now we must bear the full brunt of your encouragement. If it were my decision, she would be dismissed at once, in my opinion should have been so years ago. I called an emergency meeting and I am not ashamed to admit I will demand your resignation."

I was beyond shocked. My resignation?! What in the world was going on? What was she talking about? Was it about the class outside? The girls had gotten a little giddy, had it spurred this tirade? Who did she wish to dismiss immedately?

"What girl? I have no idea what you mean."

Mrs. Morgan emerged right then from the dining room. She took one look at me and said, "Judith, may I speak with you a moment?" She took my elbow. "Excuse us, Mrs. Strassfeld, please."

She steered me down the hall with quick steps to her private office. "This is most upsetting." She opened the door. "Come inside quickly."

My mind was reeling. What happened?

"One of the instructors found this in the road diagonally across from the park." She pulled out Ruchama's pendant, the "R" with diamonds all around.

"This is Ruchama's, is it not?"

"Yes, it is."

"You did give it to her, did you not?"

"Yes, I did."

My mind was racing. Had Ruchama gone outside grounds? Not possible. Had she hated her necklace so much that she flung it away? All the way to the street? Improbable.

"The teachers assume the necklace belongs to one of the girls and Mrs. Strassfeld is positive it's Ruchama's and is convinced she went off grounds. I didn't let on that I recognized it."

"Now I understand what Mrs. Strassfeld was saying. She wanted to dismiss someone immediately. She meant Ruchama." I grasped the seriousness of the situation. "Surely you don't think Ruchama went off grounds, Mrs. Morgan?"

"I don't know what to think. You know the girl better, can you shed light on what this could possibly mean?"

"I don't know. I need to speak to her. It's hardly feasible for her to have left grounds. We've been working together on her writing every day, every afternoon, every available moment. I can vouch for her whereabouts. I know she hated the necklace with a passion. Perhaps she threw it away." A weak suggestion, but I couldn't think of a better one.

"Very well. I believe you. I need you to find out why this necklace was off grounds. The teachers have asked for an emergency meeting, actually Mrs. Strassfeld insisted. I'm afraid her opinion is harsh and unfavorable towards you, and she has a way of being dramatic. She alleges that Ruchama went off grounds and that you encouraged her delinquency. She demands that you be dismissed."

"What?! That is so untrue! She's jumping to conclusions. Simply guessing that the necklace is Ruchama's. She doesn't know. And she has absolutely no idea how the necklace got there. Or why. And what does she mean, saying I encouraged her? She's fabricating the whole story!"

I couldn't fathom how a woman of Mrs. Strassfeld's stature and intelligence could be so wrong, so harshly judgmental. What was eating at her?

"Yes, you have a point."

"She knows nothing about Ruchama," I said. "I don't know what she has against her. The girl faces an overwhelming struggle right now. Did you know, Mrs. Morgan, that her parents are completely debilitated? That she has no home to go to, even if she could find a way to go back?"

"Yes. I had heard. It is unfortunate."

"Well, this past Shabbos, she learned about it. Her world just turned upside down and she's first beginning to come to terms with it. She wouldn't be able to withstand the teachers bearing down on her. Especially wrongly." I shuddered at the thought of Ruchama and her asthma attacks.

Mrs. Morgan looked thoughtful. "Can you find out what happened as soon as possible? May I leave it in your hands? I'll try to buy time with Mrs. Strassfeld, but you must investigate this as a priority."

"I will. I'll find out. But please promise me the teachers won't approach Ruchama."

"I'll tell them."

"May I have the necklace?" Mrs. Morgan placed it in my palm. "And can we keep it just between ourselves, that the necklace is hers?"

She blew out a breath. "Yes, I suppose that would be wise. Let's proceed to the meeting."

"Now? Must we?"

"I'm afraid so. This is the onslaught I told you was bound to happen. Remember?"

"Yes. Ages ago."

She smiled. "And I said I will stand behind you. And I will. Best prepare ourselves."

She squared her shoulders and went for the door. "Come along, best foot forward."

We went down the corridor, marching together, to fight the good fight.

"I'll need time," I said.

"I'll get it for you. Just don't waste it."

We went through the narrow hallway and into the immense formal dining room at the front of the mansion. The Limudei Kodesh teachers were seated there. The air was thick.

"Ladies," said Mrs. Morgan, steering me to a chair beside her. "I just relayed to Miss Mintz what has transpired. She assured me unequivocally that the last three days she's been working steadily, every afternoon with Ruchama, and therefore vouches for her whereabouts, thereby making it impossible for Ruchama to have gone off grounds."

"Mrs. Morgan, are you suggesting that the locket belongs to one of the other girls?" said Mrs. Strassfeld, with haughty derision.

"What other girl could afford such extravagant jewelry?" Mrs. Mark asked, looking disgusted.

"What other girl would venture off grounds?" said Mrs. Strassfeld, her teeth clamped.

"An "R" with diamonds surrounding it? I don't know any girl who would wear that to school," said Mrs. Jacobson.

"Perhaps we might suggest the possibility that someone, not from school, dropped it," said Mrs. Werner. "It is a possibility, is it not?"

"Who, pray tell? No one lives anywhere near here," said Mrs. Mark.

"There is one house across the road from the park," said Mrs. Werner.

"A dressmaker?" said Mrs. Strassfeld, with contempt. "Not likely."

"We don't know that. Or perhaps someone else. A customer, then," said Mrs. Werner. "It is worthwhile to explore the possibility that the necklace belongs to an adult, not one of our girls."

"Ladies, these are possibilities, but they are entirely irrelevant," said Mrs. Morgan. "Our task is to make sure it's not one of the girls. Therefore, although some of you jumped to the conclusion initially that it was Ruchama, we can eliminate her completely, now that Miss Mintz vouches for her."

"Miss Mintz." Mrs. Strassfeld declared my name out as if it were something despicable. "Of course she would. She cares little for the school's reputation and the quality of girl that belongs here. She encourages the girls to go outdoors, engaging in conduct that promotes irreverence toward Thornton's rules and proper refinement."

"Mrs. Strassfeld! I object! Miss Mintz obtained permission to have class on the veranda from me, and I shan't have you undermining my authority." Mrs. Morgan was clearly agitated. "In addition, you can't possibly be suggesting that Miss Mintz is not telling us the truth, that she has not spent entire afternoons working with Ruchama!"

"Mrs. Strassfeld," I said, controlling my anger, "I promise you. Every afternoon following tea I have spent hours working together with Ruchama on her writing assignments, only stopping at supper time. We've been in the sunroom in plain view. It is not possible for Ruchama to have left the school grounds. I'm sure if you wish to verify my story, you will find someone who's seen us in the sunroom doing our work."

"I can verify her story," said Mrs. Morgan, her expression resolute.

"I can, as well," said Mrs. Werner. "I've seen them doing work in the sunroom. I thought it very commendable."

"That is completely beside the point," Mrs. Strassfeld said. "The "R" diamond pendant is hers. We must confront the girl and demand answers."

"What would be the purpose in that?" I said, trying not to raise my voice. "She is innocent and yet you treat her as if she is guilty. How is that proper? How is that correct? Our task is to find out if there is a girl in our school who has broken the rules by leaving grounds. And if there is such a girl, and I truly doubt there is, then we must learn her story and help her. Not destroy her." I was close to losing my composure. "I will take on the task." I clamped my mouth shut.

Silence.

I didn't know if I had been too bold. I firmly believed in everything I just said.

"I move to confront," Mrs. Strassfeld said. "And to remove the danger from our midst." She gave me a smoldering look.

I started to shrivel.

"I agree with Miss Mintz," said Mrs. Morgan, firmly, as if

the case was closed. "We must determine if there is a girl who has broken the rules. Judith is in the best position to unearth the information. And to do it discretely, without the girls learning the details. I suggest we give Miss Mintz a day or two to investigate. Until then, no one is to breathe a word of this to anyone. Especially the girls. I must have your word on this."

I found my voice. "If you please, may I have a few days?"

"Mark my words, the girl does not belong here. And neither does the teacher who protects her," said Mrs. Strassfeld.

"I agree with Mrs. Strassfeld," said Mrs. Mark.

Mrs. Morgan pressed her lips together. "Mrs. Jacobson, Mrs. Werner, what is your opinion?"

"I think I would like to have Miss Mintz find out whatever she can with the utmost discretion."

"I, too, vote for that."

"Agreed, then," said Mrs. Morgan, firmly. "Miss Mintz shall investigate." She looked at me. "You have until Sunday morning. Please get the information and a clear understanding of the situation by then." She addressed the room. "Not a word or a whisper about this, ladies, to anyone. Best go about our work as if nothing has occurred. That is all."

Mrs. Strassfeld looked violent. She stood and shot her fiery eyes at each of us. "I hope for all our sakes that you've made the right choice."

She stalked out. Mrs. Mark hurried after her.

"Sunday morning, Judith," said Mrs. Morgan. "Do try to find out before then." She gave me a pleading look, then turned to the teachers. "Ladies, thank you for your help."

The meeting was over. Mrs. Morgan and the other two

teachers hurried away.

I got up on shaky legs. I felt faint and realized I hadn't eaten lunch. I dragged myself to the dining room, hoping there would be food on the table.

No. No food. Nobody was there.

I stumbled to the kitchen, to the place of good smells and opera singing.

"Oh, my. Look what the cat dragged in."

"You look terrible, dearie, what ails you?"

"Don't ask."

"That bad, eh?"

"Worse."

Vicky and Paula sat me down on a bench tucked into the far corner of the kitchen, their coffee spot, a miniscule table against a wall painted with a garden mural. They cooed and clucked and plied me with biscuits and yeast cakes and coffee and muttered sympathies. It helped.

I needed to speak to Ruchama. I had three days. Three days to find out why her diamond necklace was in the road. I needed to dig…with wisdom.

I needed to get rid of my headache.

Vicky and Paula hovered.

I held out my cup for more coffee.

CHAPTER 22

I waited until lights out.

I asked Ruchama to come to my room.

"Please sit down," I said, indicating the armchair.

She sat on the edge. "What is it?"

I pulled the pendant from my pocket. "This."

She looked. No reaction.

"A teacher found it in the road outside grounds."

No reaction.

"Do you know how your necklace came to be there?"

"I have no idea," she said gruffly. Her expression was tight. "And it's no business of mine." She was quiet for a moment. "Are you asking me because the teachers suspect me of going off grounds?"

I sighed. She was so smart. "There is no possibility that you lost it there?"

"No. None."

"I didn't think so. Although it's yours, isn't it?"

"Not really."

"Can you explain?"

"I gave it away."

"To a girl here?"

"I hated the necklace and had no use for it."

"And you thought another girl would want it?"

She seemed to grapple with something. "Is it necessary for you to know?"

"The school is putting pressure on me to find out."

"It's private."

"I'll keep it private. We need to work this out. Seriously."

"Because the school, or an instructor or two, jumps to conclusions and says I went off grounds and you wish to prove my innocence. Correct?"

"Partially. That is my main objective. I've already told them you couldn't possibly have gone off grounds. I vouched for you."

Her face changed. "You seem to be the only one."

"No. There are others. Mrs. Morgan supports you and stands with me. Mrs. Werner and Mrs. Jacobson have no desire to find any girl guilty."

"Yet I know there is at least one who despises me and will jump to accuse me without reason. This is an opportunity to destroy me. Why must I suffer her hating me so?" Her anguish was plain.

I was at a loss. I didn't understand it myself. "I don't have the answer. Right now, I only wish to remove all suspicion from you. And to make sure no one else is leaving without permission. Mainly so Mrs. Strassfeld will calm down."

"I didn't go anywhere. And I don't know anything else."

She set her chin stubbornly. I sighed.

"I hear you. I'm with you, Ruchama." I admired her strong convictions and her strong sense of propriety, protecting someone's privacy. I would do the same.

She stood and went to the door. "Ruchama?" She turned back and looked at me. "Remember…we face things together."

She nodded. "Good night."

I was too agitated to sleep. I looked at the necklace.

I looked at the jar of caterpillars and the other jar with the frog and bugs. The caterpillars had been good listeners. I told them everything.

My mission churned in my head, even after unloading it all on the caterpillars. I tossed and turned, sleep evading me, wondering. What could have happened?

Ruchama had apparently given the necklace to someone. But who? And where did that person go? Was it one of the girls? And if it was one of the girls, why would they go out of school grounds? There was nowhere to go. And what occurred, causing the necklace to be in the road?

Perhaps she gave the necklace to an adult? Vicky or Paula? Or Mrs. Braun? The notion seemed ludicrous.

Morning arrived without a trace of sleep. To make matters worse, I was stared at, glared at, and fumed at by Mrs. Strassfeld at regular intervals. It would have been comical, if it wouldn't have been so uncomfortable.

I looked for Ruchama. I wanted to speak to her again, to give her support. She wasn't at breakfast. I went upstairs and looked into the main room. She wasn't there.

I ran downstairs to the dining room. I asked Henchie and Blimale if they'd seen Ruchama. They hadn't. I asked Ruthie and

Miri. Neither one of them had seen her.

I began to panic. I looked out the windows. I didn't see anyone. I went outdoors, checked the garden and the front of the building. Nothing. I went down the corridor and looked into the sunroom. Empty.

My heart began to hammer. Where could she be?

I hurried back to the dining room.

"Ruthie and Miri, I can't find Ruchama. Can you help me look for her?"

They both jumped up, alarm on their faces. "We'll check upstairs." They rushed out.

I went to Henchie. "Henchie. I need your help. Please go with Blimale outside and look for Ruchama. Look in every nook and cranny."

"Yes, Miss Mintz." She jumped up and I saw her whisper to Blimale and both of them ran out.

I looked for Mrs. Morgan. She was sitting next to Mrs. Strassfeld. Not an option. I left quickly and went down the corridor and looked into each classroom. No one.

I went to the kitchen.

"Oh, no, not again. You look awful. What's troubling you, sweetie?" asked Paula.

"I can't find Ruchama. Did you see her?"

"Can't say that I did," said Paula.

"Me neither," said Vicky. "Did you look in all the unvisited corners?"

I nodded.

She lowered her voice. "You think she might have run off?"

"I'm afraid to think that," I said, feeling myself hyperventilate.

My eyes stung. "Please keep this confidential."

Vicky and Paula nodded solemnly.

"Check the fancy front area," said Vicky. "A person might go there for solace."

"I hadn't thought of that," I said, feeling a glimmer of hope. "Thanks!"

"We'll keep an eye out and holler if we see her," said Paula, bellowing after me as I ran out.

I went to find Henchie and Blimale. They were just coming in, looking a bit muddy.

"Anything?"

"Nothing at all, except the usual," said Blimale.

"We looked under rocks, not that she would be there," said Henchie.

"Thank you girls. I'll speak to you later."

"We want to help you," said Henchie.

"I'm not sure how you can help right now. I'll let you know. Girls, don't tell anyone."

"We won't."

I ran upstairs. I found Ruthie and Miri in the guest rooms, looking into closets.

"We didn't see her," said Ruthie.

"We looked everywhere," said Miri.

"What are you thinking, Miss Mintz?"

I took in a deep breath. "Please keep this confidential. Many things in Ruchama's life are extremely painful, to the point of breaking. I don't know what to think, but I'm very worried. You should probably go to class. I'll let you know if I need you."

We emerged from the stairwell and found Mrs. Strassfeld standing there, looking murderous.

"Girls, where have you been? Miss Mintz, what is the meaning of this? All three of my students are not in my Chumash class, two of whom are with you. Care to explain?"

I didn't trust myself to be civil. "Something important happened and I needed Ruthie and Miri's help. Sorry."

Her mouth clamped in a severe line. "And what about your dear Ruchama? Is she not with you?"

I felt my blood pressure rise.

Ruthie said, "Ruchama can't come today, Mrs. Strassfeld. It's just Miri and me."

She and Miri walked quickly to the classroom.

I was granted one more contemptuous look before Mrs. Strassfeld turned and left. I didn't trust myself to think kind thoughts at that moment.

I continued to search. I checked the parlor. Of course she wasn't there. I walked through the enormous dining room. No. Not in the front foyer either. I went up the spiral staircase and through the hallways, peeking into rooms. It was quiet as a tomb. I called out softly, "Ruchama?"

The place gave me the shivers.

I felt tears on my cheek. If anything happened to her, I would never forgive myself. I hurried down the stairs and knocked on the office door and tried to compose myself.

Mrs. Braun's sweet voice called, "Yes. Come in."

I entered.

"Oy. What is, Yehudis? You don't feel good?"

I broke down. "It's all my fault. A girl is missing. I think she ran away. Oh, Mrs. Braun. I shouldn't have talked to her. What should I do now? I can't find her anywhere."

"Who is it, Yehudis?"

"Ruchama Fishman."

She looked deep into my soul, her eyes concerned. She nodded. "She has many troubles for a very long time. Everything is not your fault. You care for her. She knows. She has a big nesayon. Why such a big one, I don't know. But she is a lucky girl. She has you to help her."

I crumbled right then.

I broke down and cried. Mrs. Braun patted me. She was right. It wasn't my fault. Not everything was up to me. I could only do my best to help her.

I nodded to Mrs. Braun. "Thank you. You're right."

"Yes. shaifaleh."

"Where could she have gone?"

"I'm sure we will find out. Ask Hashem to help you. You will have ideas where to look." She smiled at me. "You are a good girl, Yehudis."

I hugged her.

I went back to the corridor and knocked on Mrs. Morgan's office door. No answer.

I had to get away. I let myself out and went to the park. I sat near the water.

Time passed with little awareness on my part.

Soft footsteps approached. I looked up and saw the woman, the dressmaker. Wearing slippers. I wiped my cheek.

"Hello," she said.

"Hello," I said, quietly, not able to be friendly.

I snapped to reality. I wondered if she might know something. "Do you ever see anyone else from the school? Out here?"

"No, no one. Until you came along. But funny, just the other day, a lovely young lady from your school came by my house. Not for sewing, mind you." She gave a light chuckle. "She wanted to show me her necklace."

My heart lurched. "Do you remember her name?"

"No, I don't. Actually, I don't recall her giving her name."

"Can you describe her?"

"Oh, yes. Beautiful. Petite. Brown hair. Lovely eyes."

The description could fit many girls.

"Young?"

"Yes. Perhaps your age. A bit younger."

"Why did she want to show you her necklace?"

She chuckled again. "She had a notion to sell it. But I told her I didn't think I could help her. I told her to try her luck in the city."

I looked at my watch and realized with a jolt that I would be late for class. I needed to run. "Sorry, I have to run to class. Thank you for talking to me."

The girls were waiting for me in the sunroom when I arrived, breathless and apologetic.

"Sorry I'm late. For today's class, I have pictures and photos of various expressions." Fortunately, I had prepared them ahead. "Try to guess the emotions and situations depicted here. You may work together."

While watching the girls do the exercise, my mind churned with thoughts about Ruchama.

Where was she??

I looked at the girls in the room. Most of them were finished their descriptions and I realized they were looking at me.

"Pair up, girls, and each of you display an emotion. Each partner, do your best to 'read' each other's emotion and write what you see. Then, please create a fictitious situation that causes the person to feel this way. Bring it to class tomorrow. Unless you have questions, class dismissed."

I was dismissing them early and the class took their time filing out slowly, many of the girls making faces at each other. I smiled at them until I caught Mrs. Strassfeld staring disapprovingly through our glass window. Inwardly, I rolled my eyes. How was this helping? She had a definite problem. As far as I was concerned, she was the source of all the suffering and I fought an urge to have it out with her.

I stood up. My fists clenched.

She turned and haughtily walked away.

I went to lunch but picked at my food. Thoughts tumbled through my head. Someone from school had gone to the dress-maker with the necklace. Who was it? And why did she drop the necklace in the road? How had she gotten out? The gates were always locked.

What did Ruchama know about the girl? Was she protecting her privacy? Or was she protecting her from the teachers? Or was it a matter of principle, a conviction that it was not anyone's business.

I continued to brood. A gnawing ache settled in the pit of my stomach.

Ruchama had left school. How? Where? Had someone said

something to her? The more I thought about it, the more it seemed possible Mrs. Strassfeld or Mrs. Mark said something to her this morning.

Where was she??

Henchie was asking me something. "Maybe she went home…?"

I saw Mrs. Morgan enter and go to her seat.

"What?"

"I said, maybe she went home." Henchie scrunched her face at me, looking at me oddly.

I wasn't comprehending.

Maybe she went home. Maybe she went home. It finally penetrated.

Maybe she went home!

"Henchie, you're a genius."

I jumped up and hurried over to Mrs. Morgan.

CHAPTER 23

I spilled the story without pausing for breath.

"Do I call the Abramsons and see if Ruchama is there? If she isn't, I don't want to alarm them."

"Judith, if she isn't there, we must let the Abramsons know she's missing and begin a search for her. You say you think one of the teachers made a caustic remark, casing her to bolt?"

"I don't know. It's a thought."

"Come to my office straightaway."

We quick-marched to her office.

"Yes, hello," she said into the phone. "It's urgent that I speak to Mrs. Abramson at once. It's Mrs. Morgan from Thornton."

She tapped her nails on the desk while I paced in the small area.

"Yes? Mrs. Abramson, did Ruchama arrive at your home? She did? When? Two hours ago? You say she's not well?"

I felt a great sense of relief. Then dread. Ruchama was home, safe, but she wasn't well. Was it her asthma?

"Mrs. Morgan…" I said, trying to get her attention.

"I'm sorry?" She said into the phone. "You sent for the doctor?"

"Mrs. Morgan…" I said again, louder.

"One moment, please, Mrs. Abramson." Mrs. Morgan covered the mouthpiece. "What is it?"

"Please ask her if I may visit." I felt tight, wound up.

"Mrs. Abramson, would you mind if Miss Mintz visits Ruchama?"

She listened. I was shivering. I folded my arms and tried to calm myself.

"Fine. I'll tell her. Thank you."

She hung up. "She said you may visit after the doctor leaves. He's with her now. She will send William with the car for you after hearing from the doctor. Are you well?"

I nodded. I started to breathe. "Mrs. Morgan, I don't know how Ruchama left grounds. The gates were locked. I feel responsible. I'm sorry."

"Apparently we have gates that allow girls to slip through. Please don't berate yourself about it. There is a situation here, one I feel is intertwined with the necklace in the road. Whatever you can unearth would bring resolution to the intense and disturbing mystery."

She didn't blame me. It helped. "I'm working on it, Mrs. Morgan. Just know that Ruchama is completely innocent and at this point, we need to protect her."

I didn't need to say from whom. She knew.

"Yes. I see. Judith Mintz. Carry on. I expect to hear answers from you soon if not sooner, so we can be done with this and put it behind us."

"I'll do my best."

I was desperate to find out who had gone to the dressmaker. I had two days to find out.

I made my way to the front veranda. I was still shivering.

How could I find out who the "young lady" was? How did she and Ruchama get out of the gates?

I walked down the driveway and examined the gates carefully. There was no way anyone could get through. No one was small enough to fit through the bars. I walked along the hedges. They were thick and impenetrable.

But what was this? With a jolt, I saw a spot in the hedges that was bare. A slim girl could fit through.

No one was around. I turned sideways and slipped through and found myself on the sidewalk. I was near the corner. The park was right across the road.

This was how they had done it! I slipped back through the bushes and went up to the veranda. I sank into one of the chairs, astounded by my discovery. I felt weak and closed my eyes.

* * *

The sound of a motor car reached my ears and I shot upright. I felt my hair sticking up and my eyes blinked. I guessed I had dozed off. I scurried to the gates and there was William and the long car. I let myself out and locked the gates behind me. William jumped out and opened the passenger door for me.

I slid in and he shut the door, and we drove off. The ride felt too quiet this time without Henchie and Blimale.

Mrs. Morgan, I remembered, said something about the doctor being called. Maybe it was a blessing that Ruchama was home…she could finally get the medical care she needed.

Something niggled at me, Mrs. Morgan saying that Ruchama had arrived home two hours ago, making her arrival around ten-thirty. Ruchama had been missing at breakfast, since eight or eight-thirty. Was she outside for two hours, waiting?

"Excuse me, William?"

"Yes, madam."

"Did you drive Ruchama home from school this morning?"

"No, madam."

No. A shiver went up my spine. How had Ruchama gotten home?

We pulled up in front of the mansion and I jumped out and ran up the stairs. The door opened and to my surprise, Mrs. Abramson herself appeared. She looked terrible. Her face was blotchy, her eyes red. Her face was wet.

"She's gone. I'm so very worried." She wrung a handkerchief in her hands.

I blinked at her. What was she saying?

"Ruchama? Gone? I don't understand."

"The doctor tried to help her, but she couldn't breathe. He called an ambulance. She was rushed to the hospital." She dabbed her face.

My heart plunged into my shoes. "Was she having an asthma attack?"

"Yes. A severe one. She couldn't breathe at all." Tears coursed down her cheeks. "I'm afraid she might die."

No. No! It couldn't be! My throat closed.

"Can I go to her?" I choked.

"Yes, I suppose, you may. William will drive you."

"Mrs. Abramson, wouldn't you like to go?"

She blinked at me. "I… didn't think… I thought… I suppose I would… Yes. I would like to." She seemed to perk up. "I'll just freshen up a bit. Would you care to come inside?"

"Yes, thank you."

I went inside and caught a glimpse of myself in the ornate mirror. What a mess! I smoothed my hair into place and tucked myself in.

Mrs. Abramson emerged, very put together, her polished façade back in place. I quickly followed her to the waiting car and we drove off.

"Mrs. Abramson, do you mind telling me what happened?"

"No, of course not. It was confusing. Jeremy informed me that Ruchama was home. It was mid-morning, much after Brendon had left, perhaps ten-thirty. She looked miserably ill. I asked if she was feeling well and she could barely respond. I had Annette fetch water. The water helped somewhat and Ruchama said she would go to her room to rest. But then…she collapsed on the stairs." Mrs. Abramson looked out the window and shook her head, biting her lip. "Jeremy lifted her to her room while I phoned Dr. Gold. Annette recommended cold compresses, and took over Ruchama's care until Dr. Gold arrived." She shook her head again and cried without a sound. "It's been a nightmare."

"Did Ruchama let you know she was coming?"

"No. It came as a bit of a shock."

Who had brought Ruchama home?!

We arrived at the hospital and rushed to the emergency room entrance. We spoke to a bored nurse at the main desk, who looked up Ruchama's name and told us she had been taken to intensive care. With a sense of intense dread, I rushed with Mrs. Abramson through the hallways and up the stairs. Wasting precious moments, we waited for our visitor's pass and then located her room number. A miserable sight faced us through the glass. An oxygen mask covered Ruchama's deathly white face and a team of nurses, doctors and machines surrounded her.

A muffled sob from Mrs. Abramson reminded me that she stood at my side. "There's Dr. Gold," said Mrs. Abramson, indicating a man in a suit, a hospital gown over it.

He was speaking to another man, his expression serious. He glanced our way and came out of the room to us.

"She's still completely constricted, Mrs. Abramson," he said. "We've been giving her medication every hour and administered a bronchodilator. So far there's been minimal response. We've assisted her breathing with mechanical ventilation and oxygen."

No, please, no. She has to get better.

Mrs. Abramson put her handkerchief to her mouth, though she controlled herself. Her breathing was rapid and shallow. I was surprised at the depth of her caring for Ruchama.

Ruchama had no clue.

"How bad is it?" I asked quietly.

"Fairly serious, a full blown asthma attack." He looked at Mrs. Abramson. "Does she use an inhaler at home? Or have beta agonist medication?"

Mrs. Abramson looked lost. "No...I...I'm afraid I know nothing about her asthma. She never told me."

Dr. Gold gave her a long, hard look.

"She didn't tell anyone," I said. "She kept her condition

hidden. I witnessed one of her attacks at school, that's the only reason I know. I reported it to Mrs. Morgan, who has taken steps to find a doctor."

Mrs. Abramson looked at me in disbelief. "I should have been informed," she said, stiffly.

"Ruchama didn't wish to concern you." This conversation was becoming stressful. What was I supposed to tell her? Best change the subject. I peeked into the room. Ruchama's eyes were open. "May I go in and see her, Dr. Gold?"

"I'm afraid that would be unwise at the moment. Please wait here while I check on her condition."

"Miss Mintz," Mrs. Abramson said quietly, after Dr. Gold left us. "Was there a reason Ruchama did not tell me?"

"She didn't want anyone to know. She didn't tell anyone." How could I explain it? "She couldn't reach out. Or let anyone in." The silence was long and awkward. "What is Ruchama's full name?"

"Ruchama bas Esther."

Dr. Gold returned. "Remarkably, she's doing a bit better. I'll keep you informed."

We waited at the door. Mrs. Abramson appeared to be in deep thought. I paced, a new activity for me. What felt like hours, but was probably only an hour later, Dr. Gold emerged, a small smile on his face.

"Her breathing is much improved. She requested to leave." He chuckled softly. "You may see her now. Only keep the visit brief."

"Miss Mintz, you may go first," said Mrs. Abramson.

I entered the room. Ruchama's eyes were visible above the

black oxygen mask. All doctors and nurses except one, exited.

"It's no secret anymore," I said to Ruchama, when I was at her side. "Your asthma."

She shook her head slightly.

"Now you'll get the medicine you need." I wanted desperately to know what happened. Had someone hurt her? Why had she run home? And how had she gotten there? I dared not ask while she was still sick. "Your friends are worried about you." Her hands opened. "Henchie and Blimale. Ruthie and Miri."

She smiled. Muffled sounds came from behind her mask. I think she said, "Tell them not to worry. I'm fine."

"And what about me? Was I supposed to not worry? I looked high and low for you, racing around like a demented person."

"Sorry."

"When you get out, we do things together. Agreed?"

She nodded slowly. "When can I leave?"

"As soon as you recover. If you behave, they'll let you go home. Maybe even for Shabbos." Was I wrong to give her hope?

Her eyes looked alarmed. "Will you come?"

I had no choice. "Yes, of course."

"And Henchie and Blimale?"

I'll let them know you want them."

"Ruthie and Miri?"

"I don't know. I could ask them."

She nodded.

"Ruchama?"

She looked at me. I took her hand. "Your aunt cares about you deeply. She cried. She's very worried. She wants to help you. Will you let her?"

She closed her eyes. "I'll try." Her eyes opened. "Slowly."

Mrs. Abramson entered. Her face looked moist.

I patted Ruchama's hand. She gripped me tightly. "Stay."

I nodded.

Mrs. Abramson approached the bed. "I'm so glad you're doing better, Ruchama," her voice was hoarse. "I think we must take better care of you. You don't ask for much but..." she attempted to smile, "I'd like to do more."

An attempt at closeness. Yet I was the link.

I stayed.

I told them about the assignment we had worked on in class that day. I demonstrated a few of the exaggerated expressions the girls had displayed. Ruchama smiled. Mrs. Abramson looked on, her expression neutral.

I tried to draw Mrs. Abramson in. "May I ask, how was your week?"

"Well, we tried a new cook," she said. "But she was atrocious. I fired her this morning. Just before Ruchama arrived." She looked down at her hands.

An idea struck me with a bang.

"Mrs. Abramson, would you be interested in having a few girls from Thornton cook for you for Shabbos?"

A polite gasp escaped her parted lips and her eyes were bright. "I would be most interested. Without a cook, I feared there would be no food for us, other than biscuits and wine."

My mind began racing. "Do you have provisions in the kitchen?"

"Oh, yes. Our cooler and pantry are well stocked. We have ample food supplies for months."

I needed to speak to the girls. I looked at my watch. I couldn't believe my eyes. Five thirty! I had missed tea.

"I must get back to Thornton. Would you allow William to drive me there now?"

"Yes, of course."

We made arrangements for William to come to school Friday at twelve and drive the girls and myself to Brellenson.

I took my leave, reassuring Ruchama that I would see her tomorrow. She closed her eyes.

Mrs. Abramson escorted me to the car, conveniently waiting directly in front of the hospital, in the "reserved" area.

I sat numbly in the car the entire way back to Thornton. The events of the day had taken a toll on me. As we neared the school, I looked for the space in the hedges where I had slipped through. Yes, there it was. As I looked, I felt faint. A girl emerged. She saw the car and quickly slipped back through the hedges.

It was dark, but I had caught a glimpse of her. Had my eyes deceived me? I wasn't completely sure, but I thought…

It couldn't be!!

CHAPTER 24

"Please stop the car here!"

William braked sharply. I jumped out.

"Thank you, William. Tomorrow at twelve!"

I ran and slipped through the space in the hedge. I saw the girl go around the side of the building. I ran after her. Full speed.

She had disappeared into the building and up the stairs. I took them two at a time. I caught a brief glimpse of a skirt and shoes turning into the room. I came up to the landing. The girls were milling about. It was impossible to tell who had just come in.

"Girls," I announced, catching my breath, "we'll leave to supper in fifteen minutes. And will the girl I just followed upstairs, please come to my room to chat for a minute?"

I went to my room. I didn't wait long.

The girl appeared.

Chills went up and down my spine. I kept my breathing steady with difficulty, while I struggled to make sense of it.

How could it be? My mind refused to accept it. The reality shocked me to the core. A huge story awaited. I took a deep breath.

"Come in, Ruthie. Please shut the door."

She closed the door gently and turned to face me. She was drained of all color.

I took out the necklace. "Is this yours?" I said quietly.

Her face froze. She stared at it. She looked at me and said in a small voice, "Yes. It is. You found it." She swallowed.

"It was found in the road. By one of the teachers."

Her face flushed bright pink and she grimaced. "I was afraid of that." She blinked and seemed to be grappling with her emotions.

"Ruchama was suspected. But I knew she was innocent," I said. "She hadn't gone anywhere. Also, she told me she gave the necklace away, although she didn't tell me to whom. She was protecting you."

The depth of Ruchama's self-sacrifice was astonishing. She was ready to be punished for the sake of another girl's privacy. The greatness of the girl hit me with a force.

Ruthie swallowed again and nodded. "I know. I owe her so much. She's the most giving girl." Her eyes became huge with feeling. "No one really knows her. She said the necklace might help my family. I couldn't believe it. A priceless diamond necklace and she was giving it away."

"So what were you thinking to do with it?"

"I thought I could sell it. We needed the money desperately… for my mother's operation. I thought to spare my parents embarrassment and wanted no one to know. So I thought to go to the dressmaker across the road, perhaps she could find a buyer."

"I know. She told me."

"She told you? You mean you knew?"

"Not really. I met her in the park. She told me a girl came by with a necklace. She didn't know your name."

"I… she was nice. But she couldn't help me. I broke the rules, Miss Mintz, and it didn't even work." She sighed. "My mother's condition is quite serious now. I will have to try again. Elsewhere."

"I'm sorry. Ruthie, you meant well, but…the teachers…you took a chance. They may wish to dismiss you."

She squared her shoulders and lifted her head. She took a breath. "I wish it weren't so but if that is their choice, I'm prepared to face the charges against me. I did it for the good of my family and no other reason. I accept the consequences." She looked at me searchingly. "Must they know?"

"Not if I can help it." There were those I feared who might not take into account the extenuating circumstances. Even if it was Ruthie. I had to make sure she wasn't found out. I sighed.

Life was so complex.

"You're not upset with me, are you Miss Mintz?"

How could I explain what I felt? "Ruthie. Far from it. Actually… I admire you."

Her eyes became round and she looked down. "You understand what I'm going through." Her eyes came up, blinking.

"Yes. I do. So, what were you doing out of grounds tonight? Were you searching for the necklace?"

"Yes, I was and the last two evenings, as well. The necklace tore a hole in my pocket, it was so heavy. Must have been the weight of all the diamonds. Miss Mintz, I would like to stay in school. Will you keep my secret?"

"Ruthie. Of course. What you did was wrong, but I hear your story. I wish you would have discussed it with me, though. I could have helped you. At least I could have taken the necklace for you to the dressmaker."

She looked sheepish. She nodded. "You're right. I should have spoken to you."

"Please. From now on, let's work on this together." I took her hand and placed the necklace in her palm. "Here. This is yours. Use it as you wish. And I hope it brings you good fortune."

"Thank you, Miss Mintz. I'm…I'm at a loss how to proceed."

"Well, I've been thinking about you and an idea popped into my mind, one that might be a tad farfetched but still more doable than leaving grounds to sell the necklace. I personally think it's brilliant. If it can work."

"Please tell me. I'll do anything"

"Do you cook and bake?"

"Oh, yes, brilliantly. My sisters and I have been at the helm of our kitchen for years. Why do you ask?"

"Well, I know of a wealthy couple who is in desperate need of a cook. Ruchama's aunt and uncle. I asked Mrs. Abramson if you and a few friends might cook for Shabbos and she jumped for it. Maybe we can arrange for you to go there on a regular basis, to cook for them. They have the means to pay you handsomely. Would you be interested?"

Her eyes grew bright. "Miss Mintz, I am exceedingly interested. If it works, it would be the answer to my family's troubles."

"Then we've accomplished something good tonight." I held

up my fingers. "One. No more going off grounds. Two. Maybe a job. Now I need to convince Mrs. Morgan to let you do it."

"Miss Mintz. Must Mrs. Morgan know...about what I did?"

"I'll do my best to keep it from her, although she would be sympathetic. Ruthie, please ask Miri if she'll join you and come to the Abramsons for Shabbos. Ruchama specifically asked for you both. And Henchie and Blimale."

"Ruchama?? Miss Mintz, where is she?"

Oh, my. I had forgotten.

"Oh, dear. I forgot that I didn't tell you, sorry. Ruchama became seriously ill and had to be taken to the hospital." A picture of her in the hospital bed with the black oxygen mask over her face popped into my mind. I shuddered.

Ruthie looked devastated. "Oh, no, how awful. Can we do something?"

"I don't know. We might be able to visit her. Today, she was doing poorly. I hope tomorrow will be better. Let's pray for the best." I looked at my watch. It was late. "I think we'd better go to supper now and take care of the arrangements we need for Shabbos."

"Miss Mintz? I...can't thank you enough." Her eyes were glassy.

I couldn't help myself. I gave her a hug.

We walked down the hallway and saw that Miri had done a fine job on her own. We made our way down and I headed straight for Mrs. Morgan. Mrs. Strassfeld, unfortunately, was in the seat next to her.

Mrs. Morgan took one look at me and concern flashed across her face. "Judith. You look as though you've seen a ghost."

"May I speak to you privately, Mrs. Morgan?"

She stood up and steered me out of the room to the corridor.

"How is Ruchama?" She whispered intently.

The lines in her face were drawn. She had been worrying.

"She's in the intensive care unit."

Her hand went to her heart. "Oh, no! It can't be! What happened? Is it her asthma?"

"Yes. She couldn't breathe and they rushed her to the hospital." I felt myself shaking. Mrs. Morgan's eyes closed. "Mrs. Morgan, I need to know if you would give permission for four girls to go to Ruchama's house for Shabbos."

She looked horrified. "For pity's sake, Judith, Ruchama's in the hospital! And you want girls to frolic at her home?"

"No. This is for Ruchama. She specifically asked for them to come."

"She spoke to you?"

"Yes, behind her oxygen mask, in her own individual way. It's important for her to know we'll be there. In case she comes home." I felt my heart ache, thinking about the real possibility of her not coming home.

"If it will make her happy, by all means. But…intensive care…I can't imagine she'll be home so soon."

"You're probably right. If she can't come home, I'll stay with her for Shabbos."

"Oh, my. That would be a great sacrifice. But under the circumstances, the most supportive. You've become indispensable, Judith Mintz. The girls must be part of this and say tehillim."

"Yes, Mrs. Morgan. Also, um, I volunteered the girls to cook for the Abramsons."

Her jaw dropped. "Judith Mintz! What on earth?"

"Mrs. Abramson lost her cook and as of now, they'll have no food for Shabbos unless we help."

She shook her head and blinked. "And Mrs. Abramson agrees?"

"Enthusiastically."

She gave me a wry look.

My skin prickled and I saw Mrs. Strassfeld approach us. Her presence loomed. I inched closer to Mrs. Morgan, my breath stuck in my throat.

She spoke through clenched teeth. "Might I know what Miss Mintz has accomplished with regard to protecting our institution?" Her disdain was palpable.

Blood pounded in my head.

Before I could stop myself, I said, "Mrs. Strassfeld, you might have taken a moment to think about Ruchama's feelings before destroying her this morning." I was taking a risk, trying to find out the truth.

Mrs. Morgan's eyes popped open. "Judith! What possessed you?"

"Perhaps Mrs. Strassfeld will share with you, Mrs. Morgan, what she said to Ruchama?" I hoped I was right, hoped I was wrong, hoped that things wouldn't be the way they were.

Mrs. Strassfeld's nostrils flared with disdain. "Spare me the dramatics. I simply made a move to help her. For her own sake, I merely suggested she leave school now and avoid the embarrassment of being dismissed."

Mrs. Morgan's jaw dropped. "Mrs. Strassfeld! I specifically asked you to allow us to investigate! And not to approach

Ruchama!"

I couldn't control myself. "Especially since she is innocent! You don't know anything about her!" I was so disgusted, I felt nauseous. I clenched my teeth to hold myself in. I said quietly, "Ruchama is in the hospital right now because of your comments. Is that what you had in mind? For her own sake?"

She looked at me coldly.

"Mrs. Strassfeld," said Mrs. Morgan, her lips tight. "This is unacceptable. I demand that you make amends or… " Mrs. Morgan let her sentence hang as she breathed in and out, struggling. "I shall need to take action," she finished in a low firm voice.

Mrs. Strassfeld flinched slightly, as if she had been slapped in the face. She remained silent. Her eyes narrowed.

Without another word, she marched stiffly down the corridor and turned into the hallway that led to the front foyer.

"What is wrong with her?!" I asked.

"This situation has deteriorated to the point of no return," said Mrs. Morgan quietly, as if talking to herself. "To think that she deliberately…" She shook her head. "It's too terrible to think."

"Mrs. Morgan, would you actually fire her?"

"All depends on what she does," she said, her gaze still on the corridor. "I've said my piece. As they say in chess, 'check'." She gave me a piercing look. Then she snapped out of it. "Let's go in now and tell the girls."

"Before we do, Mrs. Morgan, do I have your permission for the girls to cook for the Abramsons?"

"Yes, yes, of course. It is a good deed. Have the girls obtain permission from their parents to go."

"Speaking of good deeds, Mrs. Morgan…" I began, but she was already marching into the dining room. I wanted to tell her about Ruthie working for the Abramsons, but instead, I followed and saw her pick up a drinking glass and spoon.

"Girls!" Clink, clink, clink, clink. The room quieted. "I'm sorry to bear sad tidings but it is important that you know. One of our girls became seriously ill today. Ruchama. She is in the hospital and needs our *tefillos*. Miss Mintz was there to visit her and tells me Ruchama is still quite ill. If you've finished here, please go into the parlor for *tehillim*. Miss Mintz will lead. I'll be in my office if you need me."

The girls were buzzing with concerns and fears. I was bombarded without pause and my head began to throb. I closed my eyes and raised my hand. Gradually, the noise subsided.

"I'll answer as many questions as I can," I said. "I visited Ruchama today in the hospital. I won't give you the details without her permission. But I can tell you that the worst is over and she is very slowly beginning to recover. I don't know how long she'll need to be in the hospital. She may need to rest for a few days at home before returning to school. My guess is she will return sometime next week, but we'll wait to hear. Her name is Ruchama bas Esther. Please find *tehillim* books in the parlor. I'll be in momentarily. Blimale and Henchie please stay. Also, Ruthie and Miri. "

Mindy's hand went up. "Please Miss Mintz, can't we do something?"

Yes, I thought. Something from the girls would be just the right thing. I thought for a moment.

"Perhaps you can write her get-well wishes?" I said.

A chorus of excited voices surrounded me, with some of the girls bouncing up and down.

"When we're done in the parlor, whoever wishes may go to the sunroom to work on it."

The girls filed out. I sensed a spirit of caring. They were good girls.

Henchie, Blimale, Ruthie and Miri gathered before me.

"You four need permission from your parents to go to the Abramsons and guess what? You'll be cooking Shabbos for them." Their faces lit up.

"They have the most humongous kitchen ever!" Blimale said.

"The cook they fired wielded a knife when she got angry," said Henchie.

"I can understand why they fired her," said Ruthie.

Shabbos would certainly be interesting. I urged the girls to call from Mrs. Morgan's office.

I led the *tehillim* for Ruchama bas Esther and used my handkerchief a number of times. I felt so sorry for Ruchama. Learning that my worst suspicions had been true and Mrs. Strassfeld had spoken harshly to Ruchama, made me sick with misery. I couldn't shake the questions away.

What had caused Mrs. Strassfeld to behave the way she did? I knew every person had a story. What could her story be?

CHAPTER 25

At last. It was time to go.

Last minute bag-closing, buckling and tucking in, shoe-finding and cupboard-shutting petered to an end. Travel bags were dragged downstairs.

I carefully packed the girls' pictures, poems and heartfelt notes for Ruchama, into my traveling bag.

William drove up at twelve o'clock, on the dot. The five of us clambered into the long car, Ruthie and Miri absorbing it with dignity and wide eyes. Henchie and Blimale assumed the role of vivacious tour guides, preparing Ruthie and Miri for the enormity of the mansion, exaggerating horrendously and bragging about roomfuls of goodies waiting to be consumed.

Jeremy, stiff and expressionless, opened the door and let us in. We went straight upstairs. Blimale and Henchie graciously offered the green room to Ruthie and Miri, maintaining their lavender room and my peach room. My room was visited briefly for refreshments and then we went downstairs to see what lay in store for us.

Mrs. Abramson was at the bottom of the stairs, formal as ever, but with a tentative, though somewhat stiff, smile on her face.

"Hello girls, I'm so pleased you could come."

"Mrs. Abramson, these are Ruchama's friends," I said. "Henchie and Blimale you met last week. And may I present Ruthie and Miri, Ruchama's classmates. Your kitchen crew for the weekend."

Her eyes were bright. "I truly appreciate this, you cannot imagine. This week has been challenging, to say the least. And now with Ruchama ill…" She looked away, her eyes downcast.

"How is she today?" I asked.

She looked at me and made an attempt at a smile. "Yes. We were there together yesterday, weren't we? During the crisis." She gave me a contemplative look. "The nurses today say she had a fairly good night, breathing a bit better. Improving, albeit slowly. I thought perhaps I might visit in a short while."

It was good to hear. Mrs. Abramson was initiating a visit to Ruchama, whereas yesterday it had been my idea. I would say things had improved. Vastly.

"May we join you?" I asked.

Her eyes darted toward the girls. "Oh. I'm not sure that they'll allow this many visitors. I'll inquire."

"Perhaps," I said, "the girls could get started now on the food preparation. Get things underway."

"Yes, of course. If you'll just follow me?"

On our way, I asked Mrs. Abramson if there was anything in particular she or Mr. Abramson liked to eat. She became animated as she led us to the meat kitchen and said that neither she nor her husband was particular but they were partial to fish, salads and soup.

Ruthie asked, "Mrs. Abramson, do you have challah rolls or shall we bake them?"

"I...don't know. We may have some in the freezer." She strained to open an enormous metal door. It seemed like her first time. She wiped her hands delicately.

"How about if we look inside ourselves?" I suggested.

"Splendid." She looked relieved.

Mrs. Abramson showed us the enormous pantry, refrigerators and stoves. The size of it all left us gaping. She offered Annette's assistance, if needed. We politely declined.

After Mrs. Abramson left us, Ruthie and Miri pulled gleaming pots off the hooks and Blimale and Henchie gleefully began hauling out chickens, fish, fruits and vegetables and loading them onto the counters. I peered into the freezer and saw loaves of bread and challahs of all sizes and shapes.

"I would say we don't need challah this week." I said. "Shall we make a menu?"

"Fish, salads, soup and something interesting for tonight," said Ruthie. "Vegetable and chicken knishes, perhaps."

"Fruit cobbler?" said Miri.

My mouth started to water.

"Yum," said Henchie.

"And for tomorrow?" I asked.

"They don't seem to be the cholent sort," said Ruthie.

"We had a sort of stew last week...not exactly cholent," said Henchie.

I tried to recall what we had eaten. Completely consumed by the serving and the stilted conversation, I couldn't really remember.

"How about if we make something simple like a mix of meat, barley, potatoes and squash?" I suggested.

"Fine with me," said Henchie. No one else seemed to care much.

The girls set about looking through the numerous drawers for knives and cutting boards. A huge pot of water was put on the flame for soup.

Ruthie had taken command, putting Henchie and Blimale in charge of cleaning, chopping and slicing. Miri was given the task of finding the fish and spices and creating pastry dough. Ruthie set another pan on the flame for sautéing vegetables.

Mrs. Abramson returned and told me it wouldn't be possible for Ruchama to have so many visitors, but I was welcome to come.

"Girls, I'll be going to the hospital with Mrs. Abramson now. I know the kitchen is in good hands."

Mrs. Abramson left the hospital's number where she could be reached. I ran upstairs and got the bundle of get-well notes and hurried downstairs and climbed into the waiting car. I took note of the time. Two o'clock. Ample time to visit and assess the possibility of arrangements for Ruchama to come back with us.

We sat in traffic. Evidently, there was an accident. William got out of the car to investigate. A pile-up ahead, he informed us.

We sat in the car. Mrs. Abramson didn't chat much. I asked her what she had been reading. She replied in a distracted manner.

I remembered the picture in the library. "Your sister...the one Ruchama resembles? Do you ever see her?"

"Er...no. I don't. They...She and her husband live in America."

"Where in America?"

"In San Francisco."

My antennae went up. San Francisco? What Jewish community was there? I looked at Mrs. Abramson, whose gaze was riveted on some unseen object of fascination outside her window. She was clearly uncomfortable. What was the story with her sister? It became warm in the car.

How far were we from the hospital?

"Mrs. Abramson, this may sound unconventional, but might we get there sooner if we walked?"

"We might. I'm not dressed for it, though."

I looked at her shoes. Elegant but flimsy, sling-back thin-heeled shoes with pointed toes. Not practical.

"It's best if I go alone," I said. "May I have directions?"

"William can direct you."

So there I was, walking through the traffic. Comments followed me, voices from vehicles saying they wished they could get out and walk and that I had the proper mode of transportation.

I walked on. In a while I could see the collision. So many cars and a large truck! Police and rescue vehicles were taking care of the injured and clearing debris. It reminded me how fortunate we were to have been a few minutes behind it. I was able to squeeze by at the side and continue on.

Suddenly, with great clarity, it dawned on me. This was probably how Ruchama had gotten home from school! She had walked! It had taken her around two hours to get home. Walking. No wonder she collapsed.

An hour's walk. That's how long it took me to reach the hospital. I made my way up to the ICU. I pitied Mrs. Abramson, still sitting in traffic.

I needed water. Badly. There was a water dispenser near the nurse's station. I must've taken ten cupfuls before I was able to breathe. I thought about Ruchama. She had probably been dehydrated by the time she arrived home. Two hours! My head was reeling! How had she done it?

"May I visit Ruchama Fishman?" I asked the nurse.

"Are you family?" She didn't look up.

"I was here yesterday together with her aunt, you remember, don't you? We got stuck in traffic and I walked here."

She looked at me without interest. "Alright, here's your pass."

I went to Ruchama's room and peeked in through the glass.

There was no one else there. Just Ruchama, sleeping.

I entered. There was no oxygen mask. That was good. I walked softly to her bedside.

Her eyes opened. "I waited for you."

I looked at the intravenous in her arm. Anything else? It didn't seem like it. "We got stuck in traffic. There was a terrible accident. It took me an hour to walk a stretch that takes fifteen minutes to drive."

She smiled. "Did the girls come?"

"They sure did."

"All of them?"

"Yes. All of them."

"I want to go home."

"What did the doctor say?"

"He said I'm recovering and must stay at least one more day. I don't agree."

"Well, what's in your arm? You can't do that at home, can you?"

"Medicine to keep my airways open. Medicine can be taken by mouth."

"Did you tell that to the doctor?"

"Yes. He didn't agree. He said he attended medical school longer than I, so his opinion is more medically correct."

"I'm inclined to agree with him." I looked at her. "Ruchama. You walked from Thornton to Prestwich yesterday, didn't you?"

"Yes. My teacher suggested it would be less embarrassing if I left on my own, instead of having the school dismiss me. So I left. On my own."

She began to wheeze in a startling way. She was getting upset all over again. I felt a sense of panic. I grabbed her hand.

"Ruchama! Look at me! She was wrong! She is the one who will be dismissed. Listen to me! Mrs. Morgan is very upset with her! She might dismiss Mrs. Strassfeld for what she said to you!"

She looked at me with wild watering eyes and gradually her gasping subsided. She was still breathing hard, though, and was unable to speak. I held her hand. I spoke soft words to calm her. I told her when her breath quieted, I would tell her about Ruthie.

After a while, her breathing returned to normal and she found her voice. "Did you say Mrs. Morgan would dismiss Mrs. Strassfeld?"

"Yes. I was there when she told Mrs. Strassfeld she would

need to take action. Mrs. Morgan told her that what she'd done to you was completely unacceptable. Mrs. Morgan told me that it depends now on what Mrs. Strassfeld does. Ruchama, Mrs. Morgan defended you and will take action for you. Can you understand that?"

"Yes. In my brain. But it'll take time to absorb here." She pointed to her heart.

I told her Ruthie's story and all about the necklace. I told her I was working on an idea to help Ruthie and her family, although I didn't tell her what it was. I wanted to wait, to see if it could work, although I knew it had to work.

"The girls are at your house now cooking for Shabbos."

"Cooking?"

"The murderous cook was let go, remember? And your aunt couldn't find a replacement. She fired another one yesterday."

Dr. Gold came in.

"Ah. I see you have company. Let's see how you're doing, young lady."

He examined Ruchama and said she was getting better.

"Doctor Gold, I must be home for Shabbos, " said Ruchama, in the sweetest voice I had ever heard. "I promise to do whatever you tell me. Rest. Drink. Take medicine. Breathe. Anything. Just please let me go."

Doctor Gold blew out a long breath. "It would be my fervent wish to allow that, Ruchama. But it would irresponsible for me to discharge you prematurely. My reputation as a good doctor is at stake."

Ruchama didn't laugh. She didn't relent either. She begged Dr. Gold to tell her what she could do so he would release her.

"You mean, what can you do in the next hour so you'll be well enough to go home?"

His comment effectively made Ruchama's request seem utterly ridiculous. She was silent.

I remembered something and debated whether it was my place to say. But I decided I had nothing to lose.

"Dr. Gold," I said, "I was wondering if there might be an additional angle to address. I'm not a doctor, but I was wondering if Ruchama might be dehydrated? She walked two hours straight yesterday and didn't taken any fluids."

"That's interesting. We did find her dehydrated. But since her arrival, our central focus has been alleviating her constricted airways. I'll have the nurse attend to it." He looked at me. "You're a relative, aren't you?"

"I'm…" What was I? Her teacher, her friend, her supporter, her mentor?

"She's the closest sister I've ever had," said Ruchama.

"And an American. An adopted sister then? " Dr. Gold chuckled lightly. "Splendid." He smiled and left the room.

Yes, I thought, *it was splendid.*

A nurse came in briskly and hung a bag of liquid on a pole. She attached the tube to Ruchama's arm.

Where was Mrs. Abramson? I looked at my watch. Four o'clock. The nurse was done and gone.

I remembered the bundle of get-well wishes I had brought for Ruchama. Her eyes grew huge with delight when she saw them and she read them one by one, showing them to me and spreading them out on the blanket. An hour passed.

"Ruchama, the girls wanted to know about you, what

happened. They know you're in the hospital. Do you mind if I tell them?"

She gave me a smirk. "Like you said, it's no secret. You may tell them."

The door opened and Mrs. Abramson entered the room, flushed and breathing rapidly. "We just arrived… were unmoving in traffic for over two hours, then inched our way for another hour. I might have done better walking. Even in these heels."

I'd never imagined I'd see her so overwhelmed.

She came over to the bed and said softly, "How are you doing Ruchama?"

"I'm fine. The doctor is fussing about me. Can you persuade him to allow me go home?"

"I'll speak to him. And then we must head home at once, an alternate traffic-free route."

She left us. A nurse came in and checked some things. She hung another bag up on the pole, attached it, patted Ruchama, and left.

What would happen now? Would I stay here with Ruchama? Was Shabbos food available for us? I had no Shabbos clothing or even a siddur with me.

And a small voice inside me was asking, how would Ruthie, Miri, Henchie and Blimale fare by themselves with the Abramsons?

CHAPTER 26

Here it was, thirty minutes to Shabbos candles, and I was frantically inquiring on every floor of the hospital about kosher food.

Things like wine, rolls, a siddur, I didn't even dream to find candles. But I had no luck finding anything. Apparently, they didn't stock kosher food. I fought a moment of panic.

There was a chaplain assigned to the Jewish patients, but he wasn't frum and basically only took care of terminally ill patients during their final days. No thanks.

I racked my brain for ideas.

How far was Manchester from here? Not too far, from what I knew. Maybe I could call Mrs. Morgan and she could send food for Ruchama and me. That was an encouraging thought.

I should have thought of it when Mrs. Abramson left. She could have sent food back for us. Or contacted Mrs. Morgan for us.

The events of the day played back in my head as I raced to the information desk for directory assistance. Mrs. Abramson had tried to convince Dr. Gold to release Ruchama. I had seen her down the hall from Ruchama's room, speaking to him intently, gesturing, tense and emphatic. Dr. Gold threw his hands out in a helpless manner and walked away.

Mrs. Abramson saw me and quickly came over. "I did my persuasive best, however Dr. Gold firmly insists there must be dramatic improvement in order for Ruchama to be discharged, which he has not seen."

"Dramatic improvement? When? We need to leave now."

"Precisely. He caught the urgency of our need yet was adamant about Ruchama's health, saying he could not discharge her as it stood."

"Maybe he could look at her now. It's possible she might have improved. She's been hydrated. Maybe it helped."

"It's possible. I did ask Dr. Gold if he might check her now, a last effort, and he consented as a favor to me, but was unavailable to do so this very moment. In the meanwhile, I sent William to bring the car around. I have no choice."

I felt dejected.

The car would leave. I would stay.

Fine. Whatever was meant to be would be. I returned to Ruchama's room.

What could I tell her? The car to Brellenson was leaving?

Without us.

I held my tongue. I looked at her. She didn't look too bad.

"How do you feel?" I asked.

"I feel fine. Can we go home now?"

Mrs. Abramson came in. "William is waiting outside. Sorry. I wish I could stay but..." She looked tense. "You'll get the care you need, Ruchama, at least that."

Ruchama looked at me. "What? I'm not sick anymore. I want

to leave now." Her chin came forward as she looked at her aunt.

"I did my best to persuade Dr. Gold, Ruchama," said Mrs. Abramson, looking awkward. "I believe I made him uncomfortable. He would do it if he could. He said you weren't ready. I wish there could be more, but I've done all I could." She sighed. "I must go now."

"Miss Mintz isn't leaving with you, is she?" said Ruchama, sending me a sharp glance.

"No, just I."

Ruchama gave me an intense look.

Mrs. Abramson took Ruchama's hand and gave it a gentle squeeze. "Ruchama, please heal quickly. We want to see you home," she said, with great meaning.

"Yes. I do too."

"The girls who came for Shabbos, Mrs. Abramson," I said. "You will let them know how pleased you are…?"

"Of course."

"Please tell them…" I didn't finish my sentence. What? That I wish I could be there with them? That I wish I could see what a good job they had done? "…that I know they would do a fine job." I felt so helpless.

Mrs. Abramson said, "Yes. Of course." She hurried out.

Ruchama and I looked at each other.

"So…" She drawled.

"So…You and me, my friend, we're in this together. Whatever the day may bring."

She snorted. "Those are your words of wisdom? This is my idea. When Dr. Gold comes," Ruchama said, with a menacing arch of her eyebrow, "you and I will convince him to let me out.

We hold him prisoner until he does."

I smirked. "Hm. Interesting idea. In the meanwhile, I'll look for food for us. So we won't starve."

And here I was, looking for food. Without luck.

The woman sitting at the desk found the number for Mrs. Hannah Morgan of Manchester. She allowed me to call.

As I listened to the phone ring, I hoped I wasn't too late.

CHAPTER 27

Mrs. Morgan answered the phone and was sorry to hear that we would need to stay in the hospital over Shabbos, but said she was not surprised. She was very concerned that we had no food and said she would take care of arranging food to be sent to us immediately. Also a siddur.

I felt a load lift from my shoulders.

I checked my watch. It was twenty minutes to sundown.

I returned to Ruchama's room.

Dr. Gold was there. He was saying, "You might wish to do better than that. Breathe in deeply, please."

Ruchama, with fierce determination on her face, did a series of grand inhales and exhales.

Dr. Gold said "Hmmmm."

I came closer and said, "May I stay?"

Dr. Gold nodded and placed a contraption over Ruchama's mouth. He asked her to do a series of exhales and looked at the numbers marked on the side.

"The other two were a bit on the pathetic side. But this one has merit. Let's try one more. Give it your best shot."

I clenched my fists and said, "Come on, Ruchama. You can do it."

Ruchama's eyes were huge as she inhaled and fiercely blew a gust that turned her entire face red.

"Mhmmm…" Dr. Gold looked at the numbers. "Not the worst. Not the best."

"Dr. Gold, I know I'm breathing," Ruchama said. "I can feel it."

He smiled. "Perhaps. Sit tight while I confer with the team."

Her hurried out. We sat somewhat tight. I wondered where his team was located.

Everything changed in an instant. Dr. Gold came rushing in and told us we were given a green light to go. A nurse would join us, bringing equipment and medication.

"Your aunt is paying for a private nurse for you."

Ruchama and I exchanged glances.

The next thing we knew, we were roaring through the streets in an ambulance. It all happened so fast.

The ride was wild and bumpy and I couldn't imagine how a deathly ill person could ride this bucking bronco and arrived in one piece. I had the feeling we were driving on the sidewalk. I looked out the window. We were.

Dr. Gold had warned the driver he had fifteen minutes to get us home. At this pace, we would probably make it in ten.

I held on. Tight. So did Ruchama. So did the nurse, who was armed with a kit, medicine, inhalers and other oxygen-monitoring equipment, all of which had been explained swiftly to us before leaving, in dizzying detail.

"It's a good thing I'm not sick," hollered Ruchama at me over the siren, "otherwise I would be half under by now."

My watch showed five minutes to sunset.

We pulled up two minutes later and screeched to a halt. The driver jumped out and pulled open the back. I climbed out. The door to the house flew open. Henchie and Blimale spilled out, squealing and waving their hands. Ruthie and Miri came down the steps as the nurse helped Ruchama from the car.

The girls surrounded us with extreme affection.

"Are we glad to see you!"

"You surely how to announce yourselves!"

"We thought you wouldn't come!"

"We'd given up all hope."

"We're so glad you're better, Ruchama."

"You can't imagine how glad!"

Their shining faces spoke volumes. Shabbos without us would have been difficult.

Mrs. Abramson stood at the doorway, a handkerchief pressed to her nose. She was a dazzling vision in rose and silver, diamonds sparkling like stars everywhere, and her patrician looks were stunning. Yet there was a new aura about her that made her seem more human. Especially because she seemed to be crying. She lowered her handkerchief and her eyes glowed.

We made our way up the front stairs, the nurse manipulating all the cumbersome equipment behind us.

"Our prayers have been answered," Mrs. Abramson said softly. "It's hard to believe."

Ruchama was fussed over. The nurse informed us that

Ruchama needed bed rest for the next twenty-four hours. Henchie and Blimale had definite opinions how best to make Ruchama comfortable, what room was ideal, how many blankets, whether she needed a drink, what sort of drink, pillows, how many pillows, books...

In the end we decided the library was the best choice to avoid her climbing the stairs. The nurse puttered about, hooking up a machine and setting out jars and tubes and medical paraphernalia. One of the couches had a pullout feature and Annette came in and efficiently made the bed. Blimale and Henchie piled on pillows and books, plumping and preening everything to their satisfaction.

The nurse, Angela, consented to Mrs. Abramson's suggestion that she stay in the parlor, right down the hall, where she could easily check on Ruchama. With Ruchama settled, I couldn't wait to sink into the couch and breathe.

A maid appeared in the doorway. "Master Abramson has arrived."

Mrs. Abramson clapped her hands lightly together. "This is so marvelous! I am quite frankly looking forward to the meal! The fragrances wafting from the kitchen have simply been heavenly."

I had completely forgotten. The girls had prepared the meals. I couldn't wait to see what the girls had done.

It was difficult to leave Ruchama. "Be back soon. Going for kiddush, Ruchama."

"Fare thee well," said Blimale. "But not for long!"

"Right," said Henchie. "We'll soon return with food for you."

"And a visit," said Ruthie.

Ruchama lay back on her plentiful pillows, a blissful look

on her face.

We were a jolly group entering the dining room.

"Brendon," said Mrs. Abramson. "Ruchama arrived by ambulance less than an hour ago." She looked radiant.

Mr. Abramson's mouth fell open. "Why, that's marvelous. It calls for celebration. Where is Ruchama?"

Mr. Abramson insisted on going to the library and greeting Ruchama. He then insisted that kiddush and challah be held there, in the library. A small table was hurriedly set up by Annette and the server. Mr. Abramson seemed completely out of character, performing a very melodious, heartfelt kiddush.

I looked at Ruchama. She looked at me. She raised her brow.

We went back to the dining room for washing and the server formallymanaged a dignified presentation of challah in the library. We bade Ruchama a quick farewell again and headed to the dining room for the meal. Ruthie and Miri excused themselves and went to the kitchen, emerging a short while later, looking pleased. They gracefully resumed their seats and watched as the server bore an immense tray of artfully arranged multi-colored salads, glazed salmon and sweet and sour whitefish. A variety of individual dips were placed alongside each serving.

I watched in wonder as Mr. and Mrs. Abramson selected one of every food that was offered, tasted it and exclaimed softly to each other, using the phrase "just like Mama made it".

Henchie and Blimale dug into their food with gusto. Ruthie and Miri watched everyone, nibbling delicately. The food was delicious and had been beautifully presented.

The Abramson's enthusiasm was a surprise. What was the "like Mama made it" phrase they kept repeating?

"Isn't this delectable, Brendon? This brings back such memories. Mmm, you must try this fish. It's utterly divine, just like Mama's."

"Yes. I agree, Ellen. Precisely like Mama's."

I caught Ruthie's eye. I nodded fiercely to her. She beamed and looked down at her plate.

"Girls, the food is absolutely gorgeous," said Mrs. Abramson. "It is a taste of home. We haven't enjoyed food like this in ages."

"I couldn't agree more," said Mr. Abramson. "To whom does the credit belong? This food is very comforting and brings back fond memories."

"Ruthie is the main one, sir," said Henchie. "She told us what to do."

"And Miri and Henchie and Blimale actually did the work," said Ruthie. "They deserve all the credit."

"I've been trying to replicate Brendon's mother's recipes for ages. Would you mind sharing your secrets with us?" Mrs. Abramson's face was positively excited.

"I don't actually use recipes," said Ruthie. "It's just what my mother taught me and my sisters. It's nothing special, really."

"She said if we sing, the food would come out better," said Blimale. "We sang. Lots."

Henchie gulped. "We hope nobody heard."

Mrs. and Mrs. Abramson looked at each other and smiled.

I thought of Vicky and Paula, who sang in the kitchen, vociferously. Maybe there was something to it since their food was fabulous.

"Would anyone mind if I brought Ruchama a portion?" I asked, thinking it might be a good time for a break.

All the girls wanted to come. We prepared a sampling of everything and paraded to the library, with cutlery, plates, and a serving tray.

We piled it onto a small table near the couch, while Ruchama looked on in amusement.

Ruchama tasted a bit of everything and nodded, looking at each girl.

"This food is good."

The girls told her how they had chopped, measured, and seasoned each dish while singing songs and dancing around the enormous kitchen.

"It's the secret to the delicious taste," said Henchie.

Mrs. Abramson entered the library and whispered a request to speak to me privately. We went out to the hallway.

"The girl, Ruthie, has the touch. We've been longing for a taste of home, ever since Brendon's mother passed away. She was my mother, as well."

I remembered her story. She had lived at her husband's home, adopted by his family. "How long ago was it?"

"It's been five years. Neither of us has been the same since. But tonight was…it was like old times. Brendon and I would love having the aura of home here at Brellenson. It would be such a comfort. Would Ruthie possibly consider coaching someone?"

This was the opening I had been hoping for.

"I know she wouldn't mind," I said, thinking I might as well tell her the whole story. "But better yet, she could cook for you. Mrs. Abramson, Ruthie is experiencing a difficult situation at home. Her mother is very ill and needs an operation that her family cannot afford. She wishes to work in order to pay for it.

Would you agree that she work here cooking for you?"

I felt sure she would agree.

Mrs. Abramson's face became a mask of horror. "That is the most abominable thing I ever heard!"

I was stunned by her reaction and felt myself stiffen.

What was ailing her? Didn't she feel sympathy for Ruthie's need? Didn't she feel concern that Ruthie's mother was deathly ill? Didn't she know there were people struggling to pay for their necessities?

I groped for words. "Mrs. Abramson, I don't understand. Can you please tell me what's upsetting you?"

Her eyes flashed. "A woman needs an operation and suffers Heaven-knows-what because she can't pay for it? Unfolding untold misery for her family while they witness her steady deterioration? That is horrific! This can't be allowed to happen. And this poor girl mustn't bear the burden of her family's needs." She inhaled deeply.

I took a deep breath and tried to absorb what Mrs. Abramson had just said. I had misread her reaction completely. Not only was she sympathetic to Ruthie's situation, she was upset that the emergency existed and wasn't being addressed. I realized how wrongly I had judged this woman.

Her chin lifted and she pressed her lips together. "I shall sponsor the operation."

I gasped. Had my ears deceived me? "Did you just say you would pay for the operation?" I said in a strange hoarse voice.

"I did. And I will. Please inquire as to the amount and let me know without delay."

My heart pounded. I was overwhelmed with excitement. It

would mean the end of Ruthie's misery. "Mrs. Abramson, that's extremely generous and most kind. I'm sure Ruthie will be eternally grateful."

But would she? Would Ruthie be pleased to accept this gift outright? I wasn't sure. "Mrs. Abramson, if Ruthie wishes, may she work for you?"

"If she wishes to, I would gladly have her. I only thought since she's still in school, she may not have the time. Perhaps she would consider coaching, once or twice a week, to train someone. It would be a favor to us."

My heart did a little dance of joy. "I'm sure she would love to. I will speak to her and let you know."

My tread was light on my way in to the library. I couldn't have worked it out better. Mrs. Abramson had created the ideal situation where Ruthie wouldn't need to come too often. A few hours twice a week for a few weeks and voila! A wonderful cook would be born! I was sure Mrs. Morgan would agree to this plan.

I watched the girls for a moment. Henchie and Blimale were singing something outrageous. Something about foods from each land, making a big mishmash of Hungarian goulash. Ruthie and Miri were shaking their heads, laughing, and Ruchama was smiling. So perfect. The beautiful Shabbos I had pictured, miraculously played out before my eyes.

Henchie declared herself ravenous again after singing the song. We returned to the dining room and the soup course was served, inducing blissful reactions again from the Abramsons.

We took a tray of soup to the library for Ruchama, who sipped slow teaspoonfuls and pronounced, "I am now completely healed." She lay back on the pillows with a small sigh.

Ruthie and Miri led the way back to the dining room to prepare their presentation of vegetable, potato and chicken dumplings. They were heavenly. And to top it all off, apple strudel.

"Our senses are very pleased," I told the girls.

Mr. and Mrs. Abramson looked like they couldn't bear any more happiness. Effusively, they expressed how much they were looking forward to tomorrow and were in a soft mood when they left the room.

We prepared a tray of dumplings for Ruchama but as we entered the library, Angela jumped up and whispered to us that she had fallen asleep. Angela took the tray from us and shooed us out.

Out in the hall, Blimale whispered loudly that she wanted to go out to the back terrace.

"Yes, let's go," I readily agreed. The need to speak to Ruthie was becoming unbearable.

We walked leisurely around the perimeter of the grounds, Ruthie and Miri and I, while Henchie and Blimale frolicked ahead. I told the two girls about the Abramsons losing their mother and why it seemed that they shared one mother. I explained how the food reminded them of home and what a huge good deed they had done for them.

"And Mrs. Abramson practically begged that Ruthie come and teach a staff member how to cook for them. Isn't that marvelous?"

Ruthie looked at me, a question in her eyes.

"And that's not even the best of it. She wants to cover your family's medical expenses, Ruthie. She asked me to find out how much is needed and to let her know as soon as possible."

"Oh, my gracious! I can't believe it!" said Ruthie. "She said that?"

Miri had grabbed onto Ruthie and they were holding onto each other for dear life.

"I promise it's true," I said.

Tears ran down Ruthie's face.

Ruthie and Miri hugged each other, crying tears of joy.

From a distance, we heard strident voices, Henchie and Blimale calling to us with frantic motions. We hurried to the terrace to see what the emergency was.

"Henchie and I must explore the pantries immediately and then go look at the stars!" Blimale said breathlessly.

I burst out laughing. I was glad to have an emergency like this.

I left the girls rummaging gleefully in the pantry and made my way to the library.

I wanted to see Ruchama. On my way, I heard voices. They were coming from the front of the mansion. I stopped a moment.

Mrs. Abramson was speaking to someone. That was odd. I had thought the Abramsons never had company. The conversation was drawing closer. Mrs. Abramson seemed to be speaking stiffly, talking about Ruchama, about her coming home minutes before sundown. Who would she be talking to about Ruchama? Was it a close friend? A neighbor? A low-toned voice asked her a question. A woman's voice.

My spine began to crawl. The voice was familiar. No. No. No. It couldn't be.

CHAPTER 28

I waited as their footsteps came steadily closer. My heart thudded in my chest. My nerves urged me to run. My curiosity told me to stay.

They appeared around the bend. There she was. My heart hammered loudly. What was she doing here?!

"Oh, Miss Mintz, this is my sister's sister-in-law. You do know her from Thornton, don't you?"

Her WHAT????

I found my tongue, though it was thick and inflexible. "Yes, of course. Mrs. Strassfeld. Good Shabbos."

She stood aloof and regarded me without feeling. "Good Shabbos. Miss Mintz." Her lips hardly moved.

"Mrs. Strassfeld came to visit Ruchama. She heard she was ill. Would you mind to have a look and see whether she's awake? I know she was asleep only a short while ago."

"Of course."

I went down the hallway, my legs wooden, my mind racing and shrieking. What was this "sister's sister-in-law" business??! What was Mrs. Strassfeld doing here?! How did she get here?

She couldn't possibly live in this ritzy neighborhood, could she?!

I peeked into the library. Angela jumped up and put a finger to her lips.

She tiptoed over to me, her finger still on her lips. "She's sleeping, she needs it, she's had a long day."

"Someone's here to visit her." Was Mrs. Strassfeld related to Ruchama? My mind recoiled at the thought and refused to accept it. As my mind cleared, I knew that it would be very destructive for Mrs. Strassfeld to visit Ruchama. She would only hurt her.

"Sorry. She needs her sleep. Not a good time for visitors," she whispered adamantly. "Perhaps tomorrow."

Good. I was glad I could honestly say that Ruchama was asleep. I returned to the hallway. Mrs. Strassfeld was standing there, large as life.

"She's sleeping," I said.

"I see."

"Would you care to visit tomorrow, since you're staying in the neighborhood?" asked Mrs. Abramson, in a tentative small voice.

I cringed inwardly. *Say no.*

"Perhaps."

I cringed again.

"Is someone walking with you?" Mrs. Abramson asked.

"Yes, my husband. He's waiting outside."

"Oh, my Heaven! Have him come in."

"No. No, thank you. He prefers to wait there. Good Shabbos." She headed rigidly toward the front door.

Mrs. Abramson escorted Mrs. Strassfeld out, while I stayed

rooted to my spot. I was losing my mind. Nothing made sense. What in the world was going on???

I heard a commotion and realized the girls were on their way to the rooftop. I wanted to go with them and air my head. It needed a good airing.

Mrs. Abramson appeared before me. My legs were trembling. I felt weak.

"Are you feeling well, dear?"

"Not very. To be frank, it's best that Ruchama is asleep."

"Whatever do you mean?"

"In my short time at Thornton, I observed great tension between Mrs. Strassfeld and Ruchama. I've seen Ruchama suffer. I don't think Mrs. Strassfeld would be the right visitor for her right now."

Mrs. Abramson took a deep breath. She seemed troubled. "There is ill feeling between us and… I wondered if it would affect her attitude towards Ruchama. I should have guessed Ruchama might become a source of bitterness for her. I didn't think."

"Is Mrs. Strassfeld actually your sister's sister-in-law?" I felt my face contort and tried to adjust it.

Happy voices approached and the girls appeared, flushed and toting baskets of goodies. How I wished I could join their carefree world.

"Oh, sorry, Miss Mintz. We didn't know…" said Ruthie, looking at Mrs. Abramson.

"Girls, it's fine," I said, "go on up. I'll be up momentarily."

The girls continued on their merry way and there remained a question hanging in midair. The disharmony Mrs. Abramson had mentioned filled me with dread. Would this troubled relationship explain Mrs. Strassfeld's antagonistic behavior? I looked at Mrs. Abramson, waiting for the answer.

"She is… unfortunately… my sister's sister-in-law. Mrs. Strassfeld's brother married my sister."

"Is this your sister who looks like Ruchama?"

"Yes."

"The one who lives in San Francisco?"

She sighed. "Yes. It is hard to believe they live in a city so distanced from Jewish life. His father is a prominent Rav in England. They don't speak of him."

I felt sad for the family and realized it was heartbreaking enough to possibly send Mrs. Strassfeld into a never-ending spiral of bad feeling. But why was it turned against Ruchama? And towards me?

"And she… Mrs. Strassfeld?"

"I shall explain, so you may understand the full story and not judge harshly... Mrs. Strassfeld has been furious ever since they married. At us, at my sister, at the world. She had been proud of her brother, a brilliant and charismatic person who showed such promise - a shining star. She's convinced that my sister prevailed upon him to move to America, to become… shall we say… free of Jewish life."

"Is that true?"

"Hardly. She was a young thing. Happy, but not attached to anything. I think the separation from my parents affected her deeply. She was a follower and she followed his lead."

It was a devastating story that explained the strong feelings. It explained Mrs. Strassfeld's fierce protectiveness of 'old world' ways and propriety. Now I understood how she was trying desperately to prevent what she feared. The breakdown of true Jewish values. The breakdown of what she held dear.

"And then they left England?" I asked.

"Yes. They had begun to display signs of leaving the fold, small things here and there and his side of the family rejected them outright. The couple didn't wish to participate in our family anymore, either. Perhaps our concern was apparent and made them uncomfortable. So they sailed to the land of the free. Cut off all ties with us, ignored the efforts I made to maintain them. And left behind great strain between the families." She gave me a sad smile.

"And I, an American, am from the country that caused Mrs. Strassfeld's brother's downfall."

She nodded and gave me an enigmatic look. "Yes, so you are."

The pieces of the puzzle were falling into place.

"And Ruchama, who bears an uncanny resemblance to your sister, becomes a target for banishment, because of the family she comes from and because of her apparent inability to become one of Thornton's girls."

Mrs. Abramson looked down at her hands. I thought I heard a small sob.

I could taste the chaos, the ill feeling. Though I understood it now, I knew it was not how things should be. A life of bitterness and hatred... how long would this go on? And Ruchama, who had done no wrong, was denied understanding and suffered so much rejection. She had no chance at all.

"It seems so pointless," I said. "It wasn't anyone's fault. What happened is a sad story, but there is still much to appreciate about the rest of the family."

"Yes, I agree. I'm heartbroken that Ruchama suffered because of it." She shook her head. "I never told her the story. I thought it best to keep it from her, to spare her. She had already been through so much."

She looked away and I saw the hurt she carried. "Unfortunately, I haven't spared her at all." She gave a soft chuckle. "The irony of it is that I was the one who suggested that Mrs. Morgan take Mrs. Strassfeld as an instructor at Thornton. I was sorry for what had happened and knew the pain she bore. I thought it would mend a broken bridge or two."

I was overwhelmed by Mrs. Abramson's kindness. Recommending Mrs. Strassfeld as a teacher was a magnanimous act and tonight, she had invited her into her home. After all she had gone through and despite the animosity she faced from Mrs. Strassfeld, she still extended herself with grace. There was a huge lesson here.

"Did Mrs. Strassfeld know?"

"I believe Mrs. Morgan told her."

I needed air. Mrs. Strassfeld's story was heavy. There was so much pain. Her family had been torn apart, wounded in a way that was ongoing. Although it shed light on the reasons for her fierceness, I felt it didn't excuse her behavior. I felt she should have treated Ruchama fairly, as an individual, not as a puzzle piece linked to her past pain. I felt she should have treated me with an open heart, judged me for who I was, not as a preconceived threat. I realized she was still burdened by her past and hadn't let it go. Yet she had come to visit tonight. Why? Was it because Mrs. Morgan had threatened her?

Mrs. Abramson's face was drawn. My heart went out to her. "Mrs. Abramson, you've been through many difficulties," I said softly.

She had lost her parents. She had lost her surrogate mother, her husband's mother. Then her sister. Her brother in Israel had become completely debilitated. Ruchama, her one hope, had been beyond reach. She had lost so much. Her aloofness took on new meaning. I realized now that she was in deep mourning. Grieving for all she had lost.

She looked at me, clearly suffering, and nodded.

"But now you have Ruchama," I said. "A new relationship will build."

"I hope so. You've brought new understanding between us."

"And I know it can continue. We'll work on it together."

I needed to get away. "If you don't mind, I'll excuse myself now, Mrs. Abramson. Good Shabbos."

"Good Shabbos, Miss Mintz," she murmured.

I managed my way up to the roof and collapsed into a chair. I looked up at the stars. They winked at me. I breathed. Happy sounds surrounded me, the girls chatting, laughing. I let it wash over me.

But my worries returned. Would Mrs. Strassfeld return tomorrow to visit? I was sure it would be harmful for Ruchama. I hadn't told Mrs. Abramson what Mrs. Strassfeld had done, the damaging words that had caused Ruchama to leave Thornton and walk all the way home. The walk that had brought on her asthma attack.

I felt sorry for Mrs. Strassfeld and what she had gone through, but I was determined to protect Ruchama. How would

I keep Mrs. Strassfeld away?

I didn't know. All I knew was that Ruchama's health was at stake and I would guard her with my life.

I closed my eyes.

* * *

It was early morning.

I awoke feeling battered as if I had fought a fierce battle. Strange dreams had plagued my sleep. I got up and went out onto the terrace. The sky was overcast, matching my mood.

What would happen today? I thought about Ruchama and renewed my resolve to shield her from harm. I had an urge to see her. I dressed and made my way to the library.

The room was quiet. I tiptoed in. Ruchama was asleep. She looked peaceful, breathing easily. I longed for peace to continue for her forever. I heard a sigh and saw Mrs. Abramson asleep in her corner chair, in her dressing gown, a *tehillim* in her lap.

She cared. Like a mother.

I felt my throat tighten with emotion.

I left the library and went back to my room. I was glad I had gotten to know Mrs. Abramson. Last week, I thought she was an ice queen who couldn't care about anyone at all. This week I found I admired her and learned from her. How different things were now.

I took my siddur. I would say every word carefully. I had the time.

I was deep in my *shemoneh esrai* when I heard feverish whispering. I strained to get to the end of my davening with my focus intact and was not surprised afterwards to find Henchie and Blimale dressed and energetic, nibbling on goodies.

"Good Shabbos, girls," I said, suppressing my laugh.

"We're ready to go outdoors." said Blimale.

"Ruthie and Miri just woke and won't need our help for another two hours," said Henchie.

It was only eight o'clock. I suggested they daven first. They rushed away.

I went back down to the library. Mrs. Abramson's chair was empty. Ruchama was still sleeping. I browsed the shelves and chose some books I thought Ruchama might like. Maybe we'd read later.

I found an elegant photo album and saw it was Mr. and Mrs. Abramson's wedding pictures. Mrs. Abramson's picture took my breath away— a gorgeous bride, bursting with happiness. Mr. Abramson's mother appeared aristocratic yet warm. It was a much happier time for them.

Ruchama was still asleep. I felt restless. I let myself out the front door and wandered down the driveway and out to the gates. They were unlocked and I let myself out and walked down the lane.

My mind was churning with last night's revelations. If Mrs. Strassfeld visited Brellenson today, I would need to confront her directly. If I spoke reasonably to her, would it help the situation? I didn't know. Could Mrs. Strassfeld listen to anything I said? An American? I had no idea. But one thing was clear. I was determined to keep her from Ruchama.

I walked on.

I tried to think of different things to say that would create more understanding, none of which seemed convincing even to me. I kept walking.

There were people walking towards me in the distance up ahead. They looked frum, wearing suits, and walking in a formal, dignified manner. I looked at my watch. Nine o'clock. I had been walking for a half hour. *Shacharis* couldn't be over yet, could it?

I turned around and headed back, wondering if I had miscalculated the timing of the meal. I reached Brellenson's driveway and looked back. I saw the man and woman only a short distance away. The man had a long beketcha, white socks and a full bushy black beard. The woman—

An icy hand clamped my heart. It was her.

I couldn't turn away and leave. They had seen me. I realized this was it. I stood and squared my shoulders, braced myself for the inevitable. I stood blocking the gates.

Say your piece, Judith.

Be polite.

CHAPTER 29

Mrs. Strassfeld approached me.

My muscles tensed, but I met her strong gaze. "Good Shabbos, Mrs. Strassfeld."

"Good Shabbos. Miss Mintz."

Her fierce expression didn't intimidate me now like it did before. Knowing her story had helped put things into a new perspective. Though strong, she was a person suffering from a blow and reacting in a flawed, all too human way.

Before I could change my mind, I carefully said, "Meaning no disrespect, Mrs. Strassfeld., but I don't think it would be wise for you to visit Ruchama. I assume that's why you're here."

Her features swelled and became angry.

I plunged ahead. "I know you're thinking it's not my place to tell you this, Mrs. Strassfeld, but I feel I must. Ruchama has been very hurt by you. Your words to her Thursday made her ill enough to put her in the hospital. She has suffered immeasurably from your constant rejection and animosity. And I'm afraid in her present fragile state, you might cause her to become ill again. If you wish to make amends, your acceptance and encouragement at school would accomplish much."

I glanced at her husband. He stood motionless, his expression frozen.

"Who are you to give orders as to how I should proceed?" Mrs. Strassfeld said, her eyes narrowed.

My chin involuntarily lifted and came forward, my shoulders tightening.

"I am Judith Mintz. A person who cares about a Jewish soul... a girl who has lost her entire family, a girl who struggles to learn, who struggles to fit in, and struggles to find someone who might understand her and guide her. I care about a girl who suffers daily from a teacher's condemnation, who is attacked for no reason at all. I protest your treatment of her and I will not allow you to see her and hurt her further." I felt my blood boil, my face hot, but couldn't stop myself.

Mrs. Strassfeld's eyes were murderous. "You protest?"

My blood pounded in my head. "Yes. I do. In the name of responsibility to my fellow Jew, I do. To protect a helpless person, I do. To prevent further damage, I do. And I would protect her with whatever I have in me, body and soul. I take responsibility for her as her teacher, as her house mother, and as her mentor and friend."

It was hard to catch my breath. Mrs. Strassfeld looked ready to strangle me. I looked at her husband. He swallowed and looked uncomfortable, his gaze shifting away.

"I think it's best that we go," he said quietly to his wife.

Mrs. Strassfeld stood still as stone. "You, an American," she said through clenched teeth, "have not the merest inkling of what it means to protect good girls from the wrong influence."

"Is that what you think?" I said, trying to control myself. "You don't know anything about me. And you know nothing about Ruchama. You don't know her story. Ruchama is a good girl. And I am protecting a good girl right now from a damaging influence." I looked at her narrowed eyes and quietly said, "You."

I shocked myself. Where had that come from? Words had spewed straight from my subconscious, unfiltered and uncensored. I was stunned that I had been so brutally honest.

Mrs. Strassfeld flinched and looked down. Her eyes blinked rapidly. Her brow furrowed and her expression underwent a drastic change. Had my rant accomplished something?

I looked at Mrs. Strassfeld's husband. His face was flushed and he looked stricken. A heavy moment of silence ensued, making the air thick.

"Please tell Ruchama we're sorry for what we said," he said quietly. "Let's go, Pessl."

He guided her away. She let him. They walked away. I stood and watched them until they disappeared.

CHAPTER 30

I leaned back on the gates for support.

The conversation played in my head. Over and over. Had I accomplished what I had set out to do? Mrs. Strassfeld had left. Did she hear me? At the end, Mrs. Strassfeld's husband had said to tell Ruchama *"we're sorry for what we said."*

He had heard me. Maybe he would talk to her. Explain it to her. Maybe she would hear it from him. I hoped.

Excited voices perked my ears. I let go the gates and followed the sounds to the back area of the house. I almost fainted.

The girls were squealing in delight. Henchie, Blimale, Ruthie and Miri were helping someone down the terrace steps. My heart leaped into my throat. It was Ruchama. Not sickly. Just wonderful.

I ran over to her and flung my arms around her. I gripped her tightly. Tears sprang from my eyes. I blinked them away and stepped back.

"Sorry. I was just so happy to see you," I said. My emotions were strung tight and I felt them ease. "You look unbelievably good. You're feeling well?"

"I told you last night, the chicken soup healed me," she said with a small smile. "I'm all better." She looked around at the girls. "I couldn't wait to see you." She looked at me. "To be with my friends."

The maid appeared and said, "Master Abramson has arrived."

"Where's Angela?" I asked.

"She pronounced my numbers perfect." She smirked. "I always wanted to be perfect at something. My aunt sent her away to her room, until we need her. I hope never."

The Abramsons beamed as we entered the dining room, their eyes full of Ruchama's presence. Mr. Abramson made a vocal kiddush again, a festive meal followed with delicious homey food and the Abramson's oohs and ahhhs of delight. A happy mood permeated mealtime, the Abramsons engaging us in conversation and the girls comfortable to share family stories with them.

Ruchama murmured to me, "I've never seen them like this. What have you done?"

"Me? I thought it was you."

It was a Shabbos to remember. We talked. We relaxed in the library, reading together, sometimes aloud to each other, we walked, we snacked. And when Shabbos was over, Mrs. Abramson gave Ruthie a check for a large amount of money for her mother's operation.

"Consider it a gift," she said. "After all, you've given us a precious gift, food for the soul. You will let me know when you're able to train someone, won't you, Ruthie?"

"Yes, I will, Mrs. Abramson. As soon as I get permission." She glanced my way.

I gave her a smile, sharing her secret in silence and knowing we had been granted a great blessing.

* * *

We left early the next morning. Ruchama was still sleeping and Mrs. Abramson felt it would be good for Ruchama to have at least one more day to rest at home.

The girls piled into the long car for our trip back. Mrs. Abramson saw us out and approached me.

"Thank you, Miss Mintz," she said. "For everything I can't put into words."

"Please," I said. "Call me Judith."

She nodded. I climbed in. There was a commotion at Brellenson's front door. Ruchama was dressed and dragging her satchel to the car while Angela protested noisily behind her.

"She won't listen, Mrs. Abramson."

Mrs. Abramson looked at Ruchama. "Are you sure about this?"

"I need to go, Aunt Ellen. I'm fine."

Mrs. Abramson studied Ruchama for a few moments, then turned to Angela. "Please fetch her medication and inhaler."

Angela went off, muttering objections.

"I'll let you go, on two conditions. One, you must call me in the morning, the afternoon, and the evening, to tell me how you're feeling, in great detail. And two, you must listen to Miss Mintz, whom I appoint as your guardian."

Angela brought the medication to the car. "Against my recommendations, but here you are."

Ruchama put them into her satchel. "Yes, Aunt Ellen. I will honor your conditions."

And we were on our way.

Blimale and Henchie chattered non-stop the entire drive. Ruthie and Miri talked with Ruchama about her aunt's generosity.

I looked out the window and was silent. I held in my worries. What would happen at school? Would Mrs. Strassfeld be kind to Ruchama and treat her decently and maybe, dare I hope, show approval? Looking at Ruchama smiling, I knew she would be stronger now, with friends surrounding her. But her health was still fragile and needed tending.

We were nearing Thornton, thirty minutes late. I saw the gap in the bushes and heaved a private sigh of relief that I wouldn't have to worry about that anymore. William drove through the open gates and down the long driveway.

Mrs. Morgan was out front waiting to greet us. My heart leaped, happy to see her. So much had happened. We climbed out and Mrs. Morgan was effusive and warm. When she saw Ruchama, she opened her arms wide.

"Oh, thank Heaven. Come here," she said. She gave Ruchama a gentle squeeze. "We must take better care of you. You're too precious to us." She looked at the other girls. "You have a story to tell, haven't you?"

The girls smiled and nodded.

"You're the most splendid girls I've ever known. You've done such a good deed. I must hear about it. But you must hurry. *Shacharis* is past and the girls are at breakfast." She looked at me and spoke into my ear, "You've been toiling all week's end, haven't you, my dear girl?"

"Is it that obvious?"

"A little birdie told me. We'll talk later."

Our close-knit group davened in the parlor and then headed to breakfast. Girls were milling about but when they saw Ruchama, a collective gasp filled the room and the girls swarmed around her, squealing with joy.

Ruchama tolerated the infusion of attention and said, "Just to let you know, I have asthma. Thursday I had a debilitating asthma attack, but my friends and their chicken soup, cured me. Thank you for your notes, I loved them all. They helped me get well."

Henchie said, "She's fine, I'm starved. May we eat now?"

Everyone laughed.

Mrs. Strassfeld was present, sitting unmoving at the end of the long table. Was she the "little birdie"? Had she told Mrs. Morgan about my strong words?

I sat down at my corner table and watched the girls, my heart swelling with affection and pride. The aroma of Vicky and Paula's delicious cinnamon breakfast rolls interrupted my doting and I succumbed.

Henchie appeared. She looked nervous. "Um, Mrs. Strassfeld asks that you come to her," Henchie said, with a grimace. "May I sit down anyway?"

"Of course, Henchie. My table is your table, you know that."

"Just being polite."

I stood. I took a deep breath. *Alright, Judith, be strong. You may have a showdown right here in front of everyone...*

I walked toward Mrs. Strassfeld with tight trepidation. All the girls were still in the room and I wished I had Mrs. Morgan there for support.

I said a small prayer, *Please please please, let this be civil.*

Mrs. Strassfeld was facing the table as I approached from behind.

"Good morning, Mrs. Strassfeld. You asked to see me?"

She turned her head and her eyes met mine. They were neutral, as if she and I hadn't exchanged strong words the day before. Or ever.

"Yes," she said, in her deep voice. "May I ask if you would mind delivering this to Ruchama." She picked up an envelope resting near her plate and extended it.

I looked at it. An envelope to give Ruchama? Was that all she wanted from me? "Yes, of course. I would be glad to."

I took the letter. I waited to see if there was anything more. Her head had turned back toward the table and she seemed to be studying her drinking glass.

I returned to my seat. Henchie's seat was empty, apparently she had her fill. Mrs. Morgan entered the dining room. "Oh, Judith, may I join you for a few moments?" She sat down without waiting for my response.

"Mrs. Strassfeld told me you were quite vehement, barring her from visiting Ruchama yesterday," she said in a conspiratorial tone. She looked at me with warm approval. "You've accomplished what none of us were able to. She said she thinks she assessed the situation inaccurately and would make amends by writing a letter to Ruchama. Did she give the letter to you?"

"I have it in my hands." I raised the letter in my hand for a brief moment. "Would it be proper for me to read it first?"

"Proper and necessary. You must be sure it is full of good verbiage and tone before giving it to Ruchama. I leave it in your hands." She studied me. "You really are something, Judith Mintz. Where giants fear to tread, Judith Mintz does tread."

"Mrs. Morgan, that's very kind of you. I hope I accomplished something lasting. Mrs. Morgan, on a different more cheerful note, I must tell you about the most unbelievable thing that happened on the weekend. Mrs. Abramson generously sponsored Ruthie's mother's surgical operation!" I watched Mrs. Morgan's mouth fall open. "Isn't that the most exciting thing you ever heard? Besides that, she and her husband went wild over Ruthie's cooking and she's begging Ruthie to train a cook in their kitchen!"

Her hand went to her heart. "Mrs. Abramson's sponsoring the surgery? What a blessing! It is quite the most beautiful news!" She sighed, then moved her face closer to mine. "Now, what was that you said afterward about Ruthie training a cook for them?"

"It's still in the planning stage, but it will be part of our *chesed* project for the girls, starting today but we were actually heading toward it last week and it's been on my mind to tell you about it but with all that was going on— "

"Judith Mintz! Slow down and tell me in coherent civilized words what sort of project you're planning."

I mapped out a tentative plan. First, the girls would propose a chesed in writing, which would be subsequently reviewed by Mrs. Morgan and then by staff members. And then, carried out by the girls.

"Ruthie's *chesed* is actually set," I told her. "The plan is for her to train a cook in the art of home-style Jewish cooking at the Abramson home, who are a very needy couple - money can't buy everything - together with another girl, who I strongly suggest be Ruchama."

Mrs. Morgan threw up her hands in a show of mock surrender. "I can't refuse this project. It is ridiculously charming. And so divinely Judith Mintz."

I bit back my smirk. "William will drive them to and fro. Neat and no problems."

Mrs. Morgan shook her head and laughed. "Quite. Any other interesting projects I need to know about?"

"Not at the moment. But you'll be the first to know." I stood. I was eager to read the letter. In private.

"There's just one thing we need to clear up before you go, Judith."

"Yes?"

"To whom did Ruchama give the necklace? And did that girl go off grounds?"

Should I tell her about Ruthie? What was there to be gained? I hesitated a moment and knew I must do the right thing.

"Mrs. Morgan, I think that mystery will remain a mystery. There's just one thing that's important for you to know. It will never happen again."

Mrs. Morgan gave me an arch look. "Case closed?"

"Completely."

"Good. I'll inform the staff, let them know the whole thing was a mistake and they may be assured that all our good girls have behaved properly."

"Yes. Absolutely true. Ta, ta." I said, with a graceful salute.

I retreated to the sunroom.

I sat down and opened the letter.

CHAPTER 31

Ruchama,

I must make amends for the times I spoke overly strongly to you, especially this Thursday past.

In my efforts to pursue what I thought best for Thornton, it seems I overlooked a few details - namely, my need to be tactful and to see the entire story of every person. I realize now that I may have perceived others in absolute terms, leaving room for mistakes— especially with you. I will work to correct it.

I hope you can forgive my error and go on to become one of Thornton's finest. You appear to have great fortitude. May it serve you well.

I am truly sorry you became ill and hope you recover fully with great strength.

Mrs. P. Strassfeld

I read the letter five times before it penetrated.

I sat in my own world, I wasn't sure how long. But when girls filed into the room, I knew it was a long, long while. Class time forced my brain to the present. I stuffed the letter into the envelope and into my pocket.

When all the girls were seated, I described the *chesed* project.

I asked the girls to think about an actual need they perceived, then to write about it in full detail including how to help alleviate the need. I divided them into groups of three or four to work together, to think, to plan.

Ruthie, Ruchama and Miri grouped together.

"This group," I spread my arms over them, "has permission from Mrs. Morgan to go to Brellenson to cook and coach cooking, or fulfill any other need there, twice a week."

They gasped and put their heads together, whispering. I lowered my head into their huddle and said softly, "The real chesed will be to help Mrs. Abramson. She's lonely."

Ruchama looked at me. I raised my eyebrows and nodded. Her eyes grew large.

"Please bring your written proposals tomorrow for my review," I announced. "I can't wait to see them. Class dismissed."

I let them go early. Ruchama lingered after the girls left.

"Just to let you know," she said, "I phoned my aunt earlier to tell her I was fine. And… Mrs. Strassfeld was civil to me today. First time. Thought you'd like to know."

I did. Mrs. Strassfeld had made good on her commitment to treat Ruchama better. I was pleased to hear it.

"That's a start. Please sit down, Ruchama. Mrs. Strassfeld wrote you a letter of apology. I looked at it beforehand, to make sure it was kosher. Here it is." I took it out of my pocket and gave it to her.

Ruchama read the letter slowly, showing me certain words she needed help with. Then she read it again. And again. And again.

Mrs. Morgan passed by our window. I left Ruchama,

hunched over her letter, and went out to the hall. "She's reading the letter. It's good. Mrs. Strassfeld asked for forgiveness, saying she would take steps to correct her mistakes."

Her mouth made an 'O' along with a great intake of breath. "Oh! Thank Heaven!! This will be a glorious year. Oh, you must come to me for Shabbos to celebrate. You may bring a friend."

"May I bring three?"

She smiled and shook her head in a doting manner. "You know, Judith, you're the daughter I wish I could have seen grow up. She had red hair just like yours."

"We'd love to come."

The rest of the week, a whole new world opened up. Mrs. Strassfeld tried to be encouraging to Ruchama and to the other girls, as well. She even initiated a "good morning" to me once, bowling me over so, I didn't have the presence of mind to respond. It would take a while to get used to her new personae, but I welcomed this particular type of challenge.

And it accomplished grand things.

Ruchama blossomed. She spoke more, sometimes with sentences of more than six words. I saw her mingling with the girls and couldn't help feeling proud.

She and I spent less time together on her reading and writing since she preferred to work on her own and the help she sought from me was minimal.

Overall, a calmer atmosphere permeated the halls of Thornton. The girls sang more and laughed more. One change had made a huge difference. Mrs. Strassfeld possessed great power and I marveled at her ability to influence the atmosphere of the school. Besides that, her ability to shift her approach was impressive, a huge lesson in how any person can change their lives, no matter their life story.

The next day, the girls presented their written *chesed* projects to me and I passed them on to Mrs. Morgan, whose reaction was ecstatic. She promptly called a meeting in the formal dining hall to unveil the idea to the teachers.

I sat patiently while the teachers read the girls' papers, with nervous hope in my heart that all would be accepted. Mrs. Strassfeld appeared to be frowning as she read. She put her papers down and stood.

"Good deeds conducted in a refined manner are the hallmark of an English girl," she said. I held my breath. "I approve of the project and am suitably impressed by these written presentations."

She then gave me a look which startled me. "Well done. Miss Mintz." I held onto my seat to keep from falling.

"Thank you," I murmured.

The consensus was unanimous.

Plans were set in motion. On Wednesday, the girls and I made the logistical arrangements and Thursday, the girls carried them out. The project wrought new dimensions in the girls and brought exciting stories to the end of the day.

Ruthie and Ruchama began their work at Brellenson. Tuesday and Wednesday they shopped with Mrs. Abramson. They cooked and Ruthie coached a new cook in the kitchen. Both girls returned to school brimming with energy, an apparent bond blossoming between them. And from what Ruchama told me, the dawning of a relationship with Aunt Ellen had softly begun.

Miri had decided to go solo to oversee a group of girls, Henchie and Blimale amongst them, who packed Vicky's and

Paula's surplus pastries into boxes and distributed them to elderly people in Manchester. Besides the pastries, the girls spent time visiting and singing with the ladies. The girls returned to Thornton flying high.

I went for Shabbos to Mrs. Morgan's home with Henchie, Blimale and Ruchama. We looked at her albums and she showed us a picture of her beautiful redhead daughter. She told us that ten years before, when her daughter was only five years old, her husband had been walking together with her daughter and they were both fatally hit by a careening car. She said that since then, she had been blessed with twenty-five daughters plus one fully-grown redhead daughter. I almost broke down and cried.

Mrs. Morgan bustled joyfully about her home, enveloping us with a beautiful Shabbos, abundant with delicious food and sumptuous desserts.

"To celebrate," she told me, offering me a piece of her luscious strawberry shortcake.

She took us out Friday night and we strolled the streets of Manchester arm in arm, meeting and greeting the neighbors. Afterwards, I stayed up late talking with her on her couch, telling her about all that had transpired the week before. Ruchama, Ruthie, the Abramsons, Mrs. Strassfeld. She listened with rapt attention, absorbed in every detail.

Mrs. Morgan woke us early the next morning and brought us to shul. We mingled afterwards with her friends, introduced as her "young ladies from Thornton." She dragged us over to the Rebbetzin, proudly telling her, "These are my remarkable girls. Aren't they remarkable?"

On the way home from shul, Blimale asked me, "Do you like the caterpillars, Miss Mintz?"

"Are you the one that keeps putting them in my room?"

"Well, I catch them, but Henchie places them in your room."

Hmm, a duo. "And the frog?"

She nodded. "Yes. It was her idea to put it into your bureau."

Mystery solved.

"Yes, Blimale. I actually do like them. They're good listeners."

Friends came by in the afternoon, women and teenage girls, who obviously had only warm affection for Mrs. Morgan. As did I.

A woman entered talking, "…and promised she would come by, and by the way, I saw her first. Where is she?" She pointed at me. "There she is!" It took me a moment to recognize her because she wasn't wearing her ostrich plume. It was Mrs. Shirley Weiss!

She marched over and I stood to greet her. I wanted to tell her that her initial warning about Thornton had been true. So much had happened since then. She pumped my hand. "Good to see you, Mrs. Weiss," I said.

"Naughty, naughty. You didn't visit and I've been waiting for weeks!"

Mrs. Weiss then gave a dramatic description, in minute detail, of our encounter at the train station, embellishing the story of her crocheted yarmulke and the almost fainting spell she had when she caught sight of my red hair.

Ruchama shot me a look.

I retuned the look.

"I never noticed your hair before."

"One of the reasons I like you."

I smiled. She smirked, her eyes gleaming.

Three weeks ago I had sailed across the Atlantic on the ship, *Brittania*.

I thought I could make a difference.

It seems I could.

ACKNOWLEDGEMENTS

Special thanks to my amazing editor, Rena Hoberman, and for her quick response to my calls for help. Thanks to my friend, Toby Cohen, who took the time to read my early chapters (which needed help) and set me straight. Thanks to my friend who hails from England, Debbie Friedman, who helped verify the authenticity of my 'English' and let me know that in England it's 'koppel' not 'yarmulka' and that summer vacation is known as 'holidays'. Thanks to the Yated for their support and helpful comments and to all my Yated readers (especially my family) who gave me the motivation to write my next book.

CPSIA information can be obtained
at www.ICGtesting.com
Printed in the USA
BVHW030205200219
540722BV00001B/8/P

9 781977 638830